Being with Brady

HART'S CREEK STORIES - BOOK FIVE

by

Suzie Peters

GWL
PUBLISHING

First Published in 2024
by GWL Publishing
an imprint of Great War Literature Publishing LLP

Produced in United Kingdom

Cover designs and artwork by GWL Creative.

ISBN 978-1-915109-43-9 Paperback Edition

GWL Publishing
Chichester, United Kingdom
www.gwlpublishing.co.uk

Dedication

For S.

Chapter One

Laurel

"Do you want any more milk?"

Addy shakes her head at me, clearly desperate to go play, and I give her a smile, helping her from her seat, then watching as she runs from the room.

Mitch doesn't even glance up from his phone as I reach for Addy's bowl, slotting it into the dishwasher, and taking a peek through the kitchen window. It looks cold enough for snow today. There's ice on the long driveway that leads to the main road, and a thick frost on the grass. It makes me relieved I don't have plans to go out at all. Addy and I can stay here in the warm, and maybe bake some cookies. She'll enjoy that.

I turn back to Mitch, who's still got his blond head buried in his phone, and I reach across the island unit for Addy's empty beaker.

"It looks freezing outside."

He raises his eyes just for a second, letting them latch onto mine. "It's January, Laurel. What do you expect?"

He has a point. It's one of the reasons I most hate this time of year. It's so damn cold all the time. Cold and dark.

"Have you got any plans for today?" I ask, closing up the dishwasher, Addy's beaker stashed inside.

"Other than working, you mean?"

I feel silly for asking now. Mitch works seven days a week. His hours are relentless, and he does it all for me and Addy. I'm grateful for that, don't get me wrong. I love the life he's given us in our beautiful home, but every so often I wish he'd find more time to share it with us.

I mean… how else are we supposed to make a brother or sister for Addy?

She's four now, and due to start school in the fall, and while some people might think I'm using that as an excuse to have another baby, that's not the case at all.

It's something Mitch and I have been talking about on and off for ages… which just goes to show that Addy starting school has nothing to do with it.

I don't know exactly when the need started, or where it came from. All I know is, I took to being a mom far better than I'd expected, and slowly but surely, I realized I wanted to do it all again… and maybe again.

I didn't naturally assume that Mitch would feel the same, though. Let's face it, Addy wasn't exactly planned, was she? That's why I broached the subject carefully, waiting until one evening, just a week or so after Addy's third birthday, when we were in bed together. He'd already made me come with his fingers, and was kneeling up, reaching over for a condom, when I grabbed his arm, stopping him.

"You know… I wouldn't mind if you stopped using those," I whispered.

That seemed like a reasonable way of raising the subject, but I sensed the tension in his body straight away as he shifted back. He didn't lean over me, like I might have expected. Instead, he settled back on his ankles, gazing down, his eyes betraying his confusion.

"What are you saying, Laurel?"

"That I want us to have another baby." I smiled up at him, although he didn't smile back. He tilted his head, his confusion still apparent.

"Even though you got so upset with me the last time?"

I don't think I'll ever forget that. The feeling of fear when the test was positive is still fresh in my mind, even now. I can remember the shocked expression on Mitch's face when I broke the news to him. He hadn't expected it any more than I had, although I suppose we ought to have realized. Having unprotected sex has consequences. And we were paying the price.

"I know, but that was different. We'd only just met, Mitch. It was a one-night stand." A very uncharacteristic one on my part. At least, I think it was uncharacteristic. It was my first time, so I hadn't worked out what was 'me' and what wasn't. "Having a baby as a result wasn't what either of us had in mind, was it?" Neither was getting married, but when Mitch proposed, I wasn't about to say 'no'. The idea of being a single mom was even more scary than the idea of being pregnant by a man I barely knew. At least he was offering to do the right thing, and when I said 'yes', he smiled and pulled me into his arms. He wanted me. He wanted us. And I was thrilled. I was so thrilled, I forgot my fear and let him sweep me off of my feet, and straight back to his bed…

"No," he said, like he was thinking things through.

"But even allowing for all that, it turned out okay, didn't it?" His hesitation was making me doubt, but the tone of my voice seemed to snap him out of his trance and he leaned over me, kissing my forehead.

"Of course it did, honey."

"In that case…"

"You wanna try again?"

I didn't think it would take much 'trying', if our first attempt had been anything to go by, but I nodded my head, and then said, "Yes," just to be sure he'd understood.

"Okay." My heart soared, and I put my arms around him, pulling him down so his body was crushed against mine.

That made him smile, and he planted a quick kiss on my lips before leaning back. "I think we ought to plan it a little better this time around, though, don't you?"

"Probably." I smiled up at him. There hadn't been any planning with Addy… other than the conversation we'd had that night, after we'd made love, for only the second time. Our plan – if it could be called that – was that I would move in with him straight away, and we'd get married as soon as possible, before anyone could notice I was pregnant.

"In which case, you're gonna need to give me some time. I'm just making a few changes at the gym, so my hours are gonna get longer, not shorter." I couldn't hide my disappointment and he noticed. "Hey… I know this isn't what you wanna hear, but I think it's gonna be better if we can wait a while."

"A while?"

"Yeah. Not forever. Just until I can get things straight at the gym. That's all."

"Okay."

Having reached an agreement, he made love to me… with a condom, clearly not ready to take chances yet.

It's been that way ever since.

I've tried mentioning it to him in between times. On the most notable occasion, I built up to it, deciding how to approach him, planning what I'd say, and choosing some sexy lingerie to distract him. Even I'd noticed that several months had passed since our original conversation, and that Mitch had shown no signs of wanting to put his words into actions. The problem was, my timing sucked. The day I chose to speak to him was the same day that Luca left. He worked for Mitch, and had done for ages, but more than that, he was my best friend's boyfriend. Mitch might have relied on him at work, but that was nothing compared to how Peony felt, and they were both surprised when he announced he was leaving town… with Stevie Pine. She was the wife of Dawson Pine, who owns the bar on Main Street, and although I've never spoken to him about what happened, I imagine he was just as shocked as everyone else. Stevie and Luca had kept their affair well hidden, according to Mitch, and while I could sympathize with his problems at the gym, I had to focus on Peony. She was devastated, and I did my best to be there for her. Of course, Luca's departure also meant that Mitch had to work even longer hours, until a replacement could be found, and it didn't take a genius to work out that there was no point in bringing up the subject of having another baby, while he was rarely even home…

Still, things are much more settled now. Not just for Mitch, but for Peony, too. She's married, as of just a few weeks ago, to a multi-millionaire. Ryan's money had nothing to do with what brought them together. She's not like that. It was love for her. Love and lust. I can still remember the tone of her voice when she told me about their one-night stand. It was just as uncharacteristic as mine had been, but at least she wasn't a virgin. She'd just failed to find out Ryan's name before leaping into bed with him. She felt terrible about it, but it didn't matter in the end, because like I say, it wasn't all about lust. There was a lot of love going on, too. Which is why he moved his entire life up here to Hart's Creek, just so he could be with her.

Now that's what I call romance.

Not that I'm complaining.

Mitch can be romantic, too.

Or he could if he was ever here.

A man called Jesse has replaced Luca, and although I don't like him very much, my opinion of the man doesn't really matter. Even if he is a little creepy, he works all the hours Mitch asks of him, which means my husband ought to be at home more.

Only he isn't.

It's unusual for him to get back before Addy goes to bed. It's unheard of, actually. Sometimes he doesn't make it home before I go to bed, but as he reminds me whenever I bring it up, the gym is open until eleven and he can't expect other people to cover the late shifts, if he's not willing to do it himself.

I understand that. I really do.

It's just that it's not much fun... and it's confusing.

After all, I sacrificed my career – or to be more accurate, I postponed starting it – so I could be a full-time mom to Addy. I didn't mind that. In fact, like I say, I've enjoyed every second of it. But I feel like I need to know what's going on now. Because if Mitch has changed his mind about us having another baby, then I need to adapt to that. I need to learn to live with the disappointment and also think about what I'm going to do with myself when Addy starts school. And if he hasn't changed his mind, then I'd like to know why we're still waiting.

Because right now, I feel like I'm living in limbo.

I've been putting off this conversation for ages, but it's only just coming up to seven. Mitch isn't due to leave for another thirty minutes, and with Addy happily settled in her playroom, I guess there's no time like the present.

I step forward, leaning against the island unit, opposite where he's sitting, watching as he takes a sip of coffee.

"Mitch?"

"Yeah?" He looks up, putting down his cup at the same time.

"Can we…?"

His phone rings, interrupting me, and he glances down at the screen. "Sorry, honey. I need to take this."

He connects the call without waiting for me to reply and I feel the disappointment sap the life out of me. There's always something… or so it seems.

"Hey, Nate," he says into the phone, smiling.

My skin tingles. Why is Nate Newton calling at this time of the morning?

"That's okay." Mitch leans back in his seat. "I wasn't doing anything. Is something wrong?" He listens for a while, his expression giving nothing away, and then he smiles again. "Not at all. They've been no trouble. We'd never even know there were construction workers here most of the time."

That's because you're never here.

If they're talking about construction workers, though, that means they're talking about the house.

Not our house. *The* house. Nate's house.

The one that's being built on the far side of our property… on a piece of land Mitch sold to him.

It's the only thing Mitch and I have ever really fought about in all the time we've been together. And even now, it still irritates me.

Why?

Because it all happened without my knowledge.

The first I knew of it was when a team of construction workers arrived a couple of weeks ago, just after Christmas. They drove up to the house and stopped, one of them getting out and coming to the door.

"We're looking for Nate Newton."

"I'm afraid you're in the wrong place. He doesn't live here."

The man frowned, looking down at the clipboard he was holding in his hand, before he turned it around and showed it to me.

"The sat/nav in the truck brought us here, but if you're saying that's not this address…" He pointed to it, and I leaned in, so I could read it, frowning myself.

"That's this address, but Nate Newton doesn't live here. He's the editor of the town's newspaper. He's got an apartment above their offices."

"I don't care where he lives, lady. We've got a contract to start work here today."

"Doing what?" I asked.

"We're building a new property," he said, flipping over the top sheet of paper on his clipboard. "It's a two-story, four-bedroom house." He looked back at me, like I was the one with the problem, which I was thinking might be the case.

"Can you give me a minute while I call my husband?"

"Sure." He shrugged his shoulders, and I left him where he was, standing on the doorstep, and went back into the house, finding my phone in the kitchen, and placing a call to Mitch.

He answered on the fourth ring, sounding a little out of breath.

"What's wrong?" he asked, rather than saying 'hello'.

"I don't know, but there's a team of construction workers here, looking for Nate Newton."

"And he's not there?" he said, sounding surprised.

"No. But why would he be?"

"Because he's the one who told me the construction work was starting today. They'll expect him to be there." He sighed, and I imagined him rolling his eyes.

"I don't understand," I said. "What construction work? And what has it got to do with Nate?"

"Everything. It's his house they're building."

"On our land?"

"No. On his land. I sold it to him."

I grabbed the back of the seat in front of me, just to steady myself. "Y—You did?"

"Yes."

"Why didn't you tell me?"

"I didn't realize I had to." I couldn't believe he was serious. He didn't realize he needed to tell me about something like this? "It's my property, Laurel," he said, when I didn't answer him.

That hurt, and I hung up before he could say another word.

It was clear something had gone on behind my back, but I couldn't keep the men waiting outside any longer, and I went back and apologized, explaining there had been a mix-up.

"Do you know where Mr. Newton is?" the man asked.

"No. I'm afraid I can't point you toward the plot of land, either. But I can give you Nate's number, if that helps?"

He checked the front sheet of paper, his eyes scrolling down to the bottom. "It's okay. I've already got it. I'll call the guy."

He gave me a nod of his head as he pulled a phone from his pocket and I closed the door, leaving him to it. Tears were already forming in my eyes and I wasn't in the mood for a witness.

Nate arrived about ten minutes later and I heard voices outside before they all drove off, further onto the property. I was glad he hadn't called by, although my relief was short-lived, because about an hour later, there was a knock on the door. It was Nate, his dark blond hair all messed up, and his shirt untucked. He looked like he'd just got out of bed.

"I'm so sorry about all that," he said. "I completely forgot about coming over this morning."

"That's okay." It wasn't, but I couldn't blame him, could I?

"I hope it won't be too much trouble, having them drive past your house every day," he said, his smile touching at his blue eyes. "One of their first jobs is to build a new access road, so hopefully the inconvenience will only be temporary."

I shrugged my shoulders. I didn't relish the idea of trucks trundling past the front door every five minutes, but it felt like the least of my problems.

"It's fine," I said, and he tilted his head.

"Is everything okay?"

"Of course." I did my best to smile and although he didn't seem convinced, Addy chose that moment to call out to me. "I'd better go, but thanks for coming by."

"That's okay. If there are any problems, just call me."

I nodded and closed the door, going to find Addy.

I hid my tears from her. She's never seen me cry, and I didn't feel like trying to answer her questions about why Mommy was upset. I could hardly tell her it was because Daddy had lied, could I? And I didn't want to lie, either. It was safer to say nothing and pretend everything was okay, even though it wasn't.

When Mitch came home that evening, Addy was already in bed. Rather than going out into the lobby to greet him like I usually would, I stayed in the kitchen and got on with what I was doing. I suppose I half expected him to come find me, but he didn't. He went upstairs, and I heard the shower running, which just made me even more angry than I already was. What right did he have to ignore me? I hadn't done anything wrong.

I was still at the kitchen sink when he came down again, although he had nothing on his feet, so the first I knew of it was when I felt his hands on my hips, and he pressed himself against me.

"Don't be mad," he said, nuzzling at my neck.

"Why not?"

"Because it's boring, Laurel."

I turned around in his arms, staring up into his face. He looked just the same as usual, but with damp hair, his baby blue eyes gazing down into mine, and his accentuated muscles shown off in a tight black t-shirt, over stonewashed jeans.

"But this is our home, Mitch."

"I get that, but it was a business deal, and you know I never discuss business with you."

It was true. He never did. And it felt petty to argue about it anymore.

"So, we're gonna have neighbors, are we?" It seemed odd. He'd always told me the reason he bought this house was because it was isolated, and he liked that.

"We are, but we won't even know they're here. Nate's house is gonna be right over the other side of the property, in that dip by the tree line."

I nodded my head, giving thanks for that. I didn't relish the prospect of being overlooked, and while I never craved the isolation that Mitch seemed to desire, I'd grown used to living out here, on our own.

"Nothing's gonna change?" I said, looking up at him.

"No, honey." He smiled, flexing his hips so I could feel his arousal. "You'll still be able to walk around naked."

I chuckled, shaking my head. "I haven't done that for years. Not since Addy was born."

"No, but maybe you should."

He unfastened my blouse, his eyes never leaving mine, and I leaned back against the sink, making it easier for him, watching as his fingers made light work of undoing each and every button.

"Oh, look… I seem to have exposed your breasts," he said, with a tease in his voice.

"You've exposed my expensive underwear."

Mitch had never held back when it came to lavishing his money on me, and I had more than enough lingerie to prove it.

He nodded his head. "I've always liked this bra... but I think I prefer it off than on." He pushed my blouse from my shoulders and let it fall to the floor, then undid my bra, releasing my breasts. "That's better," he whispered, bending to lick my nipples. I gasped, arching my back, craving the contact, just like I always had done.

Without a word, he raised my skirt, his fingers delving inside the equally expensive lace of my thong, and finding that most sensitive spot.

"Oh... yes..." I hissed out the words, parting my legs a little as he rubbed, none too gently.

"You like that?"

"Yes."

"You want more?"

I nodded my head, and he chuckled, taking my hand and pulling me toward the door.

"M—My clothes..."

"Leave them. I've gotta leave early tomorrow. I'll make sure Addy doesn't find them."

I giggled, feeling like a young lover, not a mature wife and mother, and ran with him to the front of the house and up the stairs.

We were quiet when we got to the top, for fear of waking Addy, but once our bedroom door was closed, he turned and pushed me back against the wall, unfastening my skirt and letting it pool around my ankles.

"Am I forgiven?" he asked, a smile twitching at his lips, like he already knew the answer to that question. He hadn't even apologized. Not really. Asking for forgiveness seemed a little surplus to requirements.

"I guess."

He tilted his head. "You only guess? Does that mean you need persuading?"

"It means I'd like to understand."

I realized I'd just poured cold water on the situation, the sparkle fading from his eyes in an instant as he stepped back and left me standing by the wall in my stockings, garter belt and thong.

"I told you. It's business."

"I know, but I do your accounts, Mitch. I understand enough about your business to know it's doing well. So why did you need to sell the land?"

He huffed out a sigh, pushing his fingers back through his hair, and turned away. It took two more sighs before he looked back at me. "I'm thinking of expanding, if you must know."

"You are?"

"Yeah."

"Where to?"

"I haven't decided yet. I'm not gonna build a bigger gym here. That's the last thing I need. I feel like I've tapped out the potential market in Hart's Creek. So, if I go anywhere, it'll probably be Willmont Vale."

"And when were you gonna tell me? Or weren't you gonna bother?"

"It's business," he said, narrowing his eyes.

"Maybe it is, but it impacts our lives, too, Mitch. So, when were you gonna tell me?"

"Once I'd reached a decision about exactly what I'm doing and had found a suitable property."

I felt left out, and it must have showed because Mitch moved closer again, standing right in front of me, our bodies almost touching, but not quite.

"Don't take it so personally," he said.

"How can I take it any other way?"

"Because it doesn't affect us."

"Of course it affects us. We barely see you as it is. If you open another gym in a different town, I can't see how you're ever gonna make it home." The thought crossed my mind then that we'd never have another baby, either, although I didn't say anything. It didn't seem like the right moment to drop that particular bombshell into the conversation.

His eyes raked over me, his hands following close behind, and while I wanted to tell him to stop so we could talk some more, he knew exactly where to touch, and where to kiss, and where to lick. Words died on my lips, and good intentions scattered to the four winds, while he reminded me of all the reasons I'd ever fallen for him in the first place, and then made me fall for him all over again, our disagreement forgotten…

"That's okay. Thanks for letting me know."

Mitch ends the call, putting down his phone as he looks up at me.

"That was Nate?" I ask, although I already know.

"Yeah. He wanted to let me know the access road should be completed by the end of this week. So after the weekend, there shouldn't be any more trucks coming down here by the house."

I nod my head. "Is that gonna be the permanent access to his house?"

"Yeah. I think he's planning to put a gate on it once all the work's done."

"I see."

So far, Nate's been really considerate about everything, informing us of what's going on, and when. If he carries on like this, it won't be an issue having him as a neighbor, and although I'm still confused by the way Mitch went about selling the land,

I'm not as angry about it as I was. But that's life, I guess. Time passes and other things take priority… in my case, the need to have another baby. Or at least to discuss it with my husband.

Speaking of which, it's almost time for him to leave, and I still haven't been able to talk to him.

He gets up, pocketing his phone, and giving me a smile. "What was it you were gonna say before Nate called?"

"Oh, it's nothing. You need to go."

He comes around the island unit, his six foot two body towering over me, his eyes boring into mine. "Trying to get rid of me, are you?"

"Never."

He smiles, snaking an arm around my waist and pulling me close. "Good. Now, tell me what you were gonna say?"

"It'll keep until tonight."

He frowns, pulling my body even tighter to his. "Tell me." He pauses, then says, "Is this about redecorating the bedroom again? Because you know I like it how it is."

That's something else we've talked about on and off over the years. I've never been keen on the masculine color scheme and plain decor in our bedroom, and at this time of year, I find it particularly depressing. Mitch has always refused to change it, fearful I think that I'll go overboard with floral prints… although I don't know why. I haven't done that anywhere else in the house.

"No. It's not about the bedroom. It's something completely different, and I don't want to talk about it when you're running out the door."

"Now you've got me worried, honey. You're not sick, are you?"

I rest my hands on his hard chest. "No. I'm fine. There's nothing to be worried about."

"Then tell me what you were gonna say."

"Okay. If you must know, I was gonna talk to you about whether you still want us to have another baby. We haven't discussed it for ages, and…"

"You're right," he says, interrupting me as he sighs out his words.

"I am?"

"Yes. That's not something we can talk about in a few minutes."

"No. It's not. But can I take it from your reply that you've gone off the idea?"

"Not at all. All I'm saying is, if we're gonna do it, we need to do it right."

"I know. The problem is, we're not doing it."

He chuckles. "We're doing it often enough, aren't we?"

"Yes, but…"

He puts his finger over my lips to silence me. "I'll come home early tonight."

He replaces his finger with his lips, kissing me gently. "And we'll talk?" I ask, looking up at him.

He kisses me again, pulling back this time. "Everything's gonna be just fine, Laurel. You'll see."

He steps away, giving me a wink. "Promise?"

"I promise."

He turns, heading for the door, and although I spend a second or two admiring his back, and his perfectly formed ass, I don't forget to call out, "I love you."

"Love you, too, honey."

Chapter Two

Brady

I think I'd sell my soul for some sunshine right now.

It feels as though it's been overcast and gloomy since the beginning of time, and while I know that's not true, and we're only in the second week of January, I'm craving spring and warmer weather.

That could be because it's so damn cold. The snow we had before Christmas came and went, but we've been left with deep, heavy frosts, ice, and biting winds. Frankly, I'd rather have the snow. At least it makes the place look pretty.

At the moment, it just looks gray and dismal.

Or maybe that's me.

"Cheer up. It might never happen."

I startle, almost walking in to Cooper White as he steps out of his office. He's one of my oldest friends in the town, as well as being our resident dentist. We go way back to elementary school, and before that… although I'm not sure either of us can remember anything from that long ago. At around six foot two, he's a couple of inches shorter than me, but otherwise, we could be brothers. We're not, but we have a very similar build and our coloring is almost identical.

"Who says it hasn't already?"

He pulls his coat closed, looking up at the sky. "It's freezing, isn't it?"

"I was just thinking the same thing."

"Are you busy?"

"No. It looks like all the bad guys have decided it's too damn cold to commit any crimes."

He laughs now. "My patients have decided the same thing, I think."

"That they'd rather stay on the right side of the law?"

"No… that it's too cold. I've had three cancelations already today. That's why I've come out."

"Because it's so much nicer in the freezing wind than in the warmth of your office?"

"It is when Greta keeps making threats about clearing out the storeroom."

Greta is his long-suffering assistant. He inherited her when he took over the practice and although he moans about her all the time, we all know he'd be lost without her. I think the problem is, Greta knows that too.

"That still sounds better than being out here."

"In which case, why aren't you tucked up safely at the sheriff's office?"

"Because sometimes we have to make our presence felt."

"And you couldn't do that in the comparative warmth of a car?"

"I could. But I felt like a walk."

"Do you feel like a coffee, too?"

"Absolutely."

He chuckles and we both turn toward the coffee shop, which is just a few doors down, getting there in no time at all.

Inside, it's lovely and warm, and we undo our coats, wandering up to the counter.

"Don't you guys have jobs to do?" Everly Wright, who owns this place, looks across at us. She's in her late twenties, with long blonde hair, which she ties behind her head in a ponytail while she's at work, and a slim figure that she hides behind a black apron, fastened around her narrow waist.

"Not right now," Cooper replies with a boyish grin. Everly has that effect on a lot of men, although I'm immune, for obvious reasons. "And besides, we're paying customers."

She nods. "In which case, what can I get you?"

"I'll have a flat white, please." He turns to me. "I'm buying."

"I'll have the same."

Everly nods again. "I'll bring them over."

"Thanks," Cooper says, and we make our way to a table by the window, both of us pulling off our coats and taking out our phones, putting them on the table, just in case we should get a call, because we're never off duty, it seems.

"It's not quite the same in here since Aunt Clare died," I whisper, so Everly won't hear me.

"No, it's not."

We've both known Aunt Clare all our lives, although she wasn't our aunt, she was Everly's. Even so, the name stuck with all of us who grew up around here.

"It feels different without her bustling around."

"Yeah. Do you think Everly's okay?" he asks, glancing over at her, and watching for a second while she prepares our drinks.

"Probably not. But she can hardly shut herself away and pretend it didn't happen."

"No."

Aunt Clare's stroke took us all by surprise, especially happening on New Year's Day. Obviously it was worse for Everly. Aunt Clare was like a mother to her. Everly's parents died when she was five or six. I can't remember which, but Aunt

Clare took her in, and they'd run this place together since Everly graduated high school.

"How are things with you?" Cooper asks, changing the subject. "Apart from being quiet."

"I've been helping Walker Holt with some research on that TV series he's been writing."

"Oh, yeah. I heard they'd started filming."

I nod my head. "The producer delayed it so Walker and Imogen could go on their honeymoon, and then I think there was another hold-up to do with casting, or something."

"When's it coming out?" he asks.

"I don't know, but Walker said he'd keep me informed."

He nods his head and we both fall silent as Everly comes over, bringing two cups of steaming coffee. Cooper hands her a ten-dollar bill, telling her to keep the change, and she thanks him with a slight smile in return. He seems to appreciate it, and watches her walk away, an admiring glint in his eye.

"I sure hope Seth appreciates what he's got there," he says, turning back to me.

"I imagine he does. But aren't you forgetting something?" He tilts his head, like he doesn't understand. "Isn't there a certain someone called Meredith in your life?"

"I guess."

"You only guess? Does that mean you've had another fight?"

"Not that I'm aware of."

"In that case, how does she feel about you idolizing other women?"

"I'm not idolizing anyone… and what she doesn't know won't hurt her," he says, taking a sip of coffee and smiling at me. "Besides, she's away in San Antonio, seeing her Mom and Dad."

"Ahh… and you're feeling lonely?"

He shrugs his shoulders, sitting back in his seat. "Not especially."

"How long has she been gone?"

"I don't know. Nine or ten days, I guess."

"You don't know?" He shakes his head. "Can you remember when she's coming back?"

"In about a month, I think."

"This is all really vague, Coop."

"So? We don't live in each other's pockets," he says.

"Where do you live then?"

He frowns at me. "You know where I live. Above the office."

"And Meredith? When she's not in San Antonio?"

"She lives in Willmont Vale."

I take a drink of coffee. "Still? Even though you've been together for… how long is it?"

"I don't know. A while."

I shake my head. How can he not know? "And you're okay with that arrangement? You don't want more?"

"More than what? I like things the way they are. We work and see our friends during the week, and then get together on the weekends. It's perfect. Especially with Meredith being an artist. She gets really wrapped up in what she's doing."

"Yeah. I remember you telling me."

"Exactly, and that's why I don't wanna change things. We couldn't live with each other the entire time. We'd go crazy. At least, I would. But when Friday night comes around, she forgets her latest project and devotes herself entirely to me. Show me a guy who wouldn't like that set-up."

Me. I'd hate it.

I shake my head. "But surely, if you love her…"

He holds up a hand. "Whoa… who said anything about love?"

"You mean you're not in love with her, even after all this time?"

He sits forward, clasping his hands together. "Why? Is there a procedure for falling in love? Does it work to a schedule?"

"No, but…"

"But what?"

I almost gave myself away then. I nearly said that I assumed everyone just fell… like I did. But fortunately I stopped myself, and I sit back, shaking my head. "Nothing. I'm guess I'm just surprised, that's all."

"Why would you be surprised? You know what I'm like. And personally, I think more people should live this way."

"You think the world would be a better place if we all forgot about love and romance, and limited our relationships to two days a week?" I say, smiling at him.

"Yeah. Why not? It avoids getting bored of each other."

I'm not sure that's supposed to be a priority, but I don't say that out loud. "So Meredith feels the same, does she? She doesn't want to move in with you and make things more permanent?"

"She brings it up from time to time."

"You mean, you fight about it from time to time."

"Yeah. But I think we both know it wouldn't work. She has a fantastic set up at her place. Her apartment is on two levels, and she's got a studio on the top floor. It's ideal for her. The light up there is amazing, and I can't see her wanting to give that up."

"You could live there, couldn't you? The commute back to your office would only be six miles."

He shakes his head. "I like living alone, and I like living here. Not only is it super convenient for work, but the rooms are bigger than at Meredith's place, and there's no way my bed would fit into her bedroom."

"Is that why she always comes over here on the weekend?"

"The size of my bed, you mean?" I nod my head and he smiles. "Maybe. Although Meredith likes to get away from her work. She says it helps to recharge her batteries."

"You let her get enough sleep to do that, do you?"

He smirks. "Sometimes."

"You're hopeless."

"There speaks a man who's never lived with a woman in his life."

"Neither have you… not for more than two days at time."

"That's two days longer than you've managed. So, what's your excuse?" he asks, grinning.

"Only that my situation is very different from yours."

"Why? Because you haven't found the right woman yet?" He shakes his head, like he thinks I'd be made for even trying.

"It's not that." I suck in a breath, knowing I should keep quiet, but busting to tell someone. I've held it inside for years, and should probably keep doing just that, but sometimes… *Oh, to hell with it.* "It's not that I haven't found her. It's that she's already married."

His eyes widen and his mouth drops open. "Already married? Are you serious?"

"Deadly."

"Who the hell are we talking about here?"

"Laurel Bradshaw," I whisper.

"Laurel?" I nod my head and he sighs. "I admire your taste, but she and Mitch are pretty tight."

"I know. I don't need reminding."

"In which case, what makes you think you've got a chance?"

"Nothing. I don't think I have a hope in hell with her… although I might have done if I'd acted sooner."

"What are you talking about?" He sips more coffee, leaning forward.

"I've been in love with Laurel for the last nine years."

"Jesus… how old was she back then?"

"Eighteen. It would have been perfectly legal, don't fret."

He smiles, letting out a sigh, which sounds like relief. "And you'd have been twenty-eight."

"You and I are both the same age, Coop. It's good to know you can subtract nine from thirty-seven."

He narrows his eyes at me, although I know he's not mad. Cooper's almost incapable of getting mad. Not unless he's really riled, and he's never been that with me. "You've kept it very quiet all these years?"

"Do you expect me to run around town boasting that I'm in love with another man's wife?"

"No, but she wasn't another man's wife nine years ago, was she?"

"I know. That was what I meant about acting sooner."

"Why didn't you?"

"Because I'm an idiot. I couldn't work out what she'd see in a guy who was ten years older than her, but I was bewitched… besotted…"

"I get it. You were in love with her."

"Yeah. Only by the time I plucked up the courage to ask her out, she was on her way to college. It was only a couple of months later that Dad died, and I guess I was otherwise occupied for a while."

"I know." He gives me a look, which tells me I don't need to say any more.

There's nothing more to be said, is there?

My father had a heart attack and died in the street, here in Hart's Creek. He was only fifty-six and, although he was a little overweight, he wasn't unfit, or unwell… not as far as we knew.

The shock was too much for my mom, who'd always had a weak heart herself. Her health rapidly deteriorated, and she died just two months later.

In the space of a few weeks, I'd lost the two people who meant the most to me in the entire world, other than Laurel, who wasn't even here.

I felt abandoned, so I did the only thing I could. I turned to my other family… my work family.

"You wanted to take over as sheriff, didn't you?" Cooper asks, like he's worked out the way my mind's been traveling.

"Of course. I never expected Dad to die so young, though. None of us saw that coming. I thought I'd have many more years as his deputy before I had to take on all the responsibilities that come with doing this job."

"And in the meantime, you waited for Laurel to come home?"

"Yeah. Don't get me wrong, I didn't expect her to fall straight into my arms. She had no idea how I felt about her. She still doesn't. But I'd changed while she'd been away. I hoped she'd…"

"You hoped she'd what?"

"Realize that losing Mom and Dad like that had given me a different perspective."

"In what way?" he asks, tilting his head.

"I didn't just want to date her anymore. I wanted a life with her."

"Only Mitch Bradshaw got there first."

"Don't remind me." I think that was the worst part. The thought of Laurel marrying anyone was hard… but why did it have to be Mitch Bradshaw?

Cooper finishes his coffee, pushing the cup aside. "None of us could ever compete with him, could we?"

"Nope."

"I gave up trying," he says, with a shrug of his broad shoulders. "I can remember feeling relieved when I heard he was going to college."

"Even though you were going yourself?"

"Yeah. It's not as though we were going to the same place, and somehow I thought he might be brought down to size by having a larger pool of competition. I held onto a ludicrous hope that it might turn him into a better human being."

I chuckle. "To be honest, I was surprised when he made it into college in the first place."

"Without the sports scholarship, it wouldn't have happened. The guy doesn't have the brains for it."

"I don't think brains have ever been a priority for Mitch."

"No. All he had to do was flex his muscles and tweak that twenty-four carat smile, and every girl in town would drop her panties for him."

Including Laurel… although I don't say that out loud. I don't like to think of her that way, even though I know it's the truth. They have a daughter to prove it.

"Were you surprised when he eventually came back here?" I ask, to get us off of that topic.

"Hell, yeah. I hoped we'd seen the last of him."

"So did I."

"He may not have made into it any of the major NFL teams, but he was huge in Canada. When he retired from the game, I guess I assumed he'd set up home somewhere much more exotic and luxurious than Hart's Creek."

"I know. I felt the same." As did probably every man we grew up with.

"And of course, he flashed his cash, buying that big house."

"Yeah… and then converting Donny Moore's old electronics store into a gym."

"All while keeping the single women of Hart's Creek occupied at night."

"It wasn't just at night," I remind him. "And it wasn't only the single women, if the rumors are to be believed."

"Really?"

I shake my head. "I hate the gossip that floats around this place, and I never know what to believe and what to dismiss, but when Mitch came back and bought that house, he got Sabrina Pope to redesign the interior for him."

"I know he did. For quite some time, everyone who came to see me kept talking about what he was tearing out and what he was putting in, and how much money he was spending. Of course, I don't think it was anything compared to what he spent on the gym, but that came later, didn't it?"

"It did. It took him a while to persuade Donny Moore to sell up. But did none of those people who came to see you ever mention how much time Sabrina was spending out there?"

"No." He takes a moment to realize what I'm hinting at, his eyes widening. "You mean they were having an affair?"

"I don't know for sure. But that was the rumor going around at the time."

"Do you think that's why she and Tanner split up?"

"I doubt it. The timing's not right."

He shrugs. "I guess that depends on how long it lasted, and when Tanner found out… if he ever did."

"Exactly, and I'm not about to ask him." Tanner is a couple of years younger than Coop and me, and although we're all friends, our friendship doesn't go that far.

Cooper shakes his head. "Their divorce was damn ugly. I doubt he'd thank you for raking it up."

"Especially as it's none of my business."

"I'm guessing Laurel knows nothing of Mitch's wayward past?" he says, glancing out the window, before he looks back at me and raises his eyebrows, like I'm supposed to know the answer to his question.

I shrug my shoulders. "I don't know. He might have told her…"

"Not if he had any sense. Still, at least he's calmed down now."

"Yeah. As much as I hate to say it, for all his faults, Mitch has been a good husband to Laurel."

"They're an odd match, though, don't you think?"

Of course I do. I love her. How could I think any man would be good enough for her?

"I guess the guy has hidden talents," I say, and Cooper smiles.

"Clearly, if all the stories are to be believed. But what I mean is, Mitch has a reputation for being kinda wild, and Laurel's always struck me as the quiet type."

I have to agree with him. In my mind, I've always seen Laurel as demure and sophisticated. Why on earth she fell for Mitch's charms is beyond me. The guy's good looking enough, but I've never thought of Laurel as being the kind of woman to be swayed by things like that.

Still… I've been wrong before. And I'll no doubt be wrong again.

"Perhaps there's a side to her we don't know about." It's the only logical explanation. Part of me really likes the idea of Laurel having a wild side, although I'm less keen on the idea of her sharing that with Mitch Bradshaw.

"I guess there must be. I can think of countless other women in this town who'd have fallen into Mitch Bradshaw's bed, and dozens who already have, but Laurel wouldn't have been anywhere near that list."

"I know…" I let my voice fade, the thought of Laurel in Mitch's bed filling my head, and my heart, and shattering the latter for the umpteenth time since she came back from college.

I didn't even realize she was back until I saw her coming out of Ezra Walsh's office. She was wearing a dark gray fitted suit, with a white blouse, and killer heels, and she looked really pleased with herself. I just stood and watched, smiling, as she walked down the street, her blonde hair swaying in the breeze, and a happy-go-lucky swing in her step.

God… she looked beautiful.

Her mom and dad lived in Cedar Street back then, and she was clearly headed home. I was tempted to follow her, but I didn't. I watched her until she disappeared around the corner.

That night was the opening of Mitch's new gym. Everyone in Hart's Creek seemed to be going, but there had been an accident just outside of town. It wasn't anything major, but the paperwork prevented me from attending the festivities. Not that I was particularly interested in anything Mitch Bradshaw was doing…

Unlike Laurel, it seems.

She was more than interested.

That much was obvious, because within a few weeks of the opening, she moved in with him and they stunned the town by announcing they were getting married.

Mitch Bradshaw?

Getting married?

It was beyond belief.

Hearts were broken all over town. Mine included. All my theories about Laurel not being interested in older men were shattered.

As was I.

Everyone wondered why. What had made Laurel choose Mitch, of all people? Why was he settling down all of a sudden?

And then it became clear…

Laurel was pregnant.

When their daughter Addison was born less than seven months after the wedding, everything became clearer still…

People talked.

Man, did they talk.

No-one could understand how Laurel could have been so easily persuaded into Mitch's bed.

Even fewer people could believe that Mitch had done the right thing by her.

I'll admit to being surprised by that myself.

Although I'd have been happier if Mitch had behaved true to form, and abandoned Laurel.

That might sound callous, but it's what I would have expected of him, and being completely selfish about the situation, it would have given me a chance.

Would I have been willing to raise another man's child?

Of course I would, if it had meant a life with Laurel. I'd have done anything for her. I still would.

As it was, my selfish desire meant nothing. Mitch stood by her, and they were married, their daughter was born, and they lived happily ever after, in the tradition of all good fairy tales.

I'm pleased Laurel got her happy ending. And she is happy. Anyone can see that.

As for me, my dreams of happiness died long ago.

"What about you?" Cooper says, dragging me back to reality.

"What about me?" I finish my cold coffee and put down my cup.

He shakes his head. "You can't spend the rest of your life pining for something you'll never have."

I think I probably can. "There's no-one else out there for me."

"How do you know if you don't try?"

"I have tried."

"Oh, yeah?" He grins at me.

"Yeah. I've dated since Laurel and Mitch got married."

"Dated?"

"Yeah."

"Is that all?"

I lean forward. "No. That's not all."

"And?"

"And I'm not giving you details… or names."

"I'm not asking for details, or names, but…"

"It's taught me one thing."

"Oh?"

"Yeah. That having sex with other women doesn't feel anything like as good as just looking at Laurel," I say, and his smile fades.

"Man... and you thought I had problems?"

Chapter Three

Laurel

The chocolate chip cookies came out well. They're crunchy on the outside and gooey in the middle, just how they should be.

Making them kept Addy occupied for a while, and the mess in the kitchen wasn't too bad. It wasn't anything I couldn't clean up, anyway.

It was while I was putting the mixing bowl back in the cabinet that my phone rang. I half expected it to be Mitch, telling me he wouldn't be home early after all, but it wasn't. It was Peony, and I smiled, connecting the call.

"Hello, stranger," I said, and she chuckled.

"I know, I know. I'm the worst friend in the world."

"Not quite the worst friend, but…" I let my voice fade, teasing her. "How was the honeymoon?"

"Oh. My. God." She didn't really need to say any more. Just those words, and the hushed tone in which she murmured them, was enough to fire my imagination and make me remember my own honeymoon with Mitch. It was at Niagara Falls, and although he'd been before, when he was playing pro-football up there, it was a novel experience for me. The hotel, which overlooked the falls, was perfect, and coupled with the romance he injected into our stay, I couldn't have asked for anything more.

"What was it like staying on a private island?"

"Very private," she said, and I could hear the smile in her voice. "But a little weird. There were people there to cook and clean, and fetch us anything we wanted, which felt odd. It was like having servants."

"But you enjoyed it?"

"Every second. I just can't believe I've been back for over a week already, and I haven't found the time to call you until today."

"I know. Worst friend in the world."

She giggled, and so did I. "How are you fixed today?" she asked.

"We're not doing anything at all. It's too damn cold."

"Would you like a visitor?"

"We'd love one. You could come to lunch, if you like."

"That sounds perfect."

"I'll make some soup to warm us up."

"That sounds even better."

We ended our call, knowing we could talk over lunch, and into the afternoon, and I set about making some minestrone soup. It's one of Addy's favorites and is so easy to make.

While it's cooking, I quickly tidy the house, making sure it looks spotless for when Peony arrives, which she does, at twelve on the dot.

"It's absolutely freezing," she says, giving me a hug.

"I know."

"The town is practically deserted."

"I guess everyone's decided to stay home."

"Who can blame them?" She smiles, stepping into the house and kicking off her thick-soled boots. She always wears them around the farm, and doesn't usually change when she's going out, unless it's a special occasion. Even though she's married to a multi-millionaire now, she hasn't changed at all from the girl I went to school with. Her stonewashed jeans are still torn at the knee, and her blue sweater is still several sizes too big. As for her hair… it's as wild as ever, her loose ringlets hanging over her shoulders.

I'm about to close the door when I notice the enormous red truck sitting on the driveway.

"What's this?" I say, ignoring the icy wind for a second and pulling the door back open again.

Peony glances out, a smile etched on her lips. "That was a wedding present."

"From Ryan, I presume?"

"Who else?"

I close the door, my need to be warm overriding my interest in cars.

"You didn't know he was getting it?" I ask as we make our way through to the kitchen.

"No. My old one was coming up for its sixteenth birthday, I think, and he'd been saying for months that he thought it was high time I had something more comfortable and reliable to drive around in."

"And, don't tell me, you'd been saying he shouldn't spend his money on you?"

"Something like that," she says, smiling, and watching as I put the kettle onto the stove to boil. I'm not in the mood for coffee, and I know Peony won't mind drinking tea.

"Well, it's a lovely present."

"I know."

"You won't have seen Mitch's new car, either."

She shakes her head. "I didn't know he was getting one."

"Neither did I." It came as an enormous shock when he drove home in it. I didn't know what was going on until he got out of the sleek red sports car and gave me a killer smile. "It's a Camaro, and I think it's become his most prized possession."

She chuckles. "When did he get it?"

"Last Friday."

"Have you driven it?"

"Not yet. Once the novelty wears off, he might let me, though."

She laughs, but it's cut short by the sound of footsteps, as Addy comes rushing through the door. "Aunty Pee-nee," she hollers, throwing herself into Peony's arms. I always chuckle at the way she pronounces Peony's name, and I smile, watching the two of them as Peony swings her around.

"You've grown," she says, putting Addy down on the floor again.

"I'm a big girl now. Mommy says so."

Peony looks up at me, tilting her head.

"I've been explaining to her that she'll be starting school in the fall. When I thought it through, it made sense to put the idea into her head, and keep talking about it, so it doesn't come as a surprise when the time comes."

Peony shakes her head. "I can't believe she's gonna be five this year."

"Neither can I."

I'm tempted to tell her that Mitch and I are thinking of having another baby, but I don't. Not because Addy's here and I wouldn't want her to know about it until it was happening, but because I need to wait until Mitch and I have talked it through properly.

I guess that's why I haven't mentioned it to Peony before. It's been rattling around my head for such a long time, but I've kept it to myself. Not knowing how things stood with Mitch, or whether he'd changed his mind, made it hard to talk about… as if talking about things like that is easy at the best of times.

"Mommy and I made cookies this morning," Addy says, pointing to them.

"We'll have some after lunch," I tell her, before she asks for one.

"I'm hungry, Mommy."

I smile, knowing that what she really means is she wants another cookie, but that she'll tolerate having to eat something else first.

"Okay. The soup's almost ready. I just need to make some tea for Aunty Peony and me."

"Is it the mini soup?" Addy asks, and I nod my head.

"It sure is."

"What on earth is mini soup?" Peony asks.

"Minestrone. Don't you know anything?" I say, smiling.

"I guess not." She shakes her head. "I've got a lot to learn, it seems."

"You sure have. But there's no rush."

She opens her mouth and then closes it again, giving me a smile. "Shall I set the table?"

"I thought we'd eat out here, if that's okay?"

"It's fine." She steps up to the island unit, running her hand along its smooth granite surface. "I love this."

"I do, too."

It was something Mitch put in for me last spring. I'd been asking for one for ages, telling him how much easier it would be to eat breakfast and lunch in the kitchen, rather than the more formal dining room beyond it. I don't think he could see the point when he was never here for breakfast or lunch – and sometimes not even for dinner – and I'd forgotten all about it until the workmen arrived to fit it. They laid a new floor at the same time, and although it was chaos for a few days, it looked lovely when it was done. It's so much more practical, too.

Peony lays out the silverware, while I make the tea and dish up the soup, helping Addy onto her chair. It's one of four that run down one side of the island unit, leaving the other free for preparation.

"This really is lovely." Peony leans back a little in her seat, still examining the granite countertop.

"I know you've never eaten at it, but you've seen it plenty of times, and when all is said and done, it's just an island unit."

"I know, but I'm thinking," she says as I join them, sitting the other side of Addy.

"What about?" I ask.

"That I'm gonna have to admit to Ryan that he was right."

I chuckle, taking a sip of tea before I start eating my soup. "What about?"

"Oh… he and I have been discussing what we should do with the kitchen at the farm. He's already had the roof repaired. We couldn't really wait for that, because it was leaking, but I didn't want to have major alterations done to the house while we were focused on the wedding and the construction work we were having done in the barn. Now that's all done, he's itching to get moving with the farmhouse… starting with the kitchen."

"Okay. And what is it he's right about?"

"The island unit. I've been saying it would look too modern in a farmhouse, but he disagreed. He said it didn't have to, and now I've studied this more closely, I think he has a point."

"You sound disappointed."

"Not because he's right. I'm not that petty… not most of the time." She smiles at me over Addy's head. "I just liked the idea of keeping the kitchen table."

"Why can't you do both? You could put in an island unit, and have the table beyond it, couldn't you? You've got enough space."

"We have. But if we move it out of the kitchen, it'll become a dining table, not a kitchen table… where granny used to roll pastry, and where I used to sit and drink my milk after school."

"Do you roll very much pastry, then?" I ask, trying not to smile.

"No."

"Then don't worry about it. You can still sit at it and drink milk, if you insist."

She shakes her head at me, her lips twisting upward. "Okay… I know I'm being sentimental."

"Nothing wrong with that."

"No, I guess not."

We both eat a little more soup. "Speaking of being sentimental, how are things going with your new business?"

"That's not sentimental at all. It's hard work," she says, putting down her spoon and sipping at her tea. "Who would have thought organizing weddings could be so stressful?"

"Just about anyone who's ever got married, I would have thought."

She laughs, nodding her head. "Hmm… I suppose I should have worked it out, shouldn't I?"

"Is it going okay, though?"

"It is."

"And you're enjoying it?" I ask.

"I am. We're already taking bookings for the spring and summer."

"That's not surprising. I guess most people prefer to get married when it's warmer… unlike the two of us."

Peony was only married the week before Christmas, and as for Mitch and me, we had our fifth anniversary back in November.

The timing wasn't our choice... not really. It was dictated by the fact that I was pregnant, and Mitch wanting to do the right thing. I can remember wondering if we were crazy at the time, but what choice did we have? Besides, I've got no regrets... not one.

"It sure looks that way," Peony says. "We've got six summer weddings booked in already, as well as a couple who want to re-take their vows."

"They want to do what?"

"Re-take their vows."

"Why? Didn't they mean them the first time?"

She laughs. "That's one way of looking at it, although they seemed happy enough when they came to look around the barn. I think they're seeing it as an affirmation of their love."

I roll my eyes at her. "Seriously?" She giggles, nodding her head. "Well... if it brings you some money, let them kid themselves." I know how hard things have been for Peony recently. She came close to losing everything last year... before she met Ryan, of course, and I'm thrilled this new business venture of hers is working out, although I know Ryan will be there for her, no matter what. He's that kind of guy... just like Mitch.

"I've got another two weddings that are pending, too," she says, finishing her soup and looking at me over the top of Addy's head.

"Oh? Anyone we know?"

"Yes."

I hadn't expected her to say that and I twist in my seat, facing her, despite the presence of my daughter between us.

"Who?"

"Gabe and Remi."

"I remember them from your wedding, but I didn't realize they were engaged."

"They weren't. Not then. Gabe proposed on New Year's Eve."

"Now that is romantic."

"I know. Isn't it? They're getting married sometime in the summer."

"They haven't given you a date?"

"Not yet. His parents are coming over from England in July, but they haven't confirmed exactly when, and Gabe mentioned something about a wedding he and Remi are going to in Europe in early August, and that he's thinking of tying that in with their honeymoon."

"Are his parents English?" I hadn't realized that, either.

"His mom is," she says.

"I see. And apart from Gabe and Remi, who else's wedding have we got to look forward to? It's not Everly and Seth, is it?"

"No. I doubt they've got time to think about weddings at the moment."

"You heard about Aunt Clare, did you?"

She nods. "It was such a shock."

It really was. Aunt Clare has been a fixture in the town for as long as I can remember, and her loss must be hard for Everly. I notice a glistening in Peony's eyes, and wonder if she's recalling her grandmother's death, which happened just over a year ago. It would be natural for her to associate the two events, and rather than making a fuss, it seems best to get back to happier subjects…

"So, if it isn't Everly and Seth, who is it?" I ask, and she smiles.

"Nate and Taylor. They've set the date for May, although I can't remember whether it's the fourth, or the eleventh." She frowns, like she's thinking. "The eleventh is ringing bells in my head, but that could be for something else altogether."

"It's not like you to be so forgetful," I say, and she laughs, rolling her eyes.

"It is lately. I swear, if I don't write things down, I'm lost."

"That's what marriage does for you."

"Probably."

"I'm surprised they've gone for May," I say, putting down my spoon for a second to take a sip of tea.

"Why?" Peony asks.

"Because I'd be amazed if their house is ready by then."

"According to Ryan, it depends on the weather over the next couple of months. According to Nate, he couldn't care less. They're getting married in May. Period."

We both laugh.

"Mommy…?" Addy says, and I stifle my giggles, turning to face her.

"Yes?"

"I'm finished with my soup. Can I have a cookie now?" I look down and see she's eaten almost everything I gave her, just leaving a few pieces of pasta in the bottom of her bowl. She hasn't spilled anything down her dress, either, which is nothing short of a miracle.

"Of course."

I pull over the plate of cookies, and she takes one.

"Can I go play now?"

"You can, baby girl."

I help her down, and she runs from the room, the cookie clasped in her hand.

"She's adorable," Peony says. "And so well behaved."

"I know. We're very lucky."

She twists around in her seat. "How's it been, having the construction vehicles and workers here all the time?"

"Not as bad as it could have been, I guess. The plot of land is over by the tree line, so you can't even see them from here, although they have to drive past the house all the time."

"That must be annoying."

"It could be worse. And they're putting in an access road, so according to Mitch, by next week, I won't even know there's anything going on at all." I let my head fall, studying my fingernails.

"What's wrong?" Peony asks, and I glance up at her again. "I would have thought you'd be pleased to have your privacy back."

"I am. It's just that the land, and Nate buying it, is a slight bone of contention."

"Between you and Mitch?"

"Yeah. He sold it without telling me."

"How? Surely you had to agree, didn't you? There must have been documents, and…"

I shake my head. "It's his land, Peony."

"You mean you don't have joint ownership?"

"No. The first I knew of it was when the construction workers arrived just after Christmas."

She blushes. "Do you mean I knew about the sale before you did?"

"When did you find out about it, then?"

"I can't remember exactly." I'm not sure if that's true, or if she's trying to be kind. "Ryan helped Nate negotiate the deal with Mitch and went through the planning process with him." That suggests it was quite some time ago, and she reaches over, resting her hand near my arm, although she doesn't touch me. "If I'd realized you didn't know what was going on, I'd have said something."

"It's okay."

It isn't, but what can I say? It's not her fault.

"Does Mitch really own everything? The house, the land, the gym?" she asks and I nod my head. Her eyes widen and she gets up, shifting to Addy's seat so she can lower her voice. "But what if something happened to him?"

I smile, putting my hand on her arm. "We've both made wills, leaving each other everything… not that I have much to leave. But if anything happened to Mitch – God forbid – Addy and I will be taken care of."

"I guess that's something," she says with a sigh. "Although I think I'd still want some kind of reassurance."

I can't help feeling a little put out by Peony's comment. Why would I need any kind of reassurance from Mitch? He's my husband. That's all the reassurance I need.

I guess the problem is, she hasn't been married for as long as I have.

She doesn't know how this works.

"So you're gonna tell me Ryan's signed over all his properties to you, are you?" She leans back, her face showing how much that got to her. I'm being snippy and I know it, although she doesn't give me a chance to apologize.

"No," she says, sounding hurt. "But how could he? He doesn't own a property anymore. He sold his apartment in Boston when he moved here. I've put the farm into both our names, though."

"And how did he feel about that?"

"He didn't want me to."

"But you did it anyway?"

"Yes. It's his home now, and besides, he's investing so much, I felt wrong keeping it all in my name."

I can see what she's driving at, and I don't like the seed of doubt it's sowing in my mind.

"That means you're the one making all the changes… not him." My point feels lame, but it's the only one I've got when the thought running through my head is that Mitch ought to have made those changes for me, too. At the very least, he should have offered.

"Not entirely. He's changed his bank accounts, so they're in our joint names now."

I'm stunned, and struggling to hide it. "Y—You mean he doesn't just give you money when you need it?" That's what Mitch does, and if I need more, I have to ask. I've always hated how demeaning it feels, too.

"No. Everything is ours now." I let out a sigh, and she leans closer. "Did I say the wrong thing?"

"No, but… Mitch has always kept his finances and his business to himself."

"Why are they *his* finances and *his* business? You're married. You're supposed to be a team."

"He doesn't look at it that way."

"And how do you look at it?"

"I don't know. It's not something I've really thought about." *Until now.*

"Don't you think you should? If he can sell a piece of land without telling you, what else could he do?"

"He wouldn't do anything," I say, defending him. "He felt bad enough when we fought about the land. There's no way he'd do something like that again."

"That's good… not that you fought, but that he learned his lesson."

"He did," I say, smiling, and I get up, clearing away the dishes.

As I stack them into the dishwasher, I can't help wondering, though…

Is Peony right?

Should I maybe speak to Mitch about the way things are set up?

I hate having to ask for extra cash whenever Addy needs new clothes or shoes, and it's not as though he's poor. Far from it. I shake my head, noting that I thought about Mitch's wealth as his then, not ours. Peony's right. There's got to be a better way than this, hasn't there?

A way that includes us both.

Chapter Four

Brady

It made a change to have coffee with Cooper this morning, although since I got back to the office, my day has been just as quiet as it was before.

I'm blaming the weather still, and to be honest, I'm not complaining.

The wind's got up, and I have no desire to go out, any more than anyone else, it seems.

It was good to catch up with Coop, though. We haven't had the chance for a really long talk since Peony Hart's wedding, which was before Christmas. We sat together during the ceremony, although he had Meredith with him, so we didn't get to say much then, and we weren't seated at the same table for the meal. Once that was over, though, Meredith got talking to Pierce Barton. He's a budding young artist, and I imagine he sought out Meredith, hoping to glean advice from her. I doubt she'll have been of much use to him. Her paintings are abstract, while Pierce paints landscapes… very good ones, from what I've seen. The two of them couldn't have less in common if they tried, but their conversation gave Coop and me an hour or so to catch up. Other

than that, I spent most of the time talking with Nate Newton…
when I wasn't gazing at Laurel, that is.

She was the matron of honor, and she looked divine. I
struggled to take my eyes off of her, and the figure-hugging red
dress she was wearing. Unfortunately, Mitch was there too, and
seeing them together reminded me of how lonely I am and how
– even though I'm not entirely celibate – I know there will never
be anyone for me but Laurel.

Sure, I've slept with a few women since she married Mitch, but
none of them have been serious. None of them have meant
anything, and none of them have lasted. I didn't want them to.
I wanted Laurel, and I still do, even though she belongs with
someone else.

There are times, like today, though, when I wish I'd never
fallen for her.

But that's not optional, is it?

You can't help who you fall in love with.

Any more than you can choose how it will end.

It wasn't supposed to end like this for us. When she left for
college, I was devastated, but I reasoned I still had hope. I still had
time.

Like I said to Cooper, my parents' deaths changed me.
Something like that is bound to change a person, and instead of
thinking of Laurel in terms of dating and having fun, I started
thinking of her in terms of getting married, settling down, having
kids. I felt the need for some stability in my life, and I wanted it
with her. That's not to say I didn't want to have fun too, but I
wanted more.

I waited, refusing to date anyone else, even though I had
offers, which I always declined politely, citing work, or some
other commitment, because I knew Laurel would come back
here one day. Which she did, of course.

That first Christmas, I was struck by how different she was. She seemed older, and so much more mature.

I met up with her at the Christmas fair, more by accident than intention. She looked divine, wrapped up against the cold, and somehow we spent the day together. I remember feeling relieved when she told me how immature the boys were in her class. She called them 'boys', too… not men. I liked that. It strengthened my hope.

There were other vacations… other opportunities, and I'd see her whenever I could. We'd talk, and sometimes get together. There's almost always something happening in Hart's Creek, so it's easy to bump into people, but a day at the fourth of July picnic, or an hour spent over coffee, became heaven-sent for me.

Something to look forward to…

Of course, I never followed through on any of it. Never got to let her know… to let her see what she really meant to me.

I held out for the day when she came home for good, knowing I'd be able to take my chance once we had more time.

I would have done, too, if it hadn't been for Mitch Bradshaw. Damn him.

I get up to fix myself a coffee, knowing it won't help to dwell on Laurel and her marriage any longer. It never gets me anywhere, other than into the depths of sorrow.

The coffee pot is empty and I let out a sigh, picking it up, just as my door crashes open, and Chip McGuire comes in, pulling his coat on over his uniform.

"Why don't you knock next time?" I shake my head at him, but he walks across the room, ignoring my sarcasm. He's only an inch or so shorter than me, with dark blond hair and a square jaw I know a lot of women find appealing. As a man, I believe he has a reputation for sleeping around. As a deputy, he's second to none.

"Sorry, boss, but there's been an accident about three miles out of town, southbound on the 103. It sounds like a bad one… a semi and a sports car of some kind."

"Paramedics?" I say, putting down the coffee pot, grabbing my coat from the back of my chair and shrugging it on.

"On their way."

I skirt around my desk. "We'll go in separate cars," I say as Chip follows me from the building, the wind catching my hair and biting my skin. It makes sense to do that, in case one of us needs to go on somewhere else, like the hospital. Or the morgue.

He gives me a very vague salute over the top of his car, then jumps in, although he waits to follow me, giving precedence to my rank… or maybe not wanting to be the first on scene at a bad accident, as he put it. I wouldn't blame him. I don't relish it myself.

It's got to be done, though, and with our sirens blazing, we head out of town, past the apple orchard, and onto route 103.

The crash site is easy to find.

As well as a semi, which is blocking one lane of the highway, there are several other vehicles, and dozens of bystanders. It looks like we're the first emergency responders here, though, and I climb from the car, zipping up my coat against the icy wind as Chip catches up with me.

"Find out where the paramedics are, will you?"

He nods, getting on the radio, while I rush forward, wondering where the sports car can be.

There are skid marks on the road, so whoever was driving clearly tried to stop.

"Excuse me. Clear the way, please."

People step aside, the small crowd disperses, all of them looking up at me. Some are pale-faced, others wide-eyed, a few of them relieved, all of them in shock, and I suck in a breath as the full extent of the accident comes into view, understanding their reactions.

There's a man, standing to one side, being comforted by a woman. He's distraught, but looks up and staggers over. I notice his jacket has a logo on the front that matches the one on the back of the trailer.

"I'd broken down, officer. I wasn't even moving. What was I supposed to… I mean…" He stops rambling, struggling to breathe, and I glance over his shoulder at the woman, who steps forward, joining us.

"Stay here with this lady. I'll talk to you later. Everything will be fine. Paramedics are on their way and they'll help you."

He nods, although I'm not sure he heard a word I said, and the woman puts her hand on his arm, pulling him back slightly. I give her a smile of thanks, which she acknowledges with one of her own, and I turn, taking a deep breath as I see the scene before me.

A bright red sports car is embedded beneath the rear of the semi, almost as far back as the top of the windshield.

There's a woman by the driver's window, just standing there, her head bent.

"You need to step away, ma'am," I call.

She looks up, startling, like she's just noticed where she is, and then she moves away from the car, her face calm but pale.

"I'm a nurse," she says, coming to a stop in front of me. She shakes her head, no further words necessary, and my heart sinks. "I didn't want to open the door. I wasn't even sure I could. But there's no way they could have survived."

"They?"

"There's a passenger. A woman."

She glances back at the car, swallowing hard.

"Okay. Thanks for your help," I say, smiling as best I can. "The driver of the semi is over there with that lady." I nod in their direction. "He's in shock, not surprisingly, but if you could help him until the paramedics get here?"

"Of course."

"Thank y—"

"Christ… that's Mitch Bradshaw's car." Chip's words cut into mine and I turn to face him as he approaches and the nurse drifts away.

"No, it's not. This is – or rather was – a Camaro and he drives a Corvette."

"He did until last weekend. He was showing me his new Camaro on Saturday when I left the gym… and this is it. I'm sure of it."

My heart stops, my body freezing. I can't feel a thing… not even the wind cutting through me, as I remember the passenger… the female passenger.

"No. Not Laurel." *Please, don't let it be Laurel.*

"Laurel? Laurel Bradshaw?"

"Yes. The passenger."

"What passenger?"

"In the car. It can't be her. Please… please. It can't be…"

I run for the car, although when I get there, I stop, unable to reach for the door. My hand won't move. I'm numb… torn. I want to know, and yet I don't. If it's Laurel inside, my life will be over…

"Let me." It's like Chip has realized my torment and he nudges me aside, tugging at the passenger door a couple of times until it springs open. He's blocking my view, but I'm in no hurry to learn the truth as he bends and peers inside the vehicle.

I hear him whisper, "Fucking hell," and then he stands, his eyes betraying his shock, my heart on the verge of shattering forever.

"Tell me," I whisper.

"It's not Laurel. The woman's dead, but she's not Laurel."

Nothing is quite real. I'm floating, unable to focus, or hear, or see properly. It's not Laurel. Thank God.

"Then who…?" I ask.

"You need to look for yourself."

I frown at him and he steps aside, giving me access to the vehicle, and I immediately notice a pair of female legs. They're naked, without even shoes or socks on the small feet. The toenails are painted pale pink. She must have been freezing. Who on earth would go about with nothing on their feet in this weather? I allow my eyes to wander upwards, letting out an oath when I see she's pulled up her short skirt, and isn't wearing any underwear. Her blouse is undone, too, exposing her breasts, her white lace bra covered with blood and broken glass. I raise my eyes to her face, which is a mass of cuts, some so deep the flesh is hanging off. Her eyes are wide, the pupils fixed and dilated, the brown irises staring into oblivion. Oddly, her short dark hair looks almost untouched, although I'm not sure her own mother would recognize her… not like this.

I glance over at Mitch's body. His side of the car took the brunt of the impact, his legs caught in a mangled mass of metal, his upper body spattered with blood. His face is less damaged than this poor woman, and I can make out his features. It's Mitch Bradshaw. There's no getting away from it.

"Fucking idiot," I whisper, standing up straight, my eyes locking on Chip's.

"He was clearly distracted." Chip shakes his head, and while I can see his point, that wasn't what I meant. Mitch was cheating on Laurel, the damn fool. There's no other interpretation of this.

"Yeah."

"He must have taken his eye off of the road, and failed to see the broken down semi until it was too late."

51

"You noticed the skid marks?"

"Yeah, but there's no way he'd have had time to stop. Mitch always drove too fast, and if you look at where they start…" He points to the road and I nod my head. He's right. I can only imagine how terrifying those last few seconds must have been. But Mitch shouldn't have been here in the first place. He should have been with his wife and daughter… where he belonged.

I push my fingers back through my hair. "We might have to rely on dental records to identify her," I say, nodding toward the passenger.

"Unless she's carrying some kind of ID."

"I don't want you disturbing the bodies yet. I don't want anything touched."

"I can search the car, can't I?"

I'm still confused, unable to take in what's going on here. I'm also relieved beyond words that the body we have yet to identify isn't Laurel, and that's making me slow at doing my job. "You're right," I say. "It'll be getting dark soon, and if we can ID her, we probably should."

He nods and moves to the back of the vehicle, popping the trunk.

My feet don't seem to want to move… to set the wheels in motion, because I know that part of what comes next will be informing the next of kin. At some stage today, I'll have to tell Laurel her husband is dead, and I have no idea how I'm supposed to do that.

"Boss?"

I startle at the sound of Chip's voice.

"Yeah?"

"There are some bags in here."

I get my feet to work, putting one in front of the other, and join him by the trunk, peering inside to see two black travel bags, one slightly larger than the other.

"Open them."

Chip does as I say, unzipping the one closest to him to reveal men's clothing. There are several shirts and t-shirts, two sweaters, and three pairs of jeans, as well as underwear. The one nearest to me contains dresses, skirts, blouses and lingerie… lots of lingerie.

What does this mean?

Was Mitch taking his girlfriend away for the weekend?

There seems to be too much here for that. Who needs three pairs of jeans for a weekend? Or that much lingerie, for that matter?

So, was he leaving Laurel?

I shake my head.

Why? Why would he do that?

"Boss?"

"Yeah?" I look up, surprised to see that Chip has moved away. He's standing by the passenger door again, holding a woman's purse in his hand. It's made of black leather with a long strap and a zip along the top. In his other hand, Chip's holding what appears to be a driver's license, and his face has paled a little. "What is it?"

I step over, and he hands the license to me.

I glance down at a photograph of a pretty young woman with short, dark hair. She could be the woman in the car, although her face no longer looks like this. Her date of birth shows she was twenty last month, and her address reveals that she lives – or rather, lived – in Willmont Vale.

"Kaylee Prentice," I say, shaking my head as I study her photograph. "Does that mean anything to you?"

"Yes." Chip's reply surprises me and I look up at him.

"You know her?"

He nods. "She works… I mean, she worked at the gym."

"Why don't I know her?"

"Because you never go there."

Why would I want to? Why would I choose to spend time with the man who had everything I ever wanted?

"Who was she?" I ask.

"One of the receptionists."

"You're sure?"

"Positive. I asked her out a while ago, but she refused. Probably because she was banging her boss."

He has such a way with words.

"How long had she been working for him?"

He shrugs. "I don't know. Six months... maybe eight, I guess."

That's a little vague, but I'm sure someone at the gym will be able to give us more precise information.

Either way, I can't tell Laurel about any of this. She'll be broken by the news of her husband's death.

There's no way I can inflict any more damage...

Chapter Five

>>><<<

Laurel

Peony left a while ago, once we'd had a second cup of tea. She didn't want coffee, and to be honest, I didn't either. We stayed sitting at the island unit, though, and talked for at least another hour or so, until Peony remembered she had some phone calls to make.

"I can't seem to remember what day of the week it is," she said, "let alone what I'm supposed to be doing."

"Are you getting enough sleep?" I asked, and she frowned at me, like she didn't understand. "I can still remember what it was like to be newly married."

She chuckled. "Ryan's very attentive."

"I'm sure he is, but that's why I asked if you're getting enough sleep."

Her chuckle became a laugh, and she shook her head. "I couldn't possibly say."

I knew that meant he was keeping her busy at night, and I leaned in to her. "In that case, you've got no-one to blame for your tiredness but yourself."

"I guess not."

Addy came out to say goodbye, giving Peony a hug, but then went straight back to her playroom, and I've been in the kitchen by myself ever since.

I have to admit, I'm feeling a little despondent now.

I enjoyed having Peony here, and it was good to catch up, but she's made me think about Mitch and his money.

You see? There I go again, thinking about Mitch and *his* money. Because that's what it is. It's his, not ours.

He earned it before he even met me, through his football career. Playing the game made him a very wealthy man, but he invested most of his fortune in buying this house and setting up his business. He had to work hard to get the gym to where it is, and to contemplate opening more branches, although I'll admit that was news to me. Not that anything has happened since our conversation… nothing he's told me about, anyway.

But why would he? It's business, and he never talks to me about that, does he?

I sigh, sitting up at the island unit again, feeling disgruntled. I get that it's his money and his work, but Peony's right. We're supposed to be a team.

We're not supposed to have secrets, and although I do his accounts for him, I'm wondering how much more I don't know. Are there other aspects of his work that he's keeping from me? After all, I only enter figures into an accounts program on the laptop he bought me. He's the one who provides me with all the information. My knowledge is limited to what he tells me… and it seems he likes it that way.

I gaze around the kitchen, which is much more my domain now than an office ever has been, and wonder if this is why he treats me like he does. He sees me as a wife and mother, and not an independent woman, with a brain of her own.

He forgets I graduated law school at the top of my class. The fact that I've never had a job is hardly my fault, is it?

I came back from college full of enthusiasm, bursting to make something of myself and my law degree. It was early fall by the time I got back here. I'd taken on a part-time job at a law office in the city, and had to see out my contract. Some of my class had found full-time places at firms in Boston by then, but my experience of working in an office there taught me I didn't want that. My ambitions were on a much smaller scale. But they were ambitions, none the less.

My mom didn't understand my 'small town' perspective.

"You could make so much more money if you worked in Boston," she said, when I told her of my plans.

"Maybe. But I don't particularly like living in Boston, and I don't want to feel that I'm living to work, rather than working to live."

"I thought you wanted to make a difference. That's what you always said. It's why you were so adamant about going to law school in the first place."

She wasn't wrong. I'd said almost exactly those words to her, just a few years earlier.

"I know… but is there any reason I can't make a difference here? Or in Willmont Vale? Or Concord?"

"Of course there isn't," Dad said, joining in the conversation. "There's nothing wrong with a small town law firm."

I wasn't surprised by his interruption. He was born in Hart's Creek, and had lived here all his life. Mom was from Bridgeport in Connecticut, and although she'd moved here when they got married, I don't think she'd have chosen to live in such a small town. In fact, I know she wouldn't.

As it was, she piped down, and I gave Dad a grateful smile.

A week or so after I got back, I approached Ezra Walsh at his law offices in Main Street, and asked if he'd be willing to interview me, just for the experience. With a typically friendly grin, he agreed.

Ezra is one of those people who just belongs here. He's probably in his mid-sixties, a little overweight, his waistcoat buttons always gaping slightly under the strain of his bulging stomach. He wears half-moon spectacles and has a florid complexion, with gray hair and a glorious mustache. Even though I'm sure there must have been a time when his eyesight was 20/20, his hair was a different shade, and he carried a little less weight, I can't remember him ever looking any different.

The interview went well. I enjoyed it more than I thought I would, and at the end of it, he surprised me by offering me a job.

"You want me to work here?" I stuttered out the words, unable to believe it.

"Yes."

"But I thought this was just…"

He held up his hand, and I stopped talking. "There are three other lawyers here, aside from myself, one of whom is quite junior. He's just announced he's going to be leaving in January. I know that's a few months away yet, but if you can wait, I'd really like to have you come work with me."

I couldn't think of anything I wanted more.

Ezra might look like a teddy bear with whiskers, but he knows the law better than anyone I've ever met. The thought of working with him, and learning from him… it was overwhelming.

I thanked him for the opportunity and told him I'd wait.

He nodded, happy with my reply, and leaned back in his chair.

"Of course, the secret to being a successful lawyer in a small town like this is to schmooze."

"Schmooze?"

"Yes. It pays to know everything that's going on… who's doing what with whom, and why they're doing it. I never turn down an invitation to anything. Not a single thing. So, if you get the chance between now and January, make sure to cozy up to the townsfolk."

I've always been quite a shy person, but I knew he was right, and I only hesitated for a second or two before putting on my metaphorical big girl panties and nodding my head.

"I'll see what I can do."

He smiled, shaking my hand before I left the building, with a spring in my step.

Of course, I didn't realize that an opportunity to schmooze would present itself quite so immediately, but as I looked up, I saw the sign on the front of the gym.

'Opening tonight. Everyone Welcome.'

That was an invitation if ever I'd seen one, and it seemed to me like the perfect opportunity to talk, and listen, and find out what was going on around the town... what had been happening in my absence.

As I walked home, I wondered whether I should call Peony and invite her to come with me, but then I reasoned I'd be there to meet other people, not to spend the evening talking to my oldest friend. And besides, I wasn't sure whether I was even capable of schmoozing. I certainly didn't want a witness.

So, I changed out of the business suit I'd worn for my interview with Ezra, and after debating with myself for an hour or so over whether to wear a skirt, or pants, or a dress, I chose a knee-length skirt, and a thin sweater. Looking at myself in the mirror, I still wasn't sure if attending the opening was a good idea, but at least I felt as though I'd chosen the right outfit. It was comfortable, not too casual, and not too smart.

It was just right.

When I walked through the doors later that night, there must have been about forty or fifty people in the room. It was bigger than I'd expected, filled with fitness equipment, its frosted windows overlooking Main Street. I suddenly felt nervous. There were more people there than I'd thought there would be, and I hesitated, wondering if I could duck out again, unnoticed.

"Hi." The male voice stopped me in my tracks and I looked up into scorching blue eyes. "And who might you be?"

"I'm Laurel Williams."

He smiled, revealing perfect white teeth. "Mitch Bradshaw," he said, holding out his hand. I took it and he kept a hold of me, pulling me further into the room. "I own this place."

That made sense of his bodybuilder's physique, which was just as captivating as the rest of him. "I see."

"I used to be a pro-footballer," he explained.

"Sorry. I'm not really into…"

He turned, smiling down at me. "It's okay. I'm sure you've got other thoughts occupying that pretty head of yours."

My mouth dried, my body heating beneath his gaze, and although I managed a smile, words were beyond me. I was too busy admiring him, and ruing the fact that I had so little experience with men. Was he just being friendly, or did I dare read more into it?

During the evening, he had duties to attend to, speeches to make, people to thank, but at every opportunity he came back to me. He was attentive, considerate, and paid me more compliments than I knew how to handle, and although I'd only planned to stay for an hour or so, I was the last to leave.

"I've had a lovely evening," I said as he closed up the gym, locking the doors.

"It doesn't have to end yet."

I stared up into his eyes. "It doesn't?"

"No. I bought some champagne to celebrate the opening. You could come back to my place and help me drink it, if you like?"

I'd never drunk champagne before, and I was having a good time. I saw no reason to turn him down.

"Okay."

He smiled and led me to his sports car, helping me into the passenger seat, before he sat beside me, switching on the engine and revving it a few times. He sped out of town, making me wonder where he lived, but before I could ask, he slowed, pulling into the long driveway that led to his house, and I gasped at the sight of it. Even in the dark, it was impressive… and enormous.

"What a beautiful place."

"I like it," he said, parking out front, and helping me from the car before showing me inside.

He may well have had champagne, but we didn't get to drink it. No sooner had he closed the door than he turned and kissed me. He didn't hold back, either. He wanted me and I wanted him just as much. And even if I didn't know what I was doing, it didn't matter. He did.

He certainly wasted no time in moving things to his bedroom, or in removing my clothes.

I ought to have felt self-conscious, but how could I when he was admiring me like he was, his eyes raking over my body, as he undressed and lowered us to the mattress, crawling up over me.

Everything we were doing was so out of character for me, but I didn't care. It was like I was on a rollercoaster and there was no way off. He might have been older than me, I might have only known him for a few hours, but none of that mattered, and as I lay there, looking up at him, I couldn't think of anything except what we were about to do.

I felt him enter me, surprised that it didn't hurt more, but then he stopped and looked down at me, a puzzled expression on his face.

"You're a virgin?"

I nodded, wondering if it made a difference… if he'd change his mind.

He hesitated, staring into my eyes, and then whispered "Fuck it" under his breath, slamming into me.

I cried out, feeling the pain I'd been expecting, although it only lasted a matter of moments, and once it was done, I relaxed. I felt like a woman… and about time, too.

I didn't stay the night. He offered, but the barrage of questions I'd have faced from my parents the following morning didn't bear thinking about. So, he drove me home, and while he didn't kiss me, he thanked me, with a very sexy smile on his lips.

I was disappointed, I guess, that he didn't say he'd call, or even ask for my number, but in the cold light of the following morning, I realized I couldn't blame him for that. He might not have been explicit about what he was offering, but he'd never talked of the future, or of seeing each other again.

It wasn't the way I'd envisaged losing my virginity, but I couldn't complain. I'd gone in with my eyes open.

I didn't tell a soul about what had happened – not even Peony – and it wasn't long before I'd forgotten all about it. There was no point in worrying about it, was there? It had been nice to be wanted like that, but it was over and done with, and besides, we were building up to the Fall Festival, and everyone was busy.

I suppose that was why I didn't notice my period was late. Not until the day of the festival itself.

I panicked – naturally – and when Mom and Dad had gone over to Hart's Green, I dashed to the drugstore and bought a pregnancy test, taking it home and running to the bathroom. My hands were shaking, but I did the test, feeling awash with fear when it was positive.

I thought about calling Peony. I knew she'd be kind and understanding. But it was Mitch who needed to know. He'd told me he was going to the Fall Festival to hand out leaflets for the gym, but I could hardly go there to find him, could I? Telling a man he's going to become a father isn't something that's best done in public. So I waited until the festival was over and drove up to his house. He was home, and he answered quickly when I knocked on his door. It was a few weeks since we'd seen each other and he seemed surprised to find me on this doorstep, although he invited me inside and listened while I told him my news. His face paled, and while I'd have liked to tell him he didn't have to feel obligated, I couldn't. We were both responsible in equal measure.

It took him a moment, but once he'd recovered, he pushed his fingers back through his hair and stepped closer.

"Do you wanna get married?"

I was shocked. I suppose I'd thought he might suggest a termination, so I just stared at him for a second or two, and then said, "We don't have to."

"I'm aware of that, but I'm responsible for this."

"We both are."

He shook his head. "I knew what I was doing, and you… you were a virgin." I wondered if he regretted changing that circumstance. He closed his eyes and let out a sigh, making me think he might, but then opened them again and stared down at me. "Just answer the question, will you?"

How could I? "We don't know each other. How can we get married?"

"We've got nine months to get to know each other. Stop dodging the question, and tell me, do you wanna get married?"

"I don't wanna be a single mom."

"Then we'll get married." It may not have been the most romantic proposal, but he said it with a smile, and pulled me into his arms the moment I nodded my head. Then he kissed me, and for some reason, my fears disappeared.

It wasn't what I'd dreamed of, but as he held me close, I felt safe. When he led me toward the stairs, I let him, hoping for some kind of affirmation, I guess… and he gave it to me. He didn't say 'I love you'. I'd have known he didn't mean it if he had, but he made me feel wanted again, and that was enough.

I smile, remembering the first time I said those three words to him.

I'd been living with him for a few weeks by then. It was shortly before the wedding, and the night after my first sonogram. I'd been telling him about it, and he'd been apologizing for not being able to come with me to the hospital.

"I couldn't get away," he said, holding me in his arms. "You know I'd have made it, if I could."

"You'll be there for the next one?"

"Of course I will."

"Promise?"

"I promise."

"Good." I leaned in to him and whispered, "I love you, Mitch." His body tensed and he pulled back, staring down into my eyes.

"Excuse me?"

"I said, I love you."

A smile tugged at his lips. "When did that happen?"

"It's been creeping up on me for a while now, but I think I realized it today, when I was at the hospital. I—I missed you."

"I'm sorry."

He didn't say he loved me back… not then.

He saved that for our wedding night, and the memory of his words, his touch, his love… they still make me shudder, my skin tingling, and I wonder to myself what might happen between us tonight, once we've had our talk. After all, if we're going to make another baby, there's no time like the present…

I get up, darkness shrouding the room now, and I switch on the light, and wander through to the playroom at the back of the house, to check on Addy. She's so engrossed, she clearly hasn't noticed how dark it is and I turn on the lights in here too, making her jump, although she smiles up at me.

"Thanks, Mommy."

"That's okay. Do you need anything?"

"No, thanks. What are we having for dinner?"

"I don't know. Pasta, I imagine." Mitch loves it, and he said he'd be home early.

She nods her head, going back to her dolls, all of which are laid out on the floor. I don't understand her game, but she seems happy enough and I turn away, smiling to myself.

My career may never have begun, and my life may differ greatly from the one I'd planned, but I'm a lucky woman. I really am.

I guess my only sadness is that Addy doesn't get to see as much of her grandparents as I'd like. Mitch's mom and dad are both dead, and my parents moved to Florida when I was six months pregnant. It was a wrench, but Dad had taken early retirement, and Mom was sick of the cold winters. That was what they told everyone, anyway. Deep down, I always wondered if there was more to it than that. They hadn't been exactly thrilled when I'd told them I was pregnant… and they'd been positively shocked when I'd explained who the father was. Their disappointment was obvious, and although they came to the wedding, it was with very clear reluctance and an element of embarrassment. I'd let them down. They didn't need to say the words out loud for me to realize. When they left, Dad spoke of learning to play golf and enjoying the warmer weather. It sounded less like they were leaving because of me. Since they've been gone, though, their main hobby seems to be going on cruises. We stay in touch, infrequently, and I believe they're in the Mediterranean at the moment, although I can't remember where exactly.

I wander back into the kitchen, wondering what sauce to put with our pasta, just as the doorbell rings, and I turn around again, going to the front door. Mitch didn't tell me he was expecting a delivery, and I'm certainly not, but I can't think what else it could be at this time of day.

I pull open the door, surprised to find Brady Hanson standing there, and I have to smile.

I like Brady.

I always have.

He's been good to me over the years, keeping me company when I came home from college, and always being there... like the kind, decent man he is. Even now, it's not unheard of for him to drop by the house just to check I'm okay, which I've always thought was really sweet of him. We're a little isolated here, and Addy and I spend a lot of time alone, so it's good to know he's there if we need him.

He looks absolutely frozen to the bone, and I step back slightly.

"Come on in. It's even colder than it was earlier."

He nods his head, stepping into the house, and I close the door, turning to face him. My breath catches in my throat when I look up, able to see him properly now he's standing beneath the light.

Something's wrong. I can tell by the look in his eyes.

"What is it, Brady?"

He moves a little closer. "I'm sorry, Laurel."

"What for?"

He takes a breath. "It's Mitch."

My blood freezes, my body following it, my skin turning to ice within seconds. "W—What about Mitch?"

"There was an accident earlier this afternoon."

As he says those words, my legs give way and I grab for Brady's arms. He moves forward at the same time, holding me up, his hands beneath my elbows as he opens his mouth.

"No." I raise my voice. "Don't say it. Don't you dare say it, Brady."

"I have to. I'm sorry, but I have to." He shakes his head, and a sound fills the air around us. It's like the cry of an animal in mortal pain… a loud, unending wail… and it's coming from me. "Don't," he says, pulling me against his broad chest as my tears start to fall. "Please don't."

"Then tell me it's not true. Tell me he's not dead."

"I'm sorry," he repeats. "He died at the scene." I sob even louder, although I hear him add, "He wouldn't have felt a thing."

I'm aware of powerful arms around me, of a hard chest, and steady breathing, but how am I still here? How am I standing? The floor doesn't even feel solid beneath my feet, and I grab Brady's shoulders, clinging to him, my body shutting down.

"Mommy?"

Addy's voice reaches me through the haze of pain and confusion, but I can't move. It's beyond me.

I glance up at Brady. "Do something," I whisper. "Help her."

He turns, although he keeps one arm around me, and I cling to him. "Come here, Addy," he says in the softest of whispers.

"What's wrong with Mommy?"

"Mommy's upset, but she'll be okay."

Will I? I don't feel like I'll ever be okay again.

Even as I'm leaning in to Brady, he bends, lifting Addy. She stares at me, confusion etched on her innocent face, and my heart breaks, knowing that I've got to tell her… somehow. I can't face it, though, and I bury my head against Brady's chest again, his arm coming around my shoulders as I cry my life away.

Chapter Six

Brady

I'd expected this.

This and much more, and I know it's not over yet.

The thing is, I can't care for Laurel and Addy. Not at the same time. They both need undivided attention, and I can't give them that… especially not when Laurel can barely stand.

I hold her closer to my body, balancing Addy on my hip.

"Let's go into the living room," I say, and Addy frowns, although she doesn't ask why. She doesn't say anything and, supporting Laurel as best I can, I guide her through the archway that I know leads into the living room. There's barely enough light to see anything, but I make my way over to the couch, setting Addy down in the corner, and lowering Laurel beside her before I turn and move back to the doorway, switching on the lights.

The room is illuminated and I take in the enormous space, the mustard-colored couches and two matching chairs that surround the vast fireplace, and the paler yellow walls, dotted with pictures and photographs of Addy, growing up.

She looks over at me as I make my way back, crouching between her and her mom, who's just staring into space. I don't know what to say to a four-year-old in this situation… what Laurel would want me to say, or if she'd rather tell her daughter herself. She doesn't seem capable of speaking right now, and I think it's that thought that makes me realize I need help.

I pull out my phone, looking up Peony's number, and connect a call, keeping my eyes fixed on Addy, and a smile on my lips, which I hope is reassuring.

"Hello?" Peony answers, eventually.

"Hi. It's Brady."

"Hi. Is everything okay?"

"No. I'm sorry to bother you, but can you come to Laurel's place?"

There's a slight pause. "I was only there at lunchtime."

I'm not sure that's relevant. "Okay. But can you come back?"

"Has something happened?"

"Yes."

"Give me ten minutes."

She hangs up before I do, and I put my phone away, focusing on Laurel and Addy again. I'm torn as to which of them to comfort.

Laurel is in shock. Her eyes are fixed and her body stiff. I can barely hear her breathing. She's also unaware of Addy's presence in the room, and I know that's unheard of for her. She dotes on her daughter, so she must be somewhere too far away to be reached. That scares me, because I can remember my mom reacting like this when my dad died. I recall what happened to her in the days and weeks afterwards, and I know if I can't get Laurel back from wherever she's gone, the results might be catastrophic.

I need to get her to talk, to open up, but I can't do any of that now, so I take Addy's little hand in mine.

"Mommy's upset," I say, repeating the words I used earlier.

"Why?" she asks.

"She's had a shock, but she'll be okay."

I don't know what more to say. In a situation like this, where their mother has shut down on them, most kids would ask for their father, but Addy just nods her head, letting her hand rest in mine. I'd like to hope that means she feels safe with me, because she is. There's nowhere safer right now.

I hear a car approach and get to my feet, although Addy tries to keep hold of my hand.

"I won't be a minute, sweetheart. I've just gotta answer the door."

She stares up at me for a moment, and then nods her head, letting go of me. I give her a smile, which she returns, and then I glance at Laurel, who's still lost somewhere in her own mind.

It looks like Peony's arrived just in time.

I rush to the door, opening it, as Peony approaches. Her wild blonde hair is tied up behind her head and she's wearing stonewashed jeans and a thick blue sweater, with heavy-soled boots on her feet, although I notice they're not fastened properly. She must have rushed out of the house without tying them.

"What's happened?" she asks, and I step outside so Addy won't hear me.

"Mitch has been killed in a car accident." I don't have time to dress it up, but the shock hits Peony like a wrecking ball and as she staggers backwards, I grab her. "Are you okay?"

"Y—Yes," she says, then shakes her head. "Well, no." She clamps her hand over her mouth, her eyes glistening with unshed tears. "How's Laurel?" she says, pulling her hand away.

"She's shut down. I can't get to her, and Addy's confused."

"Because she doesn't understand?"

"Because her mom is in a stupor. She has no idea about Mitch yet. I didn't know what to say, or what Laurel would want me to say, or if she'd rather tell her herself."

Peony nods. "What do you need me to do?"

"Can you take care of Addy while I try to get through to Laurel?"

"Of course."

She takes a step forward, but I stop her, putting my hand on her arm. "Are you sure you're okay?"

She pauses, takes a breath and nods her head. "I'll be fine."

I step aside, letting her enter the house ahead of me, the decision already made that I won't say anything to Peony about Mitch's traveling companion. If I can't tell Laurel, there's no way I can tell anyone else... especially not her best friend. It would be unfair of me to do so, and then to ask Peony to keep it to herself.

No... if it's going to be a secret, it's one best kept to myself.

I follow her into the house, closing the door, and we make for the living room. Once inside, Peony goes straight to Addy, although I notice her glance at Laurel as she passes. She hesitates, like she wants to do something, or say something, but then focuses back on Addy again.

"Hey," she says in the softest of voices, kneeling down in front of her. "Do you wanna come play with me?"

Addy knows Peony better than anyone, except Laurel and Mitch, but even so, she hesitates, looking over at Laurel, and then glancing up at me, which is a surprise.

"I'm just gonna talk to Mommy for a while," I say.

"And you can show me your dolls," Peony adds, sensing that some persuasion is needed.

Addy tips her head. "Okay," she whispers, and Peony stands, taking Addy's hand and helping her down from the couch.

They walk away, but Peony stops on the threshold, looking back at me. "Just come find me if you need anything," she says.

"I will."

She nods, and they leave the room.

It instantly feels quiet in here. Too quiet. And although the wind is blowing outside, that just seems to accentuate this eerie silence. It feels cold too, and I sit beside Laurel, taking her icy hands in mine. She startles, looking up at me, like she'd forgotten I was here, which I imagine she had. She'd forgotten everything else.

"Brady?"

"Yes, Laurel."

"Tell me it's not true." She hadn't forgotten everything then.

"I can't."

She shakes her head. "This… this can't be happening."

In a way, I'm relieved. She's talking, and she knows Mitch is dead. When my dad died, I had to keep telling my mom over and over, for days and days, before it finally hit home. Laurel might be broken, but broken is better than lost. Broken can be mended. Lost can't always be found. I know that much.

"It'll be okay."

She looks up at me, unconvinced. I can't blame her for that. "I feel so numb."

"I know."

"No, you don't." She leans in to me, a sob leaving her lips as she weeps on my chest. She didn't mean that to hurt, but it did. It hurt more than I'll ever be able to tell her, because I have a really good idea of how she feels. I've lived it. I've tasted it, felt it, died through it myself this afternoon, when I thought she was the passenger in Mitch's car.

And I never want to feel like that again.

She's shaking in my arms, and I hold her close against me, hating the fact that she's grieving so hard for a man who wasn't worthy of her.

I can't say that, though. I can't even hint at it.

Instead, I let her cry, because it's better than the catatonic state she was in just now. Any amount of emotion is better than the dead look she had in her eyes a moment ago, and I'll take it.

I'll take anything as long as she's not just staring at the wall, like the life's gone out of her.

"Oh… the baby," she whimpers in the most forlorn voice I've ever heard.

Baby? I know I heard her right, but not even Mitch can have been that heartless. Can he?

"Are you pregnant, Laurel?"

The sadness in her eyes breaks my heart, but I need to get used to the crushing pain in my chest. It won't be the last time that happens.

"N—No." I struggle to hide my relief as she catches her breath. "We wanted to have another baby. But I've just realized, it's never gonna happen now, is it?" That hurts. Man, that hurts, but I swallow it down, burying yet more pain… adding it to all the rest. "We were gonna talk it through properly this evening," she says. "Mitch said he'd come home early. He promised he'd…" Her voice fades, and she leans against me again, putting her feet up on the couch and laying out. In any other circumstances, sitting here like this would be a dream come true, but as it is, it's becoming more and more of a nightmare with every passing moment.

Come home early? Based on what we found at the scene of the accident, he didn't intend coming home at all.

Asshole.

I turn slightly, so I can hold her, stroking her hair, the intimacy of the moment not lost on me, although she seems oblivious to everything… including who I am. She just needs someone to cling to, and I'm okay with that.

This isn't about me.

It's about Laurel, and her grief for a man who lied to her… over, and over, and over.

*

We're still in exactly the same position when Peony comes back in. I don't know how much time has passed, and I honestly don't care. I half expected Laurel to fall asleep, but I can tell from her breathing that she's still awake, even if neither of us has said a word.

Peony doesn't bat an eyelid. She just steps into the room.

"Addy's getting tired. I need to give her something to eat and put her to bed." She glances at Laurel, and then back at me again. I nod my head.

"Can you fix her something?" I ask.

"Of course. I was just wondering if Laurel wanted anything."

It seems odd that she's talking to me when Laurel is here with us, in the room, but I guess Laurel is so inanimate, it probably seems easier.

I can't answer for her, though, so I shift slightly, leaning back, and although she takes a moment to register the movement, she lets out a sigh, looking up at me.

"Do you want anything to eat?" I ask.

She frowns, confused by my question, which just goes to show she's heard nothing of my conversation with Peony.

"Eat?"

"Yes. Peony's gonna fix something for Addy, and she wondered if you wanted anything."

"Oh… No, thank you."

She's talking to me, unaware of Peony's presence in the room, and once she's answered, she rests her head on my chest again.

I glance over her at Peony, disappointed that Laurel won't even try to eat, but grateful that Peony's here to care for Addy.

"Will you be okay?" I ask.

"I'll be fine."

She glances down at Laurel again, her eyes filling with tears, which she wipes away with the backs of her hands.

"Peony?"

She shakes her head. "I'm okay."

She isn't, but we both know, no matter how hard this is, we have to get through it. I know she'll cry her eyes out when she gets home to Ryan, and I'm relieved she's got him to lean on.

The thought of going back to my empty house and worrying about Laurel all night isn't appealing, but I'll think about that later.

For now, I've got other things on my mind.

I brush my hand down Laurel's arm, hoping to get her attention, but she just snuggles against me. It's a lovely feeling, but I can't help wondering if she's imagining I'm Mitch... and while I don't mind being her shoulder to cry on, there are limits.

"Laurel?" I whisper, and she tenses, and then sits up again, looking at me.

I'm bringing her back to reality, and I can see in her eyes it's the last place she wants to be. "Yes?" Her voice is a mere whisper, which clutches at my heart.

"You need to eat. Maybe not right now, but later. You can't go without food."

"I—If I eat, I'll be sick."

A tear trickles down her cheek, and without thinking, I wipe it away with my thumb. She gasps and I'm about to apologize when she takes my hand in hers, in the most innocent of moves.

"Thank you, Brady."

"What for?"

"Being here. Letting me do this." She releases my hand, picking at her thumbnail. "I just need to feel grounded for a while... safe. You know?" She looks up at me, that sadness breaking my heart yet again, although there's some solace in the fact that she's knows it's me she's leaning on, and not Mitch.

"You're safe, Laurel." I'll make damn sure of it. She doesn't smile, although I wish she would... wish she could. Instead, she nods her head and goes to lean in to me again. "There's something else I need to ask you." She sits back, but doesn't say a word. The effort is too much, I think. "Do you want to tell Addy about what's happened before she goes to bed?"

She pulls away now, putting more distance between us. "How? How am I supposed to tell her?" she says, shaking her head.

"Do you want me to do it?" She stills, gazing right at me, like she's giving that idea some serious thought.

"It would be so easy to say yes, and I'd love you for taking that responsibility off of my shoulders..." She doesn't mean that in the way I want her to, so I don't react to those words leaving her lips, or the effect they have on my crumbling heart. "But it's something I have to do."

"Okay. Shall I ask Peony to bring Addy in here?"

"No." She shakes her head again. "I'm not ready. I can't do it yet."

I want to ask when, but I can't. Personally, I don't think it's right for Addy to be kept in the dark, but it's not my call.

"Is Mommy better?"

Addy's voice startles Laurel out of her rest and she sits up, moving away from me slightly. She'd been leaning against me, with my arm around her for some time, hopefully feeling grounded and safe, but reality just walked back in the door, in the shape of her adorable daughter, who's now wearing pale pink pajamas, and is carrying a fluffy orange teddy bear.

"Mommy's tired," I say into the awkward silence.

Peony's right behind Addy, and she follows the little girl into the room, but stops short when Addy comes up to the couch, standing in front of Laurel.

"Are you tired, Mommy?" Addy says, looking into her mother's face, her own etched with child-like worry.

"I am a little, but I'll be okay." Laurel's reply is accompanied by a half-hearted smile, and after just a second's hesitation, she pulls Addy into her arms, hugging her close. I half expect Laurel to cry, but she doesn't. She holds it together. Just.

"Are you gonna come upstairs, and I'll read you a story?" Peony's voice cuts through the silence, and Addy leans back, a little confused, her eyes switching from Peony to her mom before she seems to make a decision and steps away.

"Goodnight, Mommy," she whispers. "I hope you feel better tomorrow."

I hear Laurel gulp. "Goodnight, baby girl."

Addy runs over to Peony, who takes her hand, leading her from the room, without a backward glance.

"Can you read the donkey story?" Addy asks.

"I can if you show me which one it is." Peony's voice fades as they go up the stairs and Laurel sits back against me.

"She loves that story."

"Do you read it to her a lot?"

"I do at the moment. I get her new ones whenever I can, but she always comes back to the one about the donkey."

"Kids like continuity, I guess." I have no idea, not having any of my own, but I imagine that's how it works.

"They do. At least, Addy does." She sits up a little. "What's she gonna say when I tell her? How's she gonna react when she finds out her daddy isn't…?" Her words are drowned by a sob and she throws herself at me. I catch her, because I always will, and hold her close against me. "I can't do this, Brady."

"Yes, you can. You're stronger than you think."

"No, I'm not."

"Then I'll help you."

She seems to calm a little, and I stroke her hair again, hoping it helps.

She's still sniffling when Peony comes back into the room.

"Addy's asleep," she whispers, and I feel Laurel relax against me. I nod my head at Peony, wondering if she'll come and sit with us now. She doesn't move, though, other than to tilt her head toward the door, making it clear she needs to see me, away from Laurel.

I sit back, and Laurel looks up at me, frowning. "I've just got to talk to Peony."

"You're not leaving?" The panic in her eyes at the thought of my departure does something toward mending my heart.

"No. I'll only be a minute or two. I promise."

She nods her head, sitting upright, and letting me stand. Her hair's a mess, her face awash with tears, and although I half expect her to lie down and rest her head again, she doesn't. She sits, like she's waiting for me to come back.

I wander over to Peony and step aside while she goes out into the lobby, following close behind her. She turns to face me, looking up into my eyes.

"Is Addy really asleep?" I ask.

"Yes. She's fine."

"Have you told her anything?"

"No. I think she's worried about Laurel, but she hasn't mentioned Mitch at all."

I nod my head. "Okay."

She takes a deep breath. "I'd like to stay and help some more… maybe even spend the night, but I really can't."

"Oh…" I'm a little surprised by that and do a poor job of hiding it.

"I'm sorry, but the thing is, I'm pregnant, and the tiredness is overwhelming." She shakes her head. "Although it's nothing compared to the morning sickness. To be honest, the thought of spending an evening away from Ryan, and then waking up without him…"

I put my hand on her shoulder, and she stops talking. "It's okay. You don't have to apologize. I should be the one doing that. If I'd realized, I wouldn't have asked you to come… or had you running around after Addy."

"You'd have managed by yourself, would you?"

"No, but…"

"It's fine, Brady. Laurel's my best friend, and I want to be here. Besides, I seem to be okay during the day, once I've thrown up for about an hour, that is. And I only start to feel truly exhausted at this time of night."

"I hope Ryan's looking after you."

She smiles. "He is. He's…" She stops talking. "It feels wrong to talk about my husband when Laurel's just lost hers."

"You can't think like that."

"Can't I?"

"No. You and Ryan have every reason to celebrate, and you should."

"I'm not sure I can now. Not when Laurel's so broken."

"Laurel will mend. It'll take time, but she'll get there, and we'll help her."

She smiles. "You're a good man, Brady," she says, and I shake my head. "You are, and even if she can't show it right now, Laurel's grateful. She knows how much she owes you."

"She owes me nothing." I stop speaking before I give myself away and step back slightly. "You go home to Ryan and get some rest. I'll be fine here."

She nods. "I can come back in the morning once I've finished being sick."

"That would be great, if you could. I'll have to go to work tomorrow, and I don't feel comfortable leaving Laurel by herself all day."

"No. But don't worry. I'll be here." That's a relief, and Peony steps away, although she stops and turns back. "I probably should have mentioned… no-one knows about me being pregnant yet, except Gabe Sullivan, and possibly Remi, if he's told her, so do you think you could keep it to yourself?"

"You haven't told Laurel?"

"No. We decided not to tell anyone until after the first scan, but Ryan felt he had to explain to Gabe why he might be absent from work from time to time."

"I see. Well… you don't need to worry. Your secret's safe with me."

There's no way I'd tell Laurel about it, given the hopes she harbored with Mitch. They might have been ill-founded, but Laurel doesn't know that, and I doubt she'd react well to Peony's news.

"Thanks," she says, heading for the door. "I'll see you tomorrow."

"Okay."

Once she's gone, the house feels quiet again, and I take a moment just to breathe, to regroup, because I have no idea what's coming next. All I know is I feel so impotent. Peony's right. Laurel is broken, and although I know she'll mend eventually, seeing her like this is killing me.

"Brady?" Laurel's voice makes me jump and I turn, going straight back into the living room.

"I'm here."

She looks up at me, sighing with something that looks like relief. "I thought…"

"You thought I'd left?" She doesn't reply, and I wander over and sit beside her, where I was before. "I told you I wouldn't."

She nods her head. "Has Peony gone?"

"Yeah, but she said she'll come back tomorrow morning." That information barely seems to register. She doesn't react at all, and I move just a little closer to her. "Can I get you anything? You've had nothing to eat or drink for hours."

"I don't want anything… other than to fall asleep and wake up tomorrow to find this has all been a bad dream."

"I can't give you that. It's not a dream."

Her eyes fill with yet more tears. "It's not, is it? He's really dead."

"Yes, he is. I'm sorry."

Her body convulses with something that looks like pain, and as she sobs, I grab her, pulling her into my arms. She comes willingly, nestling her head against my chest.

"Make it stop, Brady. Please, make it stop."

I wish I could. I wish I could take this pain from her, and if I could, I would. But even telling her the truth about Mitch wouldn't help. It would just make things worse. She's in hell now, but how would she feel if she knew the man she loved so much was abandoning her for a new life with another woman? How would she feel if she discovered the life they had together was, in reality, a lie?

I can't do that to her… and I won't, no matter how much it hurts to watch her grieve for him.

"Do you want to go to bed?" I ask. She must be exhausted, and sleep might help.

She nods her head. "I think so."

"Okay."

She sits up, and I stand, helping her to her feet. She seems to have shrunk in on herself, but that's understandable, and I take her hand in mine, leading her from the room.

"Can you manage the stairs?" I ask. "Or do you want me to carry you?"

"I think I can walk." She keeps a hold of my hand as she puts her foot on the first step, and then looks upward, like she's got a mountain to climb.

"Come here." I bend, lifting her into my arms, and before she can say a word, I climb the remaining stairs. "Which way?" I ask once we're at the top.

"That room there." She nods toward the door at the back on the left-hand side of the wide hall, and I stride over, opening it, and carrying her inside.

I set her down on the floor beside the bed, turning on the lamp, and closing the drapes before I return to her. I'd love to stay and help her out of her gray pants and pale blue sweater... but I can't, so I stand in front of her, looking down into her bewildered face.

"Will you be okay?" I ask. She looks up, something like fear crossing her eyes.

"Why? Are you going home now?"

"Do you want me to?"

"No." She reaches out, grabbing my arm. "Please don't go. Don't leave me."

Oh, God... I love you so much.

"I won't. If you need me to stay, I'll sleep on the couch."

"Th—There's a guest bedroom next door. You can sleep in there."

"If you're sure?"

She nods, turning around and studying the room like she's never seen it before. It's less feminine than I'd expected, and for a second, I wonder if this room's been changed very much since she married Mitch. The walls are pale gray, the bedding a shade darker, and the drapes even darker still.

"I hate it in here," she whispers.

"I'm sorry?"

"I hate the decor. I always did." So I was right.

"Why didn't you change it?"

She turns, staring up at me. "Because M—Mitch didn't want to. The entire house was kinda dark and drab, and although I know he paid a fortune to have it done when he moved in, I didn't like any of it. M—Mitch let me redecorate some of the other rooms, but not this one."

She's struggling over his name, taking another piece out of my heart, and while I want to tell her she can do what she likes now he's gone, it's too soon for that.

"Don't worry about it now," I say instead and she sighs, nodding again. "I'll leave you to get undressed, but I'll only be next door if you need me. Okay?"

"Okay," she whispers, sitting on the edge of the bed. There's nothing more I can do or say, and staying here is just prolonging the agony. I can't be sure what she'll do once I'm gone, but hopefully she'll get into bed, and maybe exhaustion will get the better of her, and she'll sleep for a while.

I hope so.

I make my way to the door, turning on the threshold.

"Goodnight, Laurel."

She doesn't reply, but I didn't expect her to, and I pause for a second, watching as she stares at the floor in front of her, and then I close the door quietly behind me.

Laurel isn't the only one who hasn't eaten or drunk anything for a while, and although I'm not hungry, I am thirsty.

I make my way down the stairs and into the kitchen, where I find a glass and pour myself some milk, drinking it down while I wander around checking the doors and windows are locked, and putting out the lights.

Mitch didn't build this house, so he's not responsible for the layout, which isn't as open-plan as I would have expected. Having separate rooms works, though, and they're all enormous, so it never feels enclosed at all. As Laurel said, she's put her stamp on the place since their marriage, and as I wander past the stairs and into Addy's playroom, I can't help smiling.

The walls may be a neutral off-white, but almost everything else in here is pink, including the bunting that hangs around the windows. Somehow, I can't imagine Mitch approved of that... or the fairy lights around the fireplace, but I'll bet Addy loves them.

I turn everything off, and make my way back to the living room, switching off the lights before I return, across the lobby, to the kitchen.

Peony obviously cleared away after she'd cooked dinner for Addy. This place is spotless, and I put my glass into the dishwasher, then wander through to the dining room beyond. In here, the walls are the palest of greens, and the furniture a very light beech colored wood, with a bowl of flowers in the center of the table. I hate the thought of Laurel and Mitch sharing romantic dinners in here, so rather than dwelling, I check the doors to the outside are locked and turn out the lights, passing back through the kitchen on my way up the wide, winding stairs.

I pause by Laurel's door, but there's no sound. At least she's not crying, which is something, and I head for the next room along, letting myself in.

The moment I turn on the light, I recognize Laurel's hand at work, yet again. There's nothing of Mitch's dour colors in here, and like Addy's playroom and the living and dining rooms downstairs, this room is much more pleasing to the eye. The color scheme is white, with a hint of peach, the only accent being a duck-egg blue blanket that's folded over the end of the bed. I smile as I close the door, because this is just the kind of room I would have imagined Laurel having.

The bed isn't as big as the one next door, but it's more than adequate for me, and I remove my holster, leaving it on the chair by the window, as I close the drapes. I kick off my shoes, and undo my shirt, folding it over the back of the chair, although I don't remove anything else, remaining in my pants and t-shirt, and I lie down on the bed. I don't bother getting into it, although it's a little cold, so I pull up the blanket, which is even softer than it looks, and stare at the ceiling.

I can't even think straight. My mind is in a whirl of so many emotions.

First and foremost is anger with Mitch. How could he have treated Laurel like that? There's no other interpretation for what we found at the crash site. He was clearly cheating on her. Just the way in which Kaylee Prentice was dressed was enough to give that away. I can't believe it was a recent thing, either… not given the fact that they had their bags packed and stashed in the trunk of Mitch's car.

So Mitch must have been sleeping with Kaylee for some time.

What was wrong with him?

Why would he do that?

If I were lucky enough to call Laurel mine, I'd never even look at another woman.

What am I saying? I haven't looked at another woman in ages, and Laurel is nowhere near being mine.

She wants me here, though. There's no doubt about that. But that's only because she needs the comfort and security of having a man around. Any man would probably do, although I can't help wondering if maybe it helps that I'm the sheriff. I don't mind if that's the case. If my badge gives her an added feeling of safety, I'm okay with that.

I'm just someone to lean on, and even if it breaks my heart to know I can't be anything more, I'll be that someone for as long as she needs me.

"No… No…"

I wake to the sound of screaming, and leap out of bed.

I take a moment to get my bearings. The room is in darkness, but I remember where I am, and head straight for the door, recalling the layout of the guest room.

"No…"

The piercing sound echoes through the house again, and I dart along the hall to Laurel's room, opening the door.

The light is on beside the bed and she's sitting on the edge of the mattress, wearing a skimpy white pajama top and a pair of pink shorts, her bare feet touching the floor, her hands gripping the sheets on either side of her.

I do my best to ignore the way she looks, and how I feel about her, and stride over, sitting down.

"Laurel?"

She jumps, turning to me, like she hasn't even noticed me coming into the room, her face crumpling as she bursts into tears. Her arms come around my neck and she leans against me, her breasts heaving.

I do my best to ignore that, too… although it's a struggle, and I hesitate for just a second before I put my arms around her. She clings to me, tears raining down her cheeks.

"It'll be okay," I whisper, avoiding the temptation to kiss her forehead, even though it's right by my lips. *Get a grip, man.*

She looks up, her eyes pooled with sadness. "It'll never be okay again."

I'm not sure how much more of this my heart can take.

It'll take as much as it has to. As much as she needs.

"It will be. It has to be."

"How? Why?"

"Because of Addy."

She swallows hard, then nods her head. "I have to tell her, don't I?"

"Yes."

She wipes her tears with the back of her hand. "C—Can you be here with me when I do?"

"Of course I can. But I think it might be a good idea to have Peony around too, don't you? It's gonna be hard for you, and she can help."

She nods. "She's been such a good friend."

"She has."

She looks up at me. "And so have you."

Friend? Is that what I want?

Does it matter what I want?

Not really.

"We can tell her tomorrow."

"Yes."

She sounds more certain now. Less scared.

"You need to sleep."

She nods and I stand, pulling back the covers. Without me saying a word, she lies down again, and I keep my eyes fixed on her face, rather than the way her top rides up, revealing a strip of flesh around her middle. I don't look at that at all… well, hardly at all.

I pull up the covers and she snuggles down a little.

"Do you want anything?" I ask.

"No."

"Okay."

I reach over to switch off the light, but she grabs my hand, holding on tight. "Brady?"

"Yes?"

"Thank you."

I shake my head and use my other hand to turn out the light, so she can't see the sorrow in my eyes.

Chapter Seven

Laurel

What's that smell?

I crack my eyes open, although it's a struggle. They feel swollen and scratchy, although I don't know why. The drapes are closed, but I can already tell it's gray outside, just from the lack of light in here.

That smell is driving me crazy. What the hell is it?

I sit up, resting on my elbows, and inhale.

Of course.

It's bacon.

Mitch must be cooking breakfast.

A smile touches my lips.

He hasn't done that for...

Mitch.

Oh, God... how could I have forgotten?

Tears fall, slowly at first, and then in torrents.

He'll never cook breakfast again, will he? Never stand by the stove, with that smile on his face, watching me as I fix the coffee, his eyes wandering, drinking me in.

I ache for him, even though I know there's no point in thinking like that. There's no point in anything anymore… except Addy. I let out a sigh. I have to think of Addy…

No matter how much of a struggle it is, I have to get up, too. She'll be wondering where I am, although she knows she can come find me, if she needs to.

In the meantime, though, I need a shower.

I throw back the covers and drag myself into the bathroom, catching sight of myself in the mirror as I pass. God, I look horrendous. My hair is such a mess; my face is pale and my eyes puffy, which makes sense of why it was so hard to open them.

I strip out of my pajamas, leaving them on the floor, and step into the shower, letting the water flow over me. It's a conscious effort to keep it together, but I take deep breaths, and go through the motions of washing, rinsing my hair before I step out again, the smell of bacon still wafting in the air.

Who's cooking?

It must be Brady, I guess.

He slept in the guest bedroom last night, because I asked him to. I was scared of being alone… terrified I'd wake up in the middle of the night and remember.

Which is exactly what happened.

I sat on the edge of the bed, fear overwhelming me, barely able to breathe, struggling to understand it all… and then, just when I thought I couldn't take any more, Brady was there, right beside me.

He held me and told me everything would be okay… that it had to be okay because of Addy. He was right, of course. I can't fall apart. I'm a mom. Falling apart isn't allowed.

I wrap a towel around myself, fixing it tight beneath my arms, and wander out of the bathroom, nearly jumping out of my skin when I see Brady, standing by the door to the hall.

"Oh... shit... sorry... excuse me," he mutters, averting his eyes to the window, even though the drapes are still closed.

"It's okay." Everything's covered, and I'm fairly sure there was more of me on display in the middle of the night, when he came in and comforted me. "I just took a shower."

He looks back at me again. "So I see. That's good."

Is it? It ought to be a normal function, but it felt tortuous to do it, and I nod my head, acknowledging his words, taking in the fact that he's still wearing his pants and t-shirt. I'm fairly sure that's what he had on when he came in here last night... but that makes sense, doesn't it? He was wearing his uniform when he arrived yesterday evening, and doesn't have a change of clothes. Why would he? He wasn't expecting to stay.

My brain feels like it's dragging itself through molasses today, each thought process taking ten times longer than usual, and none of them happening in the right order.

"Did you need me for something?" I ask, wondering at last why he's standing by my bedroom door.

"I just came to tell you there's some bacon and pancakes downstairs."

The smell of bacon is still driving me crazy, but it feels wrong to eat... or even think about eating.

"I'm not hungry."

He sucks in a long breath, his chest expanding to ludicrous proportions, but just when I think he's going to turn away and leave, he steps into the room, coming over and standing about two feet away from me.

"I get it, Laurel. I really do. But you're a mom. You need to think about Addy."

"I know that." I've just been telling myself the same thing. It's how I persuaded myself out of bed and into the shower, for Christ's sake.

"Then surely you know you need to eat. Aside from the fact that you need to look after yourself so you can be a mom to Addy, she needs to see you being as normal as you can be. She knows something's wrong, but you haven't told her what yet, and…"

"Okay!"

He startles at my raised voice and I burst into tears, my head falling into my upturned hands right before he pulls me into his arms.

"I'm sorry," he whispers, stroking my wet hair.

I look up, keeping my arms between us, worried that if I cling to him like I did yesterday – and like I need to now – the towel might fall.

"No. I'm the one who's sorry. I didn't mean to shout."

"It's okay."

"No, it's not. Mitch is dead." I see something that looks like sadness crossing his eyes, and I remember they were at school together. They might not have been great friends, but they've known each other most of their lives. This can't be easy for him, either.

"I get how hard this is for you," he says, his voice little more than a murmur, his dark brown eyes fixed on mine. "But you can't lose yourself in it."

He's right. I know he is, and after a few moments, I take a step back, noticing the damp patch on his t-shirt.

I reach out, rubbing my hand over it, keeping the other one firmly on the towel, and hear a slight hitch in Brady's breathing.

"I'm sorry," I say.

"What for?"

"I've made your t-shirt wet." He shakes his head, but doesn't say anything else. "I—I guess I should get dressed."

"Okay. I—I'll keep your breakfast warm downstairs."

I don't know why we've both started stammering, but I nod my head and he gazes at me for a second or two before he turns and leaves, closing the door behind him.

My hair feels cold, water dripping onto my shoulders, but I don't have the energy to dry it, so I brush it through and put it into a ponytail. That's almost unheard of for me. I've always taken pride in my hair, and usually wear it loose around my shoulders, in a crisp, neat cut. It's what Mitch liked, but he's not here, is he?

I blink back the tears that are brimming in my eyes, and wander into the dressing room, grabbing the first pair of jeans I find, along with a chunky sweater, some underwear, and a pair of thick socks, carrying it all back into the bedroom.

Before I start dressing, I open the drapes, unsurprised by the gray clouds overhead, or the chill that shudders through my body. Somehow the weather feels appropriate to what's happened, and I turn around, sitting on the edge of the bed, and pulling away the towel.

It doesn't take long to get dressed, and although I'd normally make the bed, I can't be bothered. What's the point when I'll be falling into it again later… on my own?

I fight back the tears, yet again, and wander to the door, pulling it open. The smell of bacon is even stronger out here, and I trudge down the stairs, wondering how I'm going to face the day.

"Why are you drinking tea?"

I can hear Addy from here, firing questions already. It's what she does over breakfast. Like her brain has had time to store them up overnight.

"Because I like it," Brady says.

"Not coffee?"

"No. Not with breakfast."

He's being very patient with her, considering he can't be used to being interrogated by a four-year-old first thing in the morning.

"But you like coffee too, don't you?" she asks, still talking to him as I come into the room.

"Yes. I just prefer tea first thing in the morning."

They're both sitting at the island unit, eating bacon and pancakes. Addy's still wearing her pajamas and has a glass of milk in front of her, and Brady has clearly made a pot of tea, which is on the countertop in front of him. He takes a sip, turning slightly and noticing me, putting the cup down quickly and getting to his feet.

"Hey," he says and Addy turns.

"Mommy!"

I don't want her to struggle down from her seat, so I walk over and give her a hug, holding her slender body against mine for a few moments longer than usual. She doesn't seem to mind, and when I pull back, I see Brady has retrieved a third plate of bacon and pancakes, and has placed it on the island unit, on the other side of Addy.

"Sit down," he says. "Eat it while it's hot." I do as he says, waiting while he pours me a coffee from the pot. "Addy told me you drink coffee with breakfast," he says with a smile.

"I gathered it had become a topic of conversation."

"Yeah." His smile widens, and he sits back down, looking at me over the top of Addy's head, and nodding toward the plate before me. "Eat something."

I stare at the stacked pancakes and crispy bacon, my stomach rumbling, and although I didn't think I was hungry, I pour over a little maple syrup and pick up the fork, taking a mouthful of the fluffiest pancakes I've ever eaten in my life.

God, they're good, and I glance at Brady, who gives me another smile, encouraging me to keep going, I think.

I don't need much encouragement, and I slice up some bacon, which tastes salty and sweet, and mighty fine.

I manage all the pancakes, because they're too good not to eat, but only half the bacon, and when I push my plate away, Brady glances down at it, and then looks up at me.

"Is that okay?" I ask, and he nods.

"It's better than I thought you'd do."

I feel relieved for some reason, and let out a sigh, sipping at my coffee, just as Addy twists in her seat, leaning closer to me.

"Can I have a hug, Mommy?"

"Of course."

I lift her onto my lap, holding her close, and look up to see Brady staring at us. He takes a deep breath, then gets up.

"I'll clear away."

"It's fine. I'll do it all later."

He shakes his head, ignoring me, and stacks the dishes, putting them into the dishwasher. Once he's finished, he rinses his hands, drying them off, and then pulls his phone from his pocket, wandering into the hall.

I don't know who he's calling, or why, but it must be private, and none of my business, which is fair enough. He stayed here last night, but for all I know, he could have a girlfriend… or at least someone special he needs to talk with. I might have always considered Brady as a friend, but we're not on the kind of terms where he's felt it necessary to discuss his personal life with me. I'm sure he has male friends for that, just like I have Peony for when I need to talk about…

I swallow down the lump in my throat, thinking about all the time I've spent with Peony, talking about Mitch, and how happy we've been together. I'm pretty sure she used to be jealous of my perfect marriage, especially when Luca left and she was on her own, trying to run the farm. Except that doesn't apply now, does it? She's got Ryan, and I've got…

Oh, God…

I hug Addy to me, fighting back tears, wondering about the void in my life that Mitch's death has left, and what on earth I'm supposed to do without him.

Brady's shrugging on his shirt when he comes back into the room, and I glance up at him.

"Are you okay?" he asks, noticing my tears, I guess.

I nod my head. "Are you going?"

He smiles. "I have to. I need to go home to shower and change my clothes, and then get to work. Peony's on her way over, though. I just called her to check."

I sigh out my relief. I won't be alone.

He stands on the other side of the island unit, buttoning up his shirt, his eyes dropping to Addy, who's still nestling on my lap.

"I'll be back later," he says. "We can talk things through then, if you like?"

For a moment, I wonder what he's talking about, and then I remember.

"You mean about M-I-T-C-H?" I ask and Brady nods his lead, frowning. "Don't look so confused. I often spell things out when I don't want a certain person to know what I'm saying."

"Are you talking about me?" Addy says, looking up at me.

"Maybe… maybe not."

She frowns, and I turn back to Brady to find he's smiling down at her, before he looks at me, his eyes softening even more.

"It'll be okay, Laurel," he says, his deep, mellow voice filling me with a confidence I didn't think I was capable of, and I nod my head before he leaves the room and I kiss Addy's head.

She looks up at me. "What was that for, Mommy?"

"Because I love you."

"I love you, too."

Brady returns in his full uniform, including his holster and coat, which is undone, his gun exposed, hanging from his hip. My eyes fall to it, and he follows the line of my gaze.

"I don't like wearing it around her," he says, looking at Addy.

"It's okay. It's your job."

He nods, although he looks less than convinced. "I can't be sure exactly what time I'll be back, but I'll try not to make it too late."

I nod my head. "Thank you."

"You don't have to thank me."

"Yes, I do. Not just for coming back tonight, but for being here last night, and this morning."

He steps a little closer, leaning over the island unit. "I'll be here for as long as you need me, Laurel."

It feels like I'll need him forever. The thought of standing on my own two feet seems impossible, but I can't tell him that. He'd think I was being pathetic… and I guess I am.

"Can I get you some more coffee?" he asks, when I don't reply, and I nod my head.

"Yes, please."

He takes my cup, bringing it back full, and putting it in front of me, just as the doorbell rings.

"I'll get it," he says, although Addy wriggles down from my lap, and runs after him.

"Is that Aunty Pee-Nee?" she cries, and I have to smile.

It seems some things never change…

I can't remember very much of what's happened today.

Brady left within minutes of Peony's arrival, and although I was never alone, I have to admit, I missed him almost the second he walked out the door. I know that's only because he's such a tower of strength, but I missed the feeling of safety that comes with his presence.

It's silly, I know, but that's how it is.

Peony's been fantastic, though.

She's taken care of everything, from getting Addy dressed, to doing the laundry, and cooking mac and cheese for lunch. I didn't eat very much, but it's one of Addy's favorites, and she thoroughly enjoyed it.

I haven't had to think about a thing all day, which is just as well, because I'm not capable. Every train of thought leads to Mitch, and that leads to crying… although God knows where the tears are coming from. I should be all cried out by now.

Except, every time I think of him, fresh tears form, and it seems there's nothing I can do to stop them from falling.

Peony kept Addy occupied all day, although she was able to leave her watching cartoons in the playroom for a while, just after lunch, and came to find me in the living room. I was staring into space at the time, and only realized she was there when she cleared her throat and I noticed she was already sitting at the other end of the couch, facing me.

"Are you okay?" she asked.

"No."

She shook her head. "It was a silly question, really."

"No, it wasn't. I should be coping better."

She sat forward. "Why? After what's happened…" Her voice faded, like she didn't know what to say. "I think you're entitled to fall apart." She finally found the words and let out a sigh.

"Except I'm not, am I? I've got Addy to think about."

"I can take care of Addy."

I wanted to ask how long for. There didn't seem to be any light at the end of the dark tunnel I was in, but it was unreasonable to expect anyone else – even my best friend – to put their life on hold indefinitely.

"Thank you," I said instead, and she tilted her head at me.

"I didn't realize you and Brady were such good friends."

"We're not. Not really."

"But he stayed the night, didn't he?"

"Yes. I asked him to. I didn't want to be alone."

She nodded, like she understood, and then she smiled. "I'll fix a chicken casserole for your dinner, shall I?"

"Is that okay?"

"Of course." She stood up, looking down at me. "Shall I make enough for Brady, too?"

"Yes, please." I didn't hesitate, and she didn't seem fazed by my answer, perhaps sensing that I wouldn't have been able to explain it.

The smells of onion and garlic, wine and chicken have been driving me crazy ever since. I might not be hungry, but whatever Peony has done, it's amazing.

Just like her, really.

Even so, I have to say, I'm relieved when I hear Brady's car pulling up outside.

It's getting late, and I know we have to tell Addy about her father before bedtime. I'm dreading it, but at least with Brady and Peony here, it should be easier… if such a thing can ever be called 'easy'.

Peony lets him into the house and I hear them whispering in the lobby for a minute or two before he walks into the living room.

I'd been expecting to see him in his uniform, so I'm surprised that he's wearing dark blue jeans and a cream-colored sweater.

"Sorry I'm a little later than expected," he says, sitting at the end of the couch, where I'm resting. "I thought it might be better if I changed out of my uniform before I came over."

"Is this because you don't like wearing your gun around Addy?" I ask, remembering what he said before he left this morning.

"Partly. But it's mostly because I thought she might find it easier to hear the news if we could keep it informal."

Of course. It makes perfect sense, and I could kick myself for not thinking of that myself.

"Thank you," I murmur and he shakes his head.

"You've gotta stop thanking me."

"Then you'll have to stop being so considerate."

"Never." He gets to his feet, gazing down at me. "Shall I go get Addy?"

I suck in a breath. "I guess so."

He hesitates, then crouches in front of me. "Are you okay?"

"No."

"How's today been?"

"I don't know. It feels like a blur."

He nods. "Let's get this over with, shall we?"

"Okay." He takes my hand, giving it a gentle squeeze, and then stands again, leaving the room. The empty silence is consuming. It's stifling. My nerves are on edge, raw and jagged, and I'm tempted to run from the room... to run from the house, out into the cold, and never come back.

The thought of frozen oblivion feels surprisingly warming, even welcoming, and I can't help thinking how much easier it would be if I didn't have to think, or feel anything... ever again. I shift forward on the couch, in readiness for standing up and leaving the house. I even contemplate where my shoes are, and decide I don't need them. My feet might get cold, but what does that matter when I'm searching for a frozen oblivion? The thought is so exhilarating, I can hardly wait to embrace it, but before I can move any further, Brady comes back, followed by Peony, who's holding Addy's hand, leading her into the room. The moment's lost. The thrill goes with it, and the emptiness returns.

"But I don't wanna come in here," Addy says, sulking. I can understand how she feels. I don't want to be here either.

"I know," Peony says, lifting her onto my lap. "But Mommy needs to talk to you."

Addy folds her arms, taking two attempts to get it right, and frowns up at me, although she doesn't say a word, and I wait for Brady and Peony to take a seat on either side of us.

It's like they're propping me up, which is just as well, because I feel as though I could fall at any minute.

Brady puts his arm behind me, kind of around me, and I lean against him just slightly, taking a deep breath.

"There's something I need to tell you," I whisper, and Addy looks up at me.

"What about?"

"Daddy. H—He's been in an accident." The words catch in my throat, drying my mouth as they tumble out.

"What kind of accident?" Addy asks. "Did he fall down?"

"No. It was a car accident." She nods her head, looking up at me expectantly, because she seems to know there's more to come. "I'm really sorry, baby girl, but he won't be coming home again."

I can't bring myself to say the word 'dead' to her, and even if I could, I don't think she'd understand it. She has no concept of what death means, thank God.

She stares up at me, looking confused, and while I expect her to cry, she doesn't. She simply nods her head, like this is the most natural thing in the world.

"Okay. Can I go play with my dolls now?"

I'm dumbfounded and, as she wriggles down onto the floor, I'm powerless to stop her.

"I—I'll go with you," Peony says, clearly as bemused as I am by my daughter's reaction, the two of them leaving the room.

The silence feels even more oppressive now, and I stare after them for a while, only turning to Brady when he shifts slightly in his seat.

"Is that normal?" I ask.

He shrugs. "Kids behave differently to adults. Besides, she's young, and…"

"But he's her father… or he was. No, he is." I sit back, unable to work out what I mean, or how to say it.

"Yes, but you're her rock, Laurel. You're the one she relies on, and who she spends most of her time with. Think about how she reacted yesterday when you were upset. It scared her to see you like that."

"I know, but surely she felt something for him."

"Why? I mean, when was the last time Mitch played with her, or took her out, or even made it home for dinner?"

There's an edge to his voice and I twist in my seat to face him. "He's been working long hours. It's not…"

"I get that, Laurel. I'm just saying they barely saw each other. From Addy's perspective, he was a stranger, so you can't blame her for not reacting to the news that she won't be seeing him anymore."

He has a point. "I—I guess she's gotten used to it being the two of us most of the time."

"Exactly. Her world begins and ends with you, Laurel. As long as you're here…"

"Don't." I cut him off, shaking my head and biting back my tears… yet again.

"Don't what?"

"Don't say that."

"Why not? It's the truth. Addy needs you."

"I know, but…"

"But what?"

I stare at my fingers, twisting them around in my lap. "Before you came in here with her just now, I—I was going to run away."

"Run away?"

"Yeah. I wanted to take off out there into the cold," I say, nodding to the window at the front of the house, and the icy darkness beyond it. "I wanted to end it. To end it all."

A tear falls onto my cheek, and Brady reaches over, pulling me closer to him, and holding me in his arms, my head resting on his chest.

"Never say that. You hear me? Don't even think it."

"I know… it was selfish of me. I should be putting Addy first."

"It's not that," he says, his voice hoarse for some reason. "At least it's not just that. Sure, Addy needs you, but there are other people here who care about you, too… people who love you, and who wanna help you." I lean back, looking up into his pained face. "If you ever feel like that again, come find me, talk to me. Okay? If I'm not here, call me, and I'll come over. Just don't… please don't ever…" His voice fades and he pulls me close again, letting me sob on his chest.

It's the slight backache that eventually makes me pull away, although he doesn't let go, and I stare down at his sweater for a moment.

"I've gotta stop crying on you," I say, gently patting his chest.

He shakes his head. "No, you don't. That's what I'm here for."

"Is it?"

"Yes," he says, with a soft smile.

"Why?" His smile fades, a frown forming in its place.

"Would you rather I wasn't?" He sounds a little offended, and I lean in to him.

"Not at all. It's just something Peony said earlier about you and I never having been great friends before. I guess that's true, isn't it?"

"Maybe. But that doesn't mean…"

"I'm not being critical, Brady. All I'm saying is, even if I don't fully understand why you're being so supportive, I'm glad you are. I'd be lost without you."

His smile returns. "If I'm being supportive, it's because I'm one of the many people here who cares about you." He stares into my eyes, then opens his mouth, like he's going to say something else. He doesn't, though. Instead, he snaps it closed again, and while I'd like to know what he was going to say next, I don't get the chance to find out because Peony comes into the room. I sit up and she smiles at me.

"I'm sorry, but Addy says she's hungry."

I nod my head. "She'll need a bath."

Peony bites on her lip. "I'd do it for you, but…"

I stand. "No, it's fine. I'll manage. You've done more than enough already." I step over to the door, aware that Brady is following. "How has Addy been?" I ask. "Has she talked about Mitch since I told her?"

Peony shakes her head. "She hasn't mentioned him at all. She's been engrossed with her dolls."

I let out a sigh. "This can't be normal."

"I'm not sure there's any such thing as 'normal' in a situation like this," she says.

"Do you think I should talk to her again?"

"I wouldn't if I were you. I think it's probably best to leave it for a while. We can all keep an eye on her and see how she responds over the next few days. She's so used to being away from Mitch, it might not hit her for a while."

"As long as we're here for her when it does," Brady says, and I turn, nodding my head.

"Thank you… both of you."

"I'll come back in the morning," Peony says, moving toward the front door, grabbing her purse and keys as she does. "I should be able to get here for around eight, if that's okay?"

"It's fine," I reply, only realizing then that Peony's talking to Brady, and not me. "Are you staying again tonight?" I ask him and he turns, looking down at me.

"Only if you want me to."

"I think I do. I don't like the idea of being here alone… not yet." He nods, although he doesn't smile, and a thought occurs to me. "If you've got plans, though…"

His brow furrows. "Plans?"

"Yes. I mean, if you've got a date, or something. I'm sorry, I've been making assumptions about you and your time, but you've got a life of your own, and…"

"I don't," he says, interrupting me. "I don't have… I mean, I'm not seeing anyone."

I don't think I've ever seen Brady look so embarrassed in my life, but it would be unfair to make anything of it when he's doing so much for me. "In that case…"

"I'll stay," he says, smiling at last.

Peony opens the door, a blast of icy air filtering in. "I'm going," she says with a shudder, and rushes to her car, jumping inside. Brady and I stand by the door, waving her off, and I'm reminded for a moment of my desire to run away. The very idea of it fills me with fear now. There's no warmth… no welcome exhilaration. But before I've even had time to process that thought, I feel Brady's arm come around me.

"It's okay," he whispers. "You're safe."

I've never needed to hear those words more in my life and I look up at him, hoping he can understand how much I appreciate his presence, even if I can't say anything.

Peony turns her car, driving away, and Brady pulls me back into the house, closing the door again, both of us relieved to shut out the freezing night air.

It would be nice to stand here and let Brady hold me for a while, but Addy's hungry. There are things I need to do.

"I'd better take Addy upstairs and get her ready for bed," I say, pulling back and looking up at him.

"Okay."

"We won't be long," I call over my shoulder, making my way through to the playroom.

Addy's inside, kneeling on the floor, with several of her dolls sitting in front of her in a circle.

"It's bath time," I say, and she looks up.

"Okay."

I'm surprised she's so compliant. Normally she wants another five minutes, and then another, and another, but tonight she's being much more accommodating than usual. That's a sure sign she's hungry.

She leads the way up the stairs, and I follow, taking her into the main bathroom, where I run a bubble bath, undressing her, and checking the water's the right temperature before setting her in the tub. Addy's always loved splashing, and tonight is no exception. Fortunately, though, I've learned to stay well out of the way, and although the floor has seen better days, by the time she's finished, I'm still fairly dry.

"Time to get out," I say eventually. Most nights, bath time is more about routine than washing, and she stands up holding out her arms to be lifted and wrapped up in the warm towel I've got ready for her. I take advantage of holding her and look into her upturned face. "Is everything okay?" I ask.

"Sure," she replies, confused by my question, and rather than pressing the point, I just nod my head, my confusion so much greater than hers.

Her pajamas are at the end of her bed, where Peony must have left them this morning, and I put them on my daughter, wishing I could understand why she doesn't seem to care that her father is dead.

Maybe I should have used that word, rather than telling her he wouldn't be coming home again… because let's face it, Brady was right. Mitch was hardly ever home in the first place.

"Can I go now, Mommy?" Addy says, and I realize I'm still holding on to her, even though she's ready for bed… well, ready for dinner.

"Of course." I let her go, and she tears from the room, rushing down the hall. "Be careful on the stairs," I call out as she thumps her way down them.

I follow at a slower pace, and by the time I get to the kitchen, Brady's just lifting Addy into her seat. There's silverware set out on the island unit, along with a glass of water for Addy, and wine for Brady and me.

"I hope this is okay?" he says, looking a little embarrassed. "I felt like a drink, and…"

I shake my head, and he stops talking. "I feel like one, too… so don't worry about it. And as for everything else, it's just perfect. Thank you."

He smiles, wandering to the stove. "Sit down. I've got this."

I'm not about to argue.

I know I should be coping better… should be able to fend for myself.

But I can't.

Chapter Eight

Brady

The funeral was almost as tough as breaking the news of Mitch's death.

In some ways, I think it was harder.

It was certainly more public.

Between the day of the accident and the day of the funeral, Laurel had been left pretty much to herself by the citizens of Hart's Creek. I'd made sure of it. People had stopped me in the street, asking how she was, if she needed anything, what they could do to help. It was kind of them, but I knew at least a small percentage of those concerned were more interested in finding out what was going on than they were in being of assistance to Laurel. I told them she was as well as could be expected, that Peony and I were taking care of everything, and there really wasn't anything that anyone could do. They looked at me then, with a mixture of sympathy and understanding. Again, it was kindly meant in most cases, and they asked me to pass on their condolences before going on their way. Those who were more interested in gossip pressed for more information… none of which was forthcoming. I wasn't about to tell anyone anything.

My need to protect Laurel and Addy had kicked into overdrive, and to be honest, I didn't care who knew.

Not that I think anyone guessed. I'm pretty sure everyone in town thought I was just doing my job, and maybe adding in a little extra special attention, because of the circumstances.

And I let them believe it.

I don't think most people in Hart's Creek knew that I'd been staying at Laurel's place every night, but I wouldn't have cared if they'd worked it out. At least, I wouldn't have cared anywhere near as much as I did when Laurel questioned it.

She was right when she said we'd never been 'great friends'. Those were her words, and they cut deep... not because they were true, but because I regretted the very fact of them. I'd have settled for great friendship, if that was all she was willing to offer. But we hadn't even had that. Passing acquaintance was about the best that we could muster... aside from the secret longing on my side.

What made it worse was my fear that she'd ask me to leave... that she'd realize our friendship didn't really extend to me spending so much time with her and Addy.

As it was, she didn't say any such thing. She just said she'd be lost without me, and my crumpled heart actually felt a spark of something hopeful.

Was that why I confessed to being one of the many people who care about her?

I don't know.

She didn't pick up on what I meant though, any more than she picked up on the way I nearly admitted to being one of the people who loves her... so it didn't matter.

Fortunately, Peony came in then to tell us Addy was hungry, and saved me from saying something I think I might have regretted, because even if I love Laurel more than anything in the world, I can't tell her that. Not when her grief for her lying, cheating asshole of a husband is still so profound.

It must be. Let's face it, she told me she'd wanted to end it all… to run off into the cold and never come back. It wasn't just her words that scared me, it was the desolate look in her eyes. It chilled me to the bone. I felt something similar when we were saying goodbye to Peony. That's why I put my arm around Laurel and told her she was safe. I wanted her to know I'd be there for her, no matter what, and I resolved there and then that I'd keep a closer eye on her, and call her every single day, just to make sure she's okay… and to hell with what anyone thought.

I've done that ever since.

To start with, I used the funeral as an excuse, so she didn't think my behavior was too odd, although I'm sure anyone who was thinking straight would have realized that nothing I was saying couldn't have been said over breakfast, or have waited until the evening.

Still… Laurel wasn't thinking straight.

On my days off, I gave Peony some respite and spent my time at the house with Laurel and Addy, taking on as much as I could… not just because of Peony's condition, but because I wanted to.

I'd booked the church at Laurel's request, once I knew Mitch's body was going to be released, and it was safe to set the date. The pastor was very accommodating and didn't even raise an eyebrow that he was dealing with the sheriff and not the next of kin.

"Laurel's struggling with it all," I said, and he nodded his head.

"It's understandable. I didn't know them very well, but I gather they were close."

I nodded my head, unable to give a voice to an outright lie while standing in a church. Laurel may have felt she was close to

Mitch, but there's no way Mitch could have been described as 'close' to Laurel when he was screwing one of his employees.

"It's so terribly sad," the pastor added.

"Yes, it is."

I couldn't deny that, although I doubted we were thinking along the same lines. But he hadn't held Laurel while she sobbed, or watched the grief eating away at her. He didn't know what Mitch had done, either.

Having booked the church and set the date for the funeral, Laurel needed to decide on the service she wanted. She put it off for as long as she could, but last Saturday evening, once Addy was in bed, I sat her down, explaining that decisions needed to be made.

"We've only got until Wednesday and the pastor needs to know what hymns you want… who's going to give the eulogy…"

She gazed up at me from her seat on the couch, like she didn't understand a word I was saying.

"Can't you decide?"

"Not about this, Laurel." I sat beside her. "I'm sorry, but you're gonna have to face it."

She sucked in a long breath, letting it out in stuttered pauses. It may have been nearly two weeks since Mitch's death, but she was no nearer coming to terms with it, and that broke my heart, every single day.

"I know nothing about hymns," she said. "Mitch never talked about religion, or anything like that." She spun around. "What about when you were younger? Did he go to church then?"

"Not that I can remember."

She twisted in her seat. "I keep forgetting you and he grew up together."

"We were in the same class at school." I didn't have the heart to tell her I'd done my level best to stay away from Mitch for most of my childhood and adolescence.

"What was he like?" she asked.

"Are you trying to avoid choosing hymns?" I said, smiling, while doing my best not to answer her question.

"No. I'm just interested. He never really spoke about his childhood."

She gazed into my eyes, like she was waiting, desperate for information... and I couldn't deny her, although I knew I'd have to be careful.

"I didn't know him that well."

"Really?" She seemed surprised, which was understandable. In a town like Hart's Creek, you get to know practically everyone... especially when your dad is the sheriff.

"Mitch was really into football, from quite an early age." That wasn't a lie. He was also into girls, but I wasn't going to say that.

"To the exclusion of making friends?"

I tilted my head one way and then the other, like I was having to think... which I wasn't. "I guess. He was ambitious. He wanted to make it big in the game, and I'm not sure that's a good fit with making close friends." It seemed to be a good enough fit with drifting through life, screwing around, and damaging people along the way, but that wasn't something Laurel wanted to hear.

"I never knew him when he was playing," she said. "But I think he was very different back then."

Not that different. I nodded my head. "Probably."

She turned away for a moment, and then looked back at me, moving closer. "So, he wasn't a particular friend of yours?"

"No. Why?"

She smiled, just slightly. "Because that would have made me the most selfish person in the world... focusing only on my grief and forgetting about yours."

I wanted to hold her then, to gaze into her eyes and kiss her, and tell her she had nothing to grieve for. Except that was impossible.

"You don't have a selfish bone in your body, Laurel."

"I think we both know that's not true," she said, sitting forward with purpose. "Now… about these hymns…"

Laurel found it hard, but we finally fixed everything.

We resorted to the Internet for help with the hymns and asked the pastor to give the eulogy. There was no way I was going to do it, and Laurel couldn't think of anyone else.

My only saving grace in all the immediate aftermath and planning was that Kaylee Prentice wasn't being buried in Hart's Creek. Two funerals in such close succession would have been bound to raise eyebrows, but it transpired Kaylee's parents were from Manchester, and wanted her to be buried there.

It meant there was little to no local fuss about her, and that made it easier to keep Mitch's secret.

Of course, I still can't be absolutely certain what Mitch was planning when he left town, but I have a fair idea, and I know now that it wasn't something temporary.

The quantity of clothing they'd taken with them was a fairly big hint, but a couple of days after the accident, Chip finally found the time to go through the bags we'd found in the trunk of Mitch's car. The delay was caused by several deputies being off sick with flu. Going through the possessions of accident victims wasn't a priority, but when he got around to it, Chip was surprised to make a couple of discoveries. He came to me with them, first handing over Mitch's passport.

I took it from him, and the moment I realized what it was, I told him to close my door. He did and returned to my desk.

"Is Kaylee's there as well?" I asked.

"No. That's why I brought it in. It's kinda confusing."

Okay. So, they weren't going to leave the country… at least not straight away. But it occurred to me then that if Mitch intended to start a new life, his passport might be useful.

"Check to see whether Kaylee Prentice has ever been issued with a passport, and if she has, whether it's still in date." I put Mitch's passport into my desk drawer, and although Chip raised an eyebrow, he didn't say a word. Instead, he handed me a small square envelope. "What's this?" I asked, and he frowned.

"You need to look inside."

I did as he said, my heart stopping as I opened the unsealed envelope. I didn't even need to pull out the contents to realize I was looking at a sonogram image, and I sucked in a breath, taking it in my hand and turning it around to check the date, which was printed in the top right-hand corner.

"Second of January?" I looked up at Chip and he nodded his head.

"Yes. My sister was about eight weeks pregnant when she had her first sonogram, so…"

"I can do the math…" I let my voice fade, staring down at the image before me.

"It might not have been his," Chip said and I looked up at him.

"Seriously? You think Mitch would have been going away with her… or leaving town with her, if it wasn't? Believe me, Mitch Bradshaw wasn't the type of man who'd step up and take care of someone else's problems."

He nodded his head in agreement. "Maybe he wasn't leaving after all. Maybe he was taking her to have a termination," he said, and I shook my head as I put the picture down on my desk.

"It would have been more in character, but if that were the case, he'd have made some kind of excuse to Laurel. He'd have told her he was going away and lied about the reason. Except, as far as she was concerned, he was coming home that night. In fact, he'd told her he was coming home early…" I couldn't say why. I couldn't tell him it was so they could discuss having another baby of their own. No-one else needed to know that. Just like no-one else needed to know that Mitch's stupidity hadn't just killed him and his girlfriend, but their unborn child, too. *God… what a mess.* I let my head fall into my upturned hands.

"Are you okay, boss?"

"No." I looked up at Chip, and returned the photograph to its envelope before handing it back to Chip.

"You don't wanna keep it with Mitch's passport?"

"I can't. Her family will need to be informed."

He nodded his head. "I can deal with them, if it helps."

"Thanks, Chip."

"How's Laurel?" he asked.

"In pieces."

"You didn't tell her about Kaylee?"

"No. And I'm not going to."

"What if she finds out from someone else?"

"I can't see how she will. The affair wasn't common knowledge."

"You know what this place is like, though," he said, shrugging his shoulders.

"I do. But hopefully she'll never have to know." I gave him a look which told him she'd better not hear it from him, and he returned it with one which showed he understood… perhaps more than I gave him credit for.

He left then, and I sat for a while, my emotions in turmoil. Laurel had wanted another baby with Mitch, and he'd convinced her he did, too… but all the while, he wasn't just planning on leaving her, but was having a baby with someone else.

How could he?

I was still trying to work that out, and was no further forward when Chip returned to tell me that Kaylee Prentice had never been issued a passport in her life.

That made sense of why there wasn't one among her belongings, but I was still struggling with where they were going, or for how long, or why Mitch would have wanted to leave Laurel in the first place.

What was wrong with the man?

Witnessing her pain on a daily basis was killing me, especially knowing what Mitch had done, but all I could do was keep his secret, and be there for his widow.

On the day of the funeral, the sun shone, although it was freezing cold still. Laurel wore a black coat over her fitted black dress, and Addy was in gray. She'd refused to put on the black dress Laurel had bought for her online, insisting that she wanted to wear pink instead. Luckily, Peony persuaded her into a gray dress with small pink flowers around the hem, and it seemed like a suitable compromise.

Laurel's mom and dad were there, too, having flown back from their Mediterranean cruise the day before. Laurel hadn't plucked up the courage to call them until several days after Mitch's death, and even then she'd broken down and I'd had to take over the call.

"What should we do?" her dad asked.

"Can you come back?"

"We're not due to until the end of the month."

"I think the funeral will have taken place by then, and I'm sure Laurel would like you here for that."

There was a brief silence. "Okay. I'll see what I can do."

It seemed like an odd response, but no more odd than them booking into the hotel, rather than staying at the house. Of course, their presence there would have meant I couldn't stay, so I was relieved in a way, but I sensed Laurel's disappointment.

"Do you want me to speak to them?" I suggested, but she shook her head.

"There's no point. They never approved of me and Mitch, or the way we got together. They were ashamed of it, I think."

"They do realize what century we're living in, don't they?"

She looked up at me from her seat at the island unit in her kitchen. "Sometimes I used to wonder." I got the feeling she didn't care that much anymore, and a part of me wished I hadn't persuaded her dad to come back.

They were among the many mourners at the church, though... which was full to bursting, with others standing outside. Mitch had been a popular figure in the town, although I wondered how many of them were there to gawp at Laurel.

She hadn't left the house since the day of the accident, and she sobbed through the entire day, leaning on me for support while Peony and Ryan cared for Addy.

To be honest, I was relieved when it was over. The public display was done and we could close the door on the last of the mourners.

Laurel's parents surprised me yet again by returning to Florida two days later.

"We need to check on the house," her dad said, although he wouldn't look me in the eye as he spoke. Why would he? He'd already told me they'd planned to stay away until the end of the month. The excuse was feeble, and we both knew it.

Laurel barely noticed their departure and, to be honest, I hoped it might mark a turning point for her.

With the funeral over, and her parents gone, life could return to normal... whatever that might be for her now.

Of course, a normal life might not include me. I was aware of that, even though I wanted it for her, and every day for the last couple of weeks, I've dreaded the moment when she'd realize it for herself and tell me she doesn't need me anymore. The days have passed, though, and if anything, she seems to need me more and more.

I suppose that became most obvious about four or five days after the funeral, when I arrived at her place after work, and immediately sensed an atmosphere.

It wasn't about mourning, or grief. It was different... more stifling.

Peony came out from the kitchen, grabbed her purse and keys, and left without saying a word, while I stood for a second, feeling confused. She usually gave me a quick update, or told me when she'd be arriving the next day. Not in all the time since Mitch's death had she left like that. I took a step toward the kitchen, when Laurel appeared from the living room, her face streaked with tears.

"What's happened?" I asked, and she fell into my arms. I caught her, like I always do, and she sobbed against me.

"Why?" she kept asking. "Why?"

"Why what?"

"Why is this happening?"

I wasn't any less confused, but I helped her into the living room and sat her on the couch, kneeling before her.

"Tell me what's wrong?" I said, and she sniffled, looking into my eyes.

"Peony's pregnant," she replied quite simply, and I nodded my head, doing my best to look surprised.

"I see."

"No, you don't. She's known since before... before Mitch died, and she kept it from me."

I wondered if that was the problem... if Laurel was offended because her best friend had been keeping secrets. For a second, I wondered how she'd feel if she knew about the secrets I was keeping, but I struck the thought from my mind, and focused on her saddened face.

"You can't blame her for that. She probably wanted to..."

"I don't. That's not the point. Not really."

"Then what is?"

She looked at me like I was being stupid. "You already know the answer to that. You know Mitch and I wanted to have another baby."

I did. I knew all about that, and I nodded my head to prove the point, although my broken heart was fracturing into yet more pieces. What would she say if she knew about Mitch and Kaylee's baby? That would be so much worse than this. I might have been feeling guilty for keeping things from her, but I knew then that I was right to do so. She'd never have been able to cope. "That's not Peony's fault, either," I said.

"I know, but…" Her voice faded, and she swallowed hard. "It just feels so unfair," she said, shaking her head. "I wanted another baby… so damn much, Brady."

"I know," I whispered. "I know."

"Mitch was such a fabulous father."

It was hard enough to hear her say she wanted the guy's baby, but for her to paint him as the patron saint of fatherhood was too much, and I leaned back again, releasing her. She seemed surprised by my move, but what could I do?

"Are you and Peony talking to each other?" I asked, unwilling to hear any more lies about her husband.

"Just about."

"She seemed upset when she left."

"I know." She sighed. "I'll talk to her tomorrow."

It sounded like Peony was coming back… and she did. She's been back every day since, and while things don't seem to be quite the same between the two of them, they appear to have patched up their differences.

I still call Laurel every lunchtime. The funeral no longer provides me with an excuse, but I just say I want to check she's okay, and ask if there's anything she needs. She hasn't plucked up the courage to leave the house yet, so I've gotten used to collecting her groceries and taking them over there for her when I finish work. I'll usually cook, while she gets Addy ready for bed, and then we all eat together.

Once that's done, and Addy's gone to bed, we sit and have a glass of wine, or a coffee, and every single night, I ask if she wants me to stay. She always says yes, although last Friday she added, "Sorry to be pathetic."

"You're not," I told her, wishing I could hold her. I couldn't, though, because I didn't have a reason.

I don't bring a change of clothes, because that would feel too presumptuous… too much like I was moving in. So, every morning, after I've made breakfast, I go home, take a shower and get dressed. If it's a workday, I go into the office and do my best to concentrate, knowing Peony is keeping an eye on Laurel, and if it's not a workday, I go back to Laurel's place and keep an eye on her myself.

It's not a problem.

I don't have anything better to do, and even if I did, I'd happily sacrifice it to be with her.

This may not be the life I dreamed of for us, but as I've said all along, it's not about me.

Besides, I'm realistic enough to know this can't last.

One day, Laurel will be strong enough to cope by herself. I'll ask if she wants me to stay and she'll say, "No, thanks. I'm fine tonight," and I'll have to leave.

I'm dreading it, but I know it'll happen.

Soon.

In the meantime, I'm taking it one day at a time.

Naturally enough, those days have included getting attached to Addy, not just her mom. I've been formally introduced to all her dolls, and last Saturday, when I spent the day here, she insisted that we all had to make cookies together. Laurel wasn't keen, but I persuaded her it would be good for Addy, and in the end, we all enjoyed it. The cookies tasted great, but what was best of all, was seeing a smile on Laurel's face. When I watched them pouring the chocolate chips into the bowl, and stealing some to eat, I couldn't help laughing, and recalling how I'd have married Laurel and brought up another man's child.

I'd have done it willingly, without a second's thought.

I'd do it now, given the chance... although I can't see that happening.

To Laurel, I'm nothing more than a shoulder to cry on in her hour of need.

To me, she's everything.

Tonight, I made my special lasagna, and Addy seemed to like it. Laurel's already taken her up to bed, and as I clear away the dishes, I try very hard not to think of this as my home.

It's Mitch's.

Mitch's and Laurel's.

Not mine.

Even though I've gotten used to living here, and eating here, and sleeping here over the last few weeks.

I let out a sigh, stacking the dishes into the dishwasher, just as I hear footsteps, and I turn as Addy comes rushing into the room, a teddy bear cradled in her arm.

"What's wrong, sweetheart?" I ask, crouching down.

She runs right up to me, throwing her arms around my neck. "Nothing's wrong, Brady. I just wanted to give you a goodnight hug."

I hold her close, just for a second, until she steps back. "Well, that's nice. I'm gonna sleep so much better now."

She giggles, then rushes off again, and I have to chuckle as I get back to the dishes.

It's only a few minutes later, and I've just finished wiping down the countertop, when Laurel comes back into the kitchen.

"That was so cute of Addy," I say, and she smiles.

"I know. She refused to go to sleep until she'd come down to hug you."

"She's adorable."

She nods her head. "She likes having you here."

"I like being here."

She's looking around the kitchen, a little bewildered, and I wonder if she heard me, or if she's somewhere else. It still happens from time to time, even now. "Would you like a coffee?" she asks.

"Okay." I guess my words went over her head. That happens too, sometimes, but I don't take it personally… or I try not to.

Laurel makes the coffee, and I carry it through to the living room, setting it down on the table, as she sits at one end of the couch. I sit at the other end, twisting in my seat so I'm facing her. She looks around again, with that same slightly puzzled expression on her face, until her eyes reach me, and then she smiles.

"Sorry. I was miles away."

"That's okay."

She reaches out, taking her cup, and sips from it, holding it in her hands. "I've reached a decision."

"You have?"

I know what's coming. She's gonna tell me she doesn't need me to stay anymore. Maybe Addy's attachment to me is getting to her, reminding her of what her daughter and her husband never shared. Or maybe she just feels better able to cope than she has over the last few weeks. Whatever her reason, I brace myself for the inevitable.

"Yeah. I'm gonna sell the gym."

I hadn't expected that, and I struggle to hide my relief, choking slightly. I pick up my coffee, moving a little closer to her and taking a drink, in the hope it'll help… which it does.

"Is it yours to sell?" I ask once I've recovered.

"Yes. Mitch and I both made wills leaving everything to each other. The house and gym are mine."

"You're sure about that?"

She frowns, but her reaction is understandable. She doesn't know what her husband was doing behind her back… the new life he was forging without her.

"We made our wills together when we got married. I was already pregnant, and it seemed sensible."

"And neither of you have made any changes?"

"Of course not." She looks appalled by the suggestion. "I had a long conversation with Ezra earlier in the week, and he outlined my options."

"You talked to Ezra?"

She nods her head.

This is the first I've heard of their conversation, although I don't know why I'm surprised. She doesn't owe me explanations… about anything.

"I called him, and he after we'd gone through everything, he suggested I sell the gym," she says, tilting her head. "It's not like I've got any use for it. I certainly don't want to run it myself, and as he said, the money will tide us over for a while."

The surprises are coming thick and fast tonight. "You need money?"

She nods her head again, a little more slowly this time. "We do… and more than I thought we would. Mitch might have left me everything, but it seems the house and the gym are pretty much all there was."

"He had no cash?"

"No." She frowns, moving along the couch, so she's only about a foot from me. "It's a little odd, when you think how successful the gym is, and that he'd just sold that plot of land to Nate Newton."

It's more than odd; it's highly suspicious. "Are you... are you okay? Financially, I mean. I can let you have..."

She reaches out, resting her hand on my arm. "Oh, God, Brady... don't offer to lend me money, on top of everything else you're doing."

"I wasn't going to." Her brow furrows, like she's confused. "Not as a loan, anyway."

She bites on her bottom lip, tears welling in her eyes. "You're too much, sometimes... but honestly, we're fine. We'll certainly survive until the gym is sold."

"Y—You're not thinking of selling the house as well, are you?" Fear courses through me at the thought. If she leaves, I don't know what I'll do, but even as the idea rushes through my brain, she smiles, shaking her head.

"No."

"Because you have too many happy memories?" I ask, clearly determined to inflict as much pain on myself as possible.

She hesitates, opening her mouth and then closing it shut again, which strikes me as odd. "I don't have unhappy memories," she says a little cryptically. "But I've been thinking over the last few days, and I've realized how little time we spent here as a family. This might have been Mitch's house, but Addy and I spent more time here than he ever did. I guess that's why she's finding it so easy to adapt to what's happened." She smiles, although I can tell it's an effort. "You were right about that. I'm the one she's used to having around... although she loves having you here, too."

"I love being here," I say, and this time she hears me. Her smile widens as she settles back in her seat, letting out a sigh. She seems more content in herself than she has since the accident, and I have to ask, "Do you want me to stay tonight?"

She turns. "Of course I do." She rests her hand in the space between us, maybe six inches from my leg. "I might have reached a decision about the gym, but that doesn't mean I'm feeling any stronger in myself."

"You are, you know. You're getting there." I have to encourage her, even though it's not in my interests.

"It doesn't feel like it," she whispers, and puts her feet up on the couch, leaning against me. I don't put my arm around her, but let her rest against it, neither of us saying a word.

She sighs, nestling in to me, and although I know she won't fall asleep yet, I settle down, enjoying the moment.

At least I know she won't be leaving now, and to be honest, I'm quite pleased she's decided to sell the gym. It's one less link to Mitch… and to Kaylee Prentice.

I'm just as confused as Laurel is about why Mitch didn't leave her any cash. The guy was renowned for having plenty of it to throw around, and as she said, it's not long since he sold that land to Nate Newton. I'm aware of the price of land around here, even if Laurel isn't, and Mitch won't have sold himself short. In fact, knowing him, he'll have tried to get more than it was worth. What surprises me is that she doesn't seem to want to know where the money's gone. I could probably find out if she asked me, but I hope she doesn't. It might not have been in his car, but I'll bet my house it's stashed somewhere… either in a new business, or a new home for him and Kaylee, or maybe just in a separate bank account, possibly not even in his name, to make it harder for Laurel to trace. He'll have worked things out meticulously. Let's face it, Mitch wasn't the kind of guy to leave things to chance. Not where his own welfare was concerned, anyway. He'll have known exactly what he was going to do, and how he was going to do it. I imagine Kaylee's pregnancy might have altered his well-laid plans… or at least forced him to bring them forward, so they could get away before anyone discovered their secret. But that doesn't mean this wasn't organized, down to the last letter.

The only thing he didn't bank on was dying.

Chapter Nine

❯❯❯❯❯❯❮❮❮❮

Laurel

Why is it that, even after four months, I still can't see any light at the end of that dark tunnel?

I stay in the house, going through the motions of a life I no longer have, while living in fear of practically everything.

I haven't cried for quite some time, but I'm too scared to go out now, just in case someone says something about Mitch and it sets me off again.

It sounds silly, I know, but that's how it is.

I'm vaguely aware of what's going on in the town. I know, for example, that Walker Holt is a father now. His wife, Imogen, had their baby girl a couple of weeks ago. They've called her Ava, which is lovely. You see? I might feel dead inside, but I'm capable of appreciating things like that, even though I know I'll never have them again for myself.

And maybe that's where the problem lies… at least in part.

I can't handle other people's happiness.

I think that's why I turned down the invitation to Nate and Taylor's wedding next weekend…

"I'll take you," Brady said when he called that lunchtime and I told him the invite had arrived in the morning mail. I hadn't declined yet, but I knew I would, and I told him so, shaking my head, even though he couldn't see me.

"I can't face it."

"We don't have to stay for long and…"

"I don't want to go, Brady."

He sighed. "Okay."

"Sorry. I didn't mean to snap."

"It's all right. You don't have to apologize."

I felt like I did, but he changed the subject, asking if there was anything I needed from the grocery store.

It's not Brady's fault that I can't face the world yet, and I felt guilty for biting his head off, and made a conscious effort not to do it again… even when he suggested he'd help me clear out some of Mitch's things.

"I can't," I said.

"I'll do it for you, if you like?"

"No. I'll get around to it. Just not yet."

He seemed to want to say something else, but held back, and I was relieved by that. I didn't want to explain that at least part of my reticence was because I found the bedroom such a depressing place to be.

"Why don't you and Peony go out for coffee one day?" We were standing in the kitchen after dinner one evening last week. Brady had just stacked the dishwasher, and I was waiting for the coffee to brew.

"Why?" I asked, turning to face him.

"Because I'm pretty sure Everly could do with seeing a friendly face."

I'd expected him to say it was high time I got out of the house and was surprised by his answer. "She could?"

"Yeah."

"Is this because of Aunt Clare?"

It might have been a while since her death, but I know from bitter experience that time isn't always the best of healers. As I stared at him across the island unit, I wondered if Brady thought Everly and I might become kindred spirits, sharing in our grief, or something like that. It sounded like the most awful thought in the world, but I didn't know how to say that to him.

"No. It's nothing to do with Aunt Clare." His reply surprised me yet again.

"Oh?"

"Yeah. Seth's left."

"You can't be serious."

"I can."

"Seth's left Everly?"

"Yes. It happened a couple of weeks ago, evidently."

"But they were perfect together." 'Perfect' probably wasn't a strong enough word. I'd always thought Mitch and I were well suited, but there was something about Everly and Seth. They just seemed to fit.

"They were," Brady said.

"What happened?" I asked, and he shrugged his shoulders.

"I don't know. I just heard Seth had left, that was all." He paused, leaning over the island unit. "You, Peony, and Everly were in the same year at school, weren't you?"

"Yes, but we weren't great friends, or anything like that. Everly always kept herself to herself, probably because she lost her parents when she was so young."

"Maybe, but…"

"I know you think I should be a friend to her now, Brady, but I can't. Call me selfish. Call me anything you like, but I'm not ready."

He fixed his eyes on mine and walked around the island unit, taking my arm and turning me to face him.

"It's okay. It was just an idea." I nodded my head. "And you're not selfish."

I've felt it, especially when he's been so kind, and so understanding, trying to find ways of distracting me.

Last Sunday, he suggested a walk down by the creek.

"We could take a picnic, if you like?"

"It looks like it might rain."

That wasn't true at all. Okay, so it might have clouded over, but it wasn't the kind of cloud that spelled rain. Even so, it made a good excuse not to go, and Brady didn't press me.

I know I'm being pathetic, and Brady is trying so hard to help, but the idea of going anywhere fills me with fear.

He keeps telling me I'm getting better, and I guess in some ways, he's right.

The pain has subsided a little, but it seems to have been replaced by numbness. I still feel like I'm wading through molasses, and I get through each day by not thinking. That's hardly a way to live, but whenever I think, I'm reminded of how much I miss Mitch, and the pain comes back.

When the phone rings, especially if it's late in the afternoon, my immediate thought is always that it'll be Mitch, calling to say he won't be home for dinner. When I'm cooking, I forget to cook for two instead of three. Of course, that wasn't so much of a problem to start with, because Brady was here every night, and he often did the cooking himself, while I got Addy ready for bed. But unfortunately, I had to put a stop to that…

I waited until about a month after the funeral, although 'waited' might be putting it a little strongly. That sounds like what I did was planned, and it wasn't. Not really.

The problem was, I was finding it hard to see Peony every day once she'd revealed her 'news'. Hearing that my best friend was pregnant ought to have been joyous, but all I could do was cry… loudly and uncontrollably.

Peony was naturally confused by my reaction, and because I couldn't explain it to her, I think she was hurt, and maybe a little resentful. She'd expected me to be happy for her, and I was miserable.

Brady told me to talk it through with her, and I did... the very next day. Life was tough enough without there being an awkward atmosphere between the two of us. We'd been friends all our lives, and I needed her. I thought she might need me too, under the circumstances.

"I'm sorry," I said when she arrived the next morning. "I shouldn't have reacted like that when you told me about... about the baby."

"It's okay."

I could tell it wasn't, and wondered if I should explain about the plans Mitch and I had been making to have another baby of our own. I'd told Brady, but somehow it felt cruel to tell Peony. She'd feel guilty. I knew she would, and I didn't want to steal even a moment of happiness from her... although I knew I already had.

Peony might have accepted my apology, but things had soured between us. It was my fault, not hers. She still came over every day, still played with Addy and helped around the house. I had a lot to be grateful for. But I found it hard sitting across the island unit from someone who seemed to have it all.

I felt like the worst friend in the world for feeling like that, but my dreams had been snatched from me, while Peony still had hers.

In the end, I decided the best thing was to ask her not to come over anymore... or at least, not every day. The problem I had was, how could I say that without offending my oldest friend? It wasn't Peony's fault that we'd ended up where we were, and it came to me one morning, when I was in the shower, the smell of bacon wafting up from the kitchen as Brady made our breakfast, that the only solution was to ask him not to stay over anymore, either.

That was a much harder thing to contemplate.

Brady had become a big part of our lives. He'd stayed every night since Mitch's death and in those weeks, he'd been more than someone who just cooked the dinner and made the breakfast. He'd been sounding board, a shoulder to cry on… a rock. I'd asked a lot of him, and he'd done it. All of it. He'd talked into the early hours, fixed things around the house, played with Addy. He'd held me when I'd cried… and sometimes when I hadn't, but just needed to be hugged.

Could I really push him away?

It was the last thing I wanted, but what choice did I have?

If things had carried on as they were, I'd have had to keep seeing Peony every day, watching her bump grow, her pregnancy develop, and face the constant reminders of everything I'd dreamed of… and lost.

Logic told me that, even if I wasn't ready to move on yet, I'd never be able to do it at all if I couldn't at least put my dreams behind me.

So that night, when Brady arrived, I asked Peony if she'd wait. "Of course."

She seemed surprised by my request, but that was understandable. She usually rushed off once Brady got here, keen to get back to Ryan.

Brady raised an eyebrow, too, but they both joined me in the living room. Addy was watching cartoons, and organizing her dolls in the playroom, but I knew we didn't have long. She'd have heard Brady arrive, and I knew she'd come to find him soon. She always did.

"I've reached a decision," I said. None of us had sat down, and they both turned to face me.

"Oh, yes?" Brady had a smile on his face, but I understood that. I'd said those words to him before, when I was talking about selling the gym.

"Yes." I looked at Peony, because I knew it would be easier. "I've decided it's time for me to stand on my own two feet."

She frowned. "What does that mean?"

"It means that I appreciate everything you've both done, but you don't have to babysit me anymore. You've both got lives of your own." I stepped closer to her. "You've got a lot going on, Peony. The farm needs more attention than you're able to give it when you're spending so much time here."

"Ryan helps," she said. "And I don't mind…"

"No. Really. I've decided."

I heard her sigh of relief, even though she tried to hold it in. "In that case, I'm pleased for you."

I could tell she meant that. It wasn't a selfish comment, born of her desire to get back to living her own life. She was genuinely happy – and maybe even a little proud – that I seemed to be on the road to recovery… even if it was all an act on my part.

I smiled, and then turned to Brady, the look on his face surprising me. There was no happiness or pride there. His face was a mixture of disappointment, sadness, and shock.

"Is that okay with you?" I asked when he didn't respond.

"Sure. If it's what you want."

"I'm really grateful to you, Brady…"

"I don't want your gratitude."

He was angry, as well as disappointed, sad, and shocked. I stepped back, but Brady's eyes locked on mine and the hurt I saw there took my breath away.

He didn't stay that night. He didn't even ask… not like he usually did, and I have to admit, I missed him. That look in his eyes haunted me, and something about it made me wonder if sending him away might have been the stupidest decision I'd ever made.

Addy missed him, too. We had dinner alone, Brady having already left, and when she asked why he wasn't there, I had to explain that he couldn't stay with us forever.

"He's got his own life," I said, surprised by how much that thought alarmed me. I'd wondered about Brady's personal life before, but never like that. Never in a way that made me fear what we'd do without him.

What was wrong with me?

I shouldn't have been thinking like that, should I? And yet, I couldn't seem to stop myself.

I was reminded of Addy's emotionless response to her father's death, contrasting it to the way she only just held back her tears, staring at Brady's seat in the kitchen… or the seat she'd grown used to him using, anyway.

"Did I do something wrong?" she asked, breaking my heart.

"Of course not, baby girl."

How could I explain to her that I'd sent him away? How could I give her a reason when I didn't have one? Not one that made sense, anyway.

It had been really comfortable having Brady here. He'd fitted in with us perfectly, and I enjoyed having a man around the house. I enjoyed having someone I could turn to and rely on. I wish I could say that was because it reminded me of Mitch, but Mitch was never here as much as Brady. And although I hate to say it, he was never as reliable, either.

Brady's departure made one thing easier… and only one thing. It meant I could move out of the bedroom Mitch and I had shared, and into the room Brady had been using. The downstairs of this house is significantly larger than the upstairs, as a result of which, despite its size, there are only four bedrooms here. One of them was converted into an office when Mitch had the place refurbished, and with Addy in her pink bedroom, and Brady in the guest room, I was stuck in that drab gray hole. It wasn't the reminders of Mitch so much as the color that was driving me crazy. Redecorating is beyond me right now, and while I enjoyed having a dressing room – or the half of the dressing room that was mine – giving it up was a small sacrifice.

The guest room is so much nicer. My clothes fitted in perfectly, and I managed to avoid even looking into Mitch's closets when I moved everything around. The bed is smaller, but there's still an adjoining bathroom... and, oddly enough, even though he didn't stay for that long, I noticed when I first moved in there that it smelled of Brady. And I liked that.

He still stays in touch, all these weeks later. He calls me once a day without fail. We talk for a while. He asks after Addy and makes sure I'm okay. Then he asks if I need anything. If I don't, he promises to call the next day. If I do, he brings it over after work. I haven't yet been tempted to tell him I need something, even if I don't... but I'll admit I look forward to the evenings when he drops by, and I always invite him to stay for dinner.

So far, he's said, "Yes," every single time.

Addy loves having him here, and makes a point of asking me during the afternoon if Brady will be coming over. When I say, "No," there's no doubting the sadness in her eyes, and although I wish I could have seen the same devotion about Mitch, I can't re-write history, can I?

As for Peony... we talk on the phone, and I'm up-to-date with her pregnancy, even though I don't want to be. So, I know that she and Ryan have almost finished decorating the nursery... in yellow, because they don't know whether they're having a boy, or a girl. I was surprised when she told me they weren't going to find out in advance, but she explained that she wasn't sure she wanted to know, and Ryan was adamant he didn't... so the decision was made.

She still comes by at least once a week. In fact, she's due here this morning, and I've made cookies. The days merge into each other, but I know it's Saturday, because Peony made a point of saying how nice it was not to have a wedding booked for today. Her business is doing really well... so well, she's just employed someone else to run the apple orchard. I'm fairly sure her pregnancy had something to do with that. The work is quite physical, and there would have come a point when she couldn't do it anymore, so it made sense to get someone in.

I put the kettle on the stove to boil, remembering that Peony still can't stand the smell of coffee, and set out the cookies on a plate, just as I hear a car pull up outside.

Addy beats me to the door, yanking it open, and Peony greets her with a hug.

"I swear you've grown since last week," she says, and Addy giggles.

"No, I haven't."

Peony steps back, looking down at her. "I think you have."

Addy takes her hand, dragging her into the house, and Peony looks up, smiling at me.

"How are you?" she asks, and I smile back.

"I'm fine."

I do my best to avoid looking at her neat little baby bump, and to ignore the stiff atmosphere between us. It never used to be like this, and although I know it's my fault, I don't know what to say, or how to feel.

I turn, going back into the kitchen, and they follow, Peony helping Addy onto a chair, before sitting herself, while I finish making the tea, bringing the pot over.

"Can I have a cookie, Mommy?"

"What's the magic word?"

"Please?" she says and I nod my head, offering her the plate. She takes a cookie and, with Peony's help, jumps down from her chair, rushing off toward her playroom.

Almost the moment she's gone, a stony silence descends. I take my time pouring the tea, adding milk to both cups before I sit beside Peony at the island unit.

"How's everything going?" she asks.

"Not too bad. The sale of the gym should be completed by the end of the month."

"It's taken a while, hasn't it?"

"Yes. I didn't realize there would be so much to negotiate."

"Was that to do with the employees?" she asks.

"Partly. All their contracts had to be renegotiated. But there was also something to do with the memberships having a value, which had to be added to the price, and then bartered over." To be honest, I left Ezra to deal with most of it, and I'm grateful for everything he's done.

Money's been a little tight, because of the unexpected delay, but Brady refuses every offer I make of paying for my own groceries, and I have to admit, that has really helped. Without him, I'd have had to borrow from either Peony or Mom and Dad... and neither of those prospects bear thinking about.

She nods, and we both take a sip of tea.

"Are you going to Nate and Taylor's wedding?" she asks.

"No." I shake my head, although I feel reluctant to explain.

"How's their house coming along?"

"It's a couple of months away from being finished, I think."

"Like Ryan said, that's the problem with starting the construction work in the depths of winter."

"Probably. The last I heard, they're gonna carry on living at his apartment for now."

Peony nods her head, sipping at her tea as another silence falls. She's run out of questions, and I can't think of a single thing to say. I hate this. We used to be able to talk about anything, and now – thanks to me – we're like strangers.

"This is horrible."

"We need to talk."

We both speak at the same time, and Peony puts down her cup, giving me a smile. "You go first."

"I don't know what to say. I know I reacted badly when you told me you're pregnant, but…"

"It's okay," she says, resting her hand on her bump. "I get how hard this must be for you."

I don't see how she can. Not really.

"Do you?" I say, unable to keep my doubts inside.

"Luca left me," she says, tilting her head. "And my grandmother died not long afterwards. I understand how it feels to lose people."

"I appreciate how hard it was for you, Peony, but are you honestly telling me that either of those situations comes close to my husband being killed?"

"Of course not. I'm just saying…" She stops talking and sits up, taking a breath. "Why are you blaming me, Laurel? Why is it my fault?"

She rests both hands on her bump, like she feels the need to protect her unborn child… although I'm not sure what from.

"It's not. But can't you see?"

"See what?"

"You've got everything, Peony, and I've got nothing."

I burst into tears, knowing how selfish I'm being, and I hear a chair scraping across the floor.

She'll leave now. I know she will. I've gone too far.

I startle, feeling her arm come around my shoulder, and I look up to see her familiar face, tears welling in her eyes.

"What do you want me to do?" she says. "Do you want me to leave Ryan so we can both be miserable?"

"Of course not."

"Good… because I wouldn't do it, anyway. Not even for you."

I chuckle, unable to help myself, and she joins in, the ice broken at last.

I lean in to her hug. "I'm sorry. You must hate me. I've been such a terrible friend."

"I could never hate you, and you've got nothing to apologize for. You're grieving. It's hard. I understand that. That's all I was trying to say. I wasn't comparing—"

"It's okay. I know what you meant." She sits down again and I roll my shoulders. "I need something to focus on, other than the past."

"The future?" she says and I smile.

"That seems logical, but I don't feel like I have one right now."

Peony shakes her head. "What happened to that crusader… that righter of wrongs, who was gonna rock the legal world with her brilliance?"

"I don't know. I can barely remember her."

"I can. Maybe it's time you found her again."

I sip my tea, thinking about that… about how I used to be. Sure, I was shy, but I had goals…

"I guess I could try. I'll need to find a job soon, anyway."

"You will? What about the money you'll get from selling the gym?"

"It won't last forever, and anyway, Addy's due to start school in the fall, and I can't sit around here all day doing nothing."

Peony puts her hand over mine. "Make that your focus, then."

"Finding something to do?"

"Yes."

I nod my head, although I'm still not sure I can put those words into any kind of action. It's been such a long time since I even opened a law book, let alone thought about working in the profession.

Still, what choice do I have?

Chapter Ten

Brady

Before Mitch died, I used to cherish my days off, whenever they fell, just so I could catch up at home, and get some sleep… maybe go out with Cooper, and enjoy myself. It was good to behave like a man, not the town sheriff, just for a couple of days a week.

In the aftermath of Mitch's death, my days off became so much more.

I'd spend them with Laurel and Addy, doing whatever they needed. I didn't care about catching up, or sleeping, just so long as I could be with them… and be there for them.

Now, I dread my days off.

I've even tried swapping shifts a few times, with mixed results, depending on what everyone else has got planned.

This weekend, no-one was interested, which is why I'm sitting in my kitchen on a Saturday afternoon, trying to work out what to do with the rest of the day.

I called Laurel at lunchtime, but she said she didn't want anything from the grocery store. I hate it when that happens, but what can I say?

Nothing.

Because she doesn't need me anymore.

I knew the day would come. I'd feared its arrival long enough.

When it came, though, it still took me by surprise.

It would have been about six weeks after Mitch's death. I'd just arrived at Laurel's place, and she surprised me by asking Peony to wait, rather than leaving straight away. Things between the two of them were still strained, and I wondered if she wanted to discuss it, and maybe needed me there for moral support... or to act as referee.

It was nothing to do with that, though.

She announced she'd reached a decision, and I recalled the way she'd told me about selling the gym not long after the funeral. I knew she wouldn't sell the house. She'd already made that clear. So what else did she have in mind?

She was focused on Peony, and I felt at ease, until the words, "I've decided it's time for me to stand on my own two feet," left her lips.

They were clearly aimed at both of us. Otherwise, why was I there?

I couldn't answer her, though. Couldn't say a word, in case I gave away how hurt I was.

She and Peony were talking.

"... you don't have to babysit me anymore. You've both got lives of your own."

How could she say that? Didn't she realize she was my life? Didn't she know that everything I was and ever wanted to be revolved around her and Addy?

My mind went blank for a second or two, and then I heard Peony say, "I don't mind..."

"No. Really. I've decided."

Laurel sounded adamant, and Peony seemed relieved.

I wasn't. I was devastated.

Laurel turned to me a moment or two later, and no matter how hard I tried, I couldn't disguise my feelings.

"Is that okay with you?" she asked, looking up at me.

"Sure. If it's what you want." What else was I supposed to say? Was I supposed to beg her not to discard me? I would have done, if I'd thought it might have worked.

"I'm really grateful to you, Brady…"

Just for a second, I saw red. "I don't want your gratitude," I snapped. *I want you.*

I couldn't say that though, and as I had no reason to stay, I left.

I still see her several times a week, but it's not the same. It's not like it was when I was there every day, cooking dinner, preparing breakfast, playing with Addy, sitting with Laurel in the evenings, sleeping in the guest bedroom…

It's nothing like that at all.

I call her every lunchtime, just like I used to, to check if she needs anything.

Sometimes – like today – she says she doesn't, and I have to accept I won't be seeing her. Other times she says yes, and I collect whatever she's asked for, taking it to her when I've finished work. She always asks me to stay for dinner, and I always say, "Yes."

Why wouldn't I?

It's the best I can hope for these days, and I'll take it.

I miss the times we used to have together, but I can't begrudge her this. I can't resent her coming out of the gloom of her grief. It's something I've encouraged her to do, right from the beginning, and I haven't stopped… even now. All my suggestions have been greeted with a firm, "No," from Laurel, and while I'd have loved to take her shopping, or on a picnic, there's one thing I'm relieved she vetoed.

It was a while ago, and although I don't know what possessed me, I asked if she wanted to clear out Mitch's things. Laurel shook her head, but for some bizarre reason, I persevered. Why, I don't know, because, if she'd agreed, she'd almost certainly have discovered some of his clothes were missing. That thought didn't occur to me until later, and I could have kicked myself for being so blind. Fortunately, she hasn't mentioned it again… and neither have I.

I've encouraged her in other ways, though. I keep telling her how well she's doing… because she is. She smiles more and cries less, although she still occasionally sheds a tear for the husband who didn't care enough about her to stay true. When that happens, if I'm there, I always hold her. I can't do anything else.

It would kill me to watch her cry and do nothing.

She doesn't talk about him as much as she used to. He comes up more by accident now… like the other evening, when Addy came running into the kitchen not long after I got there, holding out one of her toys.

"It's not working, Mommy," she said, as Laurel took it from her. It appeared to be a child's tablet, although the screen was frozen.

"Do you want me to take a look?" I said, and she gave me a smile.

"It's okay. The screen sometimes locks, if Addy tries to switch between games too quickly, and I've discovered the best thing to do is to turn it off, wait ten seconds, and turn it back on again."

"How did you work that out?"

"Trial and error." She shook her head, waiting for the device to restart. "And necessity, I guess. Mitch was never here, so anything that went wrong, I had to deal with it."

I watched as the screen sparked back to life, feeling relieved that Laurel still had no idea why Mitch was never home, and resolving to keep it that way.

There are only two people who know the truth about what happened that afternoon… me and Chip. I might never have said so in as many words, but there have been looks and glances, and I'm fairly sure he's worked out that my feelings for Laurel go deeper than friendship. I won't confirm or deny, and he knows me well enough not to ask outright. He knows I've always kept my private life to myself, and I figure the less I say to anyone, the better.

He dealt with everything related to Kaylee Prentice, just like he said he would, and I made a point of dealing with Laurel. That way, we were able to keep the two sides of the story completely separate, although they're linked within the files, because they have to be. He obviously knows about Mitch's affair, and Kaylee's pregnancy, but other than that, he knows nothing about Mitch's and Laurel's relationship, and I've kept it that way, because the files don't need to mention that. Like everyone else in Hart's Creek, he has no idea I've been spending time with her, and as far as I'm aware, the case is something he's consigned to the record books.

Laurel has no reason to come to my office, and it's highly unlikely she and Chip would meet anywhere else. He's only twenty-three. He hangs out mostly in Concord, with a much younger group of friends. I doubt anything that happens in Hart's Creek even features on their radar… and in any case, he knows better than to gossip about work.

I feel like I've done everything I can to protect her from ever finding out what really went on that day, or what Mitch was planning.

The secret's safe.

I check my watch. It's nearly three-thirty. I can't just sit here doing nothing.

I get up, just as my phone rings, making me jump and I grab it from the countertop, my heart stopping when I see Laurel's name on the screen. She's never called before, so something must be wrong.

"Is everything okay?" I ask, the moment the call connects.

"Yes. I'm sorry to trouble you."

There's something almost playful in her voice and my heart races, a smile catching at my lips, my cock twitching. I haven't allowed myself to respond to her like this since Mitch died, but the tone of her voice makes it impossible not to. It's beyond my control.

"You're not troubling me." *You never could.*

"You might not say that when you hear why I'm calling."

"Oh?"

"Yeah. You know I said the other night about how good I am at handling things that go wrong?"

"Yeah…"

"Well, it seems I'm not."

"Why? What's happened?"

"Promise you won't laugh?"

"I promise."

She pauses for a second and then says, "I can't get the garage doors to open."

I do my best not to laugh, because I promised. "Would you like me to come over and take a look?"

"You don't mind?"

"Of course not. I can be there in ten minutes."

I grab my keys before I've even ended the call, and run from the house, driving straight to Laurel's place. It's the first time I've felt needed by her in weeks, and while the problem might be trivial, I'm not about to pass up an opportunity to spend some time with her.

She's standing by the door when I pull up outside, and I have to smile, taking in her skin-tight jeans and pretty floral blouse. Her hair is tied up in a ponytail, and she's leaning against the doorframe, her arms folded, and a slight smile on her lips.

"Are you waiting for me?" I ask, climbing from my car.

She nods her head, a blush creeping up her pale cheeks, and she opens her mouth to say something, just as Addy comes charging out.

"Brady!" she yells and promptly falls flat on her face.

There's a moment of calm before her cry rips through the air, and I run forward, getting to her before Laurel.

"Hey… let's see," I say, turning her over. There's a cut on her right knee and a graze on her left. Laurel crouches on the other side of her, but Addy reaches for me. I glance at Laurel and she nods her head as I lift Addy into my arms.

"Bring her into the kitchen," Laurel says, leading the way, and I follow, kicking the door shut behind me.

"Where shall I put her?" I ask once we've joined Laurel.

"Over by the sink is probably best."

I sit Addy up on the countertop beside the sink and she stares up at me, tears still trickling down her cheeks.

"It's okay," I murmur, stroking her head. "We'll soon make it better."

Laurel comes, bringing a first-aid kit, and removes Addy's shoes, twisting her round and putting her feet into the sink.

"Let's see what we're dealing with," she says, studying her daughter's knees, before looking up at me. "Could you get some paper towels?"

"Sure."

I fetch a roll from the other side of the kitchen, bringing it back, and Laurel wets a few sheets under the faucet, dabbing at the wounds on Addy's knees. They're really not bad at all, and clean up easily, after which Laurel puts a Band-aid on the cut, leaving the graze to heal by itself.

Addy seems a lot better now. She's stopped crying and appears to be amused by the fact that she's sitting with her feet in the sink.

"Do you want me to clean up?" I say as Laurel packs away the first-aid kit.

"If you like."

The faucet is one of those fancy ones, with a spray hose, and I pull that free, turning on the water, which splashes Addy's feet, making her giggle.

"You want to try?" I say, and she nods, taking the hose from me. I realize my mistake a second too late as she turns the hose on me, dousing me with cold water.

"Addy!" Laurel comes flying over, removing the hose from Addy's grip and shutting off the water before she turns to face me. "Oh, God... I'm so sorry."

I smile down at her. "It's okay. It was my fault."

Her eyes alight on my chest, her teeth nipping at her bottom lip. "Y—You're soaked."

"Only so as you'd notice."

"We'd better dry your t-shirt. You can't wander around like that all day."

"No. I guess not."

I tug my t-shirt off over my head as she puts the hose back into place. When she turns around, I hear her sharp intake of breath and notice how she almost stumbles backward.

"Are you okay?" I say, reaching for her.

"I—I'm fine."

Her eyes wander south, widening as they go, and I struggle not to smile.

"I never realized."

"Never realized what?"

"That you had a tattoo." She moves a little closer, studying it. For a moment, I wonder if she'll realize the significance of the pattern, which comprises roses and laurel leaves, starting on my chest and drifting up over my shoulder. But she doesn't say a word and just swallows hard and looks up into my eyes. "When did you have it done?"

"About nine years ago." *Not long after you left for college… when I found out your middle name is Rose, and decided to make something of it.*

"I can't believe you stayed here all that time and I didn't notice."

"You never saw me without a top on."

She shakes her head. "No, I suppose I didn't."

"What shall I do with this?" I say, nodding toward my dripping t-shirt, clutched in my hands.

"I'll put it in the dryer." She takes it from me, disappearing into the laundry room at the back of the kitchen. When she returns, she's empty-handed, but she stops on the threshold, her eyes fixed on mine. "I—I'll find you something to wear. I'm sure one of Mitch's t-shirts will fit."

"I don't think I want to…" I stop speaking, unable to finish my sentence, and she nods her head.

"No. Sorry. I didn't think."

She probably assumes I'm unwilling to wear a dead man's clothes, and while I'll admit, I'm reticent, my restraint has more to do with who he was and what he did to her, than the fact that he's no longer here.

"There's nothing to apologize for. I'll be fine like this… as long as you don't mind."

"Not at all," she says, far too quickly, her cheeks flushing bright red, and I have to fight really hard not to smile.

To make it easier – for both of us, I think – I turn around, tilting my head at Addy.

"Now, young lady… shall we dry off your legs and get you out of there?"

She nods her head, and I grab a towel, twisting her around and drying her off, before I lift her down to the floor. She limps, exaggerating her injuries, and looks up at me.

"I think I'm gonna need a cookie."

Laurel chuckles. "I guess you deserve one for being so brave."

I crouch down by Addy as Laurel fetches a cookie from the jar. "Shall I carry you through to the playroom? You can sit and watch a cartoon while I help Mommy with the garage doors."

Addy nods her head, and I lift her, standing up, and turning to Laurel, who's smiling at us.

"Can Mommy bring my cookie?" Addy says.

"It's probably for the best. If I had to carry that as well, I don't think I could manage."

She giggles and rests her head on my shoulder as I start toward the back of the house, making my way to the playroom. There are toys scattered around, but I've seen worse, and I set her down on the small couch along the side wall, while Laurel puts on the TV in the corner, finding a cartoon for her to watch, and finally handing Addy the cookie.

"Are you gonna be okay for a little while?" Laurel asks.

Addy nods her head, already engrossed by the furry critters on the screen.

"We'll only be in the garage, and we'll leave the front door open. Okay?"

She looks up, just briefly. "Okay."

The TV captures her attention once more and Laurel shakes her head, the two of us leaving the room.

We head back to the front door, but when we get there, Laurel hesitates before opening it.

"Thank you," she whispers, gazing up at me.

"What for?"

"Being here."

I move just a little closer, noting the quickening of the pulse in her neck. "Being here has never been a problem for me, Laurel."

She sucks in a stuttered breath, and we stare at each other for a perfect moment, before she comes to her senses and opens the door, the bright sunlight blinding me to everything but my love for her.

"What's wrong with the doors?" I ask as we walk over to the garage.

Laurel pulls a remote device from her jeans pocket, looking at it for a second. "I don't know. They just won't open."

She presses the button as we approach, but nothing happens, and she hands the device to me.

"I take it there's no other way in?"

She shakes her head. "No. I always told Mitch it was a a dumb way to design a garage, but it was how this place was built, and he never got around to changing it."

I have to agree with her. It was a stupid piece of design. As for why Mitch didn't change it… I guess he was otherwise occupied.

I press the button, copying Laurel's actions. Again, nothing happens and I turn to face her, smiling when I see she's studying my chest. Not just my tattoo, but my chest. I don't comment or do anything. It would spoil something special, as far as I'm concerned.

"I take it you've checked the batteries?"

Her eyes dart up to mine, and while she blushes again, I know it's got nothing to do with the way she was scrutinizing me.

"Oh… Oh… I didn't think." She raises her hand to her forehead. "I should have done that before I called you."

"It's not a problem."

I take off the back of the device to find it takes a single triple-A battery.

"I've got some of those," she says, and darts back into the house, returning seconds later with a small box of batteries. She takes one out, handing it to me, and I switch them over, replacing the cover, and press the button once more.

The doors open with no trouble at all, and Laurel sighs. "God… I feel like such an idiot. It never occurred to me to check the battery."

"Why should it?"

"Because it's the most obvious thing to think of. I haven't been in the garage for months. I haven't used my car since Mitch died."

"Were you gonna use it now?" I ask. I'd be surprised if she was, considering she's declined every attempt I've made to get her out of the house.

"No." She turns, glancing at her car, which is parked in the garage. "I'm not ready for that yet. It's just that I was talking to Peony this morning..."

"You were?"

She nods, smiling, a light touching her eyes. "She came over. We... We cleared the air at last."

"That's great, Laurel."

"I know. It's taken far too long, but I feel like we're back on track at last."

I nod my head. "I'm really pleased."

"So am I. I hated the atmosphere between us."

"I'm sure she did, too."

She sighs. "It was my fault."

I reach out, touching her arm. "It doesn't matter about that now. What matters is you're friends again."

"I know. She was saying I need to look to the future, not the past."

"I couldn't agree more."

She smiles. "She also reminded me that when I came back from college, I had plans."

"You were gonna practice law, weren't you?"

"I was." She seems surprised that I remember, but what she doesn't realize is, I remember everything about her.

"Is that what you still want to do?"

"It's the only thing I'm qualified for."

"That's no mean feat, Laurel."

She smiles. "I know. But I've never had a job, let alone one in my chosen profession, and it's been years since I've even thought about legal work. All my old law books are in here." She nods toward the open garage. "So, I thought I could go through them and see if I can actually remember anything."

I nod my head, handing her the remote.

"Do you want me to help you find them?"

"Would that be okay?"

"Of course it would. I can carry them inside for you."

"That'd be great. Thanks."

It's taken us over an hour to find all the boxes, and I carry them back into the house. They weigh a lot... but books do, and although Laurel initially said I could leave them in the lobby, she changed her mind and asked if I'd put them upstairs, in the room that's used as an office.

It's no trouble, and once I've done that, I go back to the kitchen, where Laurel's waiting, clutching my t-shirt in her hands.

"It's dry," she says, holding it out to me.

I take it from her, hesitating for a moment or two before I put it on, wondering if this is her way of saying 'thanks and goodbye' for the day. I hope not. Something feels different between us, and although I'm not sure what it is, I'm not ready for it to end.

"Thanks," I whisper as I pull it over my head, noting the slight disappointment in her eyes when I cover myself. I'm not seeing things. It's there, I know it is.

"Would you like to stay for dinner?" she asks.

"I'd love to."

"I'm making chicken with potato salad, and a green salad on the side... not that I expect Addy will eat much of that."

"Neither will I… not if there's potato salad on offer."

She giggles and I do my best to control my response to her, although it's a struggle.

"I'll check Addy's okay, and then I'll make a start."

"Okay."

While she's gone, I take a look around the kitchen. I might stop here for dinner maybe once or twice a week now, but I haven't had time to really look at the place since I was staying here. Laurel hasn't changed a thing, and I'm relieved to see the wine fridge is pretty much intact. At least she hasn't been drinking alone, which is something.

"She seems okay," she says, coming back into the room and going straight over to the refrigerator.

"Why did you choose to study law?" I ask, as she pulls out some chicken and turns back around again.

"I don't know. It's not in the family, or anything like that. I think I just wanted to do some good… or as Peony put it earlier, to right wrongs. You know?"

"I do."

She smiles. "Of course you do. It's what you do every day."

"I try." She fetches some potatoes, dumping them on the countertop. "Can I help?"

She shakes her head. "I wouldn't dream of it. I owe you a free dinner after getting you over here for no good reason."

"You don't need a reason, and you don't owe me anything, Laurel."

She stops, staring at me, our eyes locked for a moment or two before she coughs and turns away again.

Was it a mistake to say that? It didn't feel like one.

I sit in silence, watching the way she moves around the kitchen, grateful the island unit is hiding my erection from her sight, and once everything's cooking, she turns to face me.

"I know I said I wouldn't ask you to cook, but as you're here, could you just keep an eye on everything while I take Addy upstairs and get her ready for bed?"

"Of course I can."

The sparkle in her eyes makes me smile, and she returns the gesture, biting on her lip and letting out a slow sigh before she leaves the room.

I can't have read that wrong... can I?

Dinner is amazing.

I've had Laurel's potato salad before, but I don't think it's ever tasted this good. Maybe it's not the potato salad that's different, though. Maybe it's that we're both more relaxed than we've ever been in the past.

The wine might be helping with that. We opened a bottle of Chardonnay, and although I was reminded of a conversation I once had with Laurel about Mitch's wine choices – which didn't align with mine, or with Laurel's, it transpired – I kept quiet for tonight, and just enjoyed the company instead.

Addy's been yawning for the last five minutes, and doesn't raise the slightest argument when Laurel says it's time for bed.

I help her down from her chair, but she clings to me, her tiny arms tight around my neck.

"Are you okay?" I whisper, and she nods her head.

"Just saying goodnight."

I smile. "Goodnight, sweetheart."

"I like it when you call me that."

"I like it too."

I glance up at Laurel, whose eyes are glistening, and I mouth the word, "Okay?" at her. She nods her head, smiling, and I put Addy down on the floor. She lets me go, running to her mom, and the two of them leave the room.

My heart might belong to Laurel, but Addy's made a home there, too, and although I'm trying desperately not to read too much into anything that's happened today, I can't help hoping that one day, there might be a future for us... all three of us.

Dreaming about the future won't clear up the kitchen, though, and I load the dishwasher before wiping down the countertops.

I'm almost finished when Laurel comes back down, her sigh alerting me to her presence.

"Is everything okay upstairs?" I ask.

"She fussed about her knee a little, but she's fast asleep now."

"That's good."

She comes further into the room, and we both reach for her empty wineglass at the same time, our hands touching. To me, it feels like a bolt of electricity charging through my body. Judging by the way Laurel jumps, I think she might feel the same, and I turn to her.

"Sorry."

"It's okay. I was just gonna have another glass, that's all."

"Oh. Okay."

"Do you want some more?"

"I can't. I won't be able to drive home."

"You could always stay," she whispers, and my heart stops in my chest.

"Stay?"

"Yes. It's not like you haven't done it before."

I suppose that's true, and overthinking won't help. Neither will holding my breath, and I let it out, hoping she won't notice.

"Okay. I'll have another glass, thanks."

She smiles, fetching the wine from the fridge, and pours us both a glass, putting the bottle down on the countertop.

"Can I ask you something?" she says, pushing my glass closer to me, although I don't pick it up.

"Sure."

"If you were in my shoes, would you move away?"

My heart beats a little too fast now, fear washing over me.

"Move away?"

"Yeah."

"I thought you said you were gonna stay. You said it's Addy's home, and you didn't wanna leave."

"I know. But I was just watching her fall asleep, and I was wondering if what I'm doing is the best thing for her."

"Why wouldn't it be?"

"Because there might be better opportunities elsewhere."

"Professional ones?"

"Yeah."

At least she's not saying this is personal. She's not talking about finding someone else as a father-figure for Addy. That's something. But it's still a tough question for me to answer.

"You have to do whatever feels right for you," I say eventually.

"I wish it was that easy. When I think about what feels right professionally, it feels at odds with what feels right personally."

"So you want to stay here?"

"Of course I do." She shakes her head. "I love it here. It's just… It's so complicated, Brady."

"What is?"

"Life."

I chuckle. "Ain't that the truth."

"No, I'm serious. I went to college intending to become a hot-shot lawyer, then I came back here, got pregnant with Addy, and married Mitch. My career had to take a back seat, and I was okay with that. Being a mom was so much better than I ever thought it would be, and I love every second of it."

"You're good at it, too."

She smiles. "Thank you. The thing is, it wasn't supposed to be like this. I wasn't supposed to wind up on my own."

"You're not on your own."

"I've got Addy, but…"

"You've got me."

Her eyes widen, and she takes a sip of wine while I watch her, wondering what she'll say next. "You've been the best friend I could ever hope for, Brady." I open my mouth to tell her I'm a lot more than a friend, but before I can say anything, she beats me to it. "I had such plans," she whispers, putting down her glass. "Only I've just realized, plans are a waste of time. I mean… look at me…"

"I am. I love looking at you, Laurel. You're the most beautiful woman in the world."

Chapter Eleven

Laurel

"Don't be silly."

I wave away his compliment, my skin flushing, my body on fire. It's been that way for most of the afternoon, ever since he pulled off his wet t-shirt, revealing that perfectly toned chest, the stunning tattoo taking my breath away... and if that makes me shallow, I honestly don't care.

I haven't been blind over the last few months. Brady is an extremely handsome man. He's taller than Mitch, and surprisingly – given what Mitch did – he's in better shape, too. I hadn't realized exactly how much better until I caught sight of his rippling abs and firm pecs. The tattoo just added to the overall masculinity, I think. It gave him an edginess that I never realized existed, and suddenly I found myself in the middle of a full-blown inferno, centered right at my core, and although I knew I shouldn't even be looking, the view was too good to miss.

And now, this man is calling me beautiful?

Me?

I don't think Mitch ever called me beautiful.

He might have occasionally said I looked nice, or called me pretty... but beautiful?

"I'm not," Brady says, and my eyes meet his.

Is this the wine talking? We've only had a glass each, so it can't be that, can it?

Whatever the cause of his temporary insanity, I need to get us back on topic.

What were we talking about? I can't remember...

It was something to do with plans... work... moving.

I take a breath, gulping down some wine, although I'm not sure alcohol is a good idea.

"I need to decide."

"What about?"

"The future. Is it better to put my personal life ahead of my professional one?" That's it. That's what we were discussing. "I know I should make Addy my priority and stay here, where she knows everyone, but what if I can't get a job?"

He moves a little closer, and that inferno heats up even more. If I'm not careful, I'm going to melt and form a puddle at his feet.

"Do you have to decide now?"

"No. But Hart's Creek isn't exactly overflowing with career opportunities for me."

"Have you tried talking to Ezra?"

"Not about this, no. He's been handling the sale of the gym, but I haven't discussed the prospect of working for him. Obviously, he offered me a job when I came back from college, and I accepted, but then had to turn it down when I found out I was pregnant."

He nods his head. "And you think he might have second thoughts about making a similar offer?"

"I don't know. It's possible that he'll feel I let him down, though, don't you think?"

"There's only one way to find out. Ezra's a fair man. He doesn't hold grudges, so I'm pretty sure he'll want to hear from you."

"He might not need anyone, though."

"Maybe not, but if he doesn't, you could always look a little further afield. Alan Barton has a law practice in Willmont Vale."

"I—I know he lives here, but I he's not someone I'm familiar with. He's my dad's age, and I…"

"I know him, Laurel. I can introduce you, if you like?"

"Could you?"

"Of course. And if that doesn't work out, there are several law firms in Concord. That's only a twenty-minute drive from here."

I suck in a breath, nodding my head. "You're right."

"I know I am. You need to relax."

"It's hard sometimes. The future feels so uncertain."

"I get that, Laurel."

I stare up into his eyes. They're like molten chocolate, and I study them for a second. "Do you have any regrets about staying here?" I ask.

He looks confused. "I've never considered leaving."

"You don't think you could've made more of your career if you'd moved away?" He frowns and I realize what I just said, reaching out and placing my hand on his arm. "I'm sorry. That came out wrong. I didn't mean to belittle what you do. You're…"

He shakes his head, smiling. "It's okay. I get what you mean, and in answer to your question, I don't have any professional regrets at all. I like my job, and what I do. It's good knowing practically everyone here by their first name, and I can't imagine living anywhere else. If that makes me boring or lacking in ambition, then I guess that's who I am."

"It doesn't make you any such thing… but it's interesting to know." I sip a little more wine. "You said you don't have any professional regrets. Does that mean you have personal ones?"

I'm not sure that's the most sensible question that's ever left my lips, given the way he makes me feel, but it's out there now.

"Just one." I nod my head, mesmerized, and he stares at me a little longer, like he's expecting me to ask for more details. I can't possibly do that, though, can I? My original question was intrusive enough, but to ask for more would be downright nosy. "Do you want me to tell you what it is?" he asks. I can't answer and he steps even closer, so we're almost touching, and looks down into my eyes. "I regret not taking my chances with you."

I didn't expect that, and for a second I can't think straight. I'm struggling to breathe, too. "Wh—What chances?" I whisper, unable to speak properly.

"When we were younger."

"We were never younger. Not at the same time."

"No. I'm talking about when you were younger, I guess. Just before you went to college, and… and afterwards."

I feel like someone just pulled a rug from under my feet… except I know there are no rugs in my kitchen, and I'm standing on solid ground.

"Are you saying you wanted to be with me back then?"

He nods his head. "I was convinced you'd never give me a second glance – not romantically."

"Why not?"

"Because of the age gap. I was twenty-eight to your eighteen. I didn't think I stood a chance. But I loved the brief times we spent together whenever you came home."

"I didn't realize."

He tilts his head. "Why would you? You saw me as a friend. How were you supposed to know I longed to walk right up to you, place my hands on your cheeks, tip your head back, and kiss you?"

I blink, my breath catching, my heart fluttering. It's a struggle to control the shudder that rocks through my body at the thought of being kissed like that… being touched like that, and knowing he's felt that way all this time. He stayed here for weeks, slept in the room next to mine, and did nothing. A thought races through my mind. I've invited him to spend the night, but now I've switched bedrooms, I'm not sure how we're going to manage it. I can't imagine he'll want to sleep in the room I used to share with Mitch, which leaves the couch, or my bed. *My bed...* My body tingles at that thought, and I gaze into his sparkling eyes. It seems to be what he wants, and now I come to think about it, it doesn't feel like such a bad idea to me, either.

"Why don't you?" I whisper.

"Don't you mean 'why didn't I'? I already explained, I didn't think you'd be interested in me."

"I know, but I didn't say why *didn't* you. I said why *don't* you?"

"You mean now?"

"Yes."

He moves closer still. We're maybe an inch apart – no more – and I stare up into his eyes, melting under the heat of his gaze. I could still step back… still say 'no', or 'stop', and he would. I know that. But I need this. I need to feel wanted.

He dips his head, clasping my face between his hands, and tips my head so it's at just the right angle when his lips meet mine.

There's nothing gentle about his kiss. He claims me, like he's been holding back forever, and as his tongue flicks against my lips, I open to him willingly. He delves, discovering me, and I delve back, wanting more.

He walks us backwards, until I hit the island unit, moving his feet either side of mine, and a low growl fills the space around us as he flexes his hips, his arousal pressing hard against my hip.

There's no turning back. Okay, so there is. He'd let me, if I wanted to. But I don't. I want him.

I reach between us, tugging at his belt buckle and he repeats that growl, a little louder this time, pulling my blouse from my jeans…

Chapter Twelve

Brady

Laurel's already undone my belt and the button on my jeans, but rather than going further, she shifts her attention to my t-shirt. We're both breathless, our tongues dancing, hips grinding, and she pulls it up, letting her hands roam freely over my chest.

The feeling of her skin on mine is too much. I need more.

I need to see her… to touch her… to be inside her.

How we got here is beyond me, but having taken every chance she's offered today, I can't let this one go.

I won't live with any more regrets.

I lift her into my arms and dump her onto the countertop behind her, making her squeal as I break the kiss, looking down at her. She's breathing hard, her eyes on fire, although I think she knows she only has to say the word and I'll stop. Her silence is all I need to hear, and as she reaches for my zipper, I take her hands, holding them behind her back with one of mine.

"Not yet, baby."

She's panting, her breasts heaving, and I unfasten her jeans, pulling them down a little and delving inside. There's a piece of lace that forms an almost non-existent barrier between my fingers and their destination, and I push it aside, finding her swollen clit. She bucks against me, moaning softly as I circle my finger around her.

"Oh, yes," she whispers, and I release her hands, waiting while she lifts her ass so I can pull down her jeans to reveal a lace thong, which makes my cock ache to be inside her… although there are other things to be done first. I remove her jeans completely and lay her down across the island unit, pulling her ass to the edge, and parting her legs as wide as they'll go. She's breathing hard, even though I'm not touching her, and I can't help smiling as I push the lace aside and run my fingers down her folds, finding her entrance. She's dripping and lets out a sigh of satisfaction when I insert two fingers into her, turning my hand so the palm is facing upwards, as I start to move. The action isn't so much in-and-out, as up-and-down, and within seconds, she grabs my wrist.

"What are you doing?" she asks, her eyes betraying her confusion.

"Making you come."

"But it feels so…"

"So what?"

"Different."

"In a good way?"

"In a spectacular way."

I start to move again, and she releases my wrist, slapping her hands down onto the countertop, her body writhing in ecstasy. I don't relent. The motion needs to be hard and fast, and I keep it that way until I sense a tension in her.

"Don't fight it, Laurel."

She shakes her head. "I—I can't do… I can't. It's too…"

"Let it happen. Give yourself to me."

She stutters out a breath, then moves her hand up, covering her mouth as she comes, spurting hot, clear liquid in an arc that hits the floor by the sink. She's thrashing hard, her body succumbing, but I keep up the pressure, until eventually, she grabs my wrist again, and I stop, slowing the movements, rubbing my thumb gently across her clit, which makes her tremble and twitch through the dying embers of her orgasm.

"Wh—What the hell just happened?" she whispers.

"You came."

"I've never come like that before," she says, shaking her head as she leans up on her elbows, still struggling to catch her breath. "The floor's soaked."

"So are you."

I smile down at her and gently pull my fingers from her, raising them to my lips and licking them. She tastes sweet, and I suck my middle finger into my mouth. Her eyes widen and she gasps when I pull her upright and lift her into my arms.

She wraps her legs around me, tilting her head as I lean in and kiss her again, letting her taste herself. There's an urgency to this. Her tongue flicks over mine, swirling into my mouth, and I support her with one arm, while I hold the back of her head with the other hand, controlling the kiss.

Man, she's hot, and just as wild as I'd hoped.

I carry her through to the living room. It's still light outside, and I move to the couch, wishing I had a free hand, so I could pinch myself, just to make sure this is really happening.

It is, though. I can feel her breasts pressed into me, her fingers twisting in my hair.

I contemplate sitting on the couch, with Laurel on my lap, but instead, I set her down on the floor, breaking the kiss, to give her another chance to back out, if nothing else. She looks up into my eyes, and the fire I see in hers tells me that backing out is the last thing on her mind. She proves that, reaching out and putting her fingers in the top of my jeans, pulling me closer. I watch as she lowers my zipper, then pushes down my jeans and trunks, my erection popping into her waiting hand.

"Fuck…" I whisper, and she gasps, lowering her gaze, her eyes widening as she looks up at me again.

"That's… that's…"

"That's what?"

"Huge."

I smile. "It's yours."

She grins, stroking me from base to tip and back again, over and over. I put my hand behind her neck, pulling her into a bruising kiss, my lips crushed to hers. She moans, her hand moving faster and faster, until I have to pull back.

"I—I can't take much more."

"Yeah, you can," she whispers, and drops to her knees, her eyes never leaving mine as she leans in, licking the tip of my cock, then swirling her tongue around it before taking me in her mouth.

I grab her ponytail as she bobs back and forth, and while I desperately want to hold her still and fuck her mouth, I restrain myself, watching her lips as she takes me deeper with every stroke. I'm hitting the back of her throat, but she doesn't gag, and I know if I don't stop this soon, it'll be too late.

I pull my dick from her mouth and lean over, kissing her and pulling her to her feet at the same time. Her hand returns to my cock, but I grab her wrist, pulling it away, only for her to replace it with her other hand. There's a desperation about her, but I can't come yet, so I pull both of her hands behind her back, just like I did in the kitchen, and hold them there.

"Wait," I murmur, towering over her, and she looks up at me, breathing hard and fast, her eyes wide, and then she nods her head.

I release her, quickly undoing her blouse, and pushing it off of her shoulders, letting it fall to the floor. Her bra follows, and I take a moment to enjoy the sight of her perfectly rounded breasts, her nipples hard and pink, before I bend and lick one. She gasps, then cries out when I bite on it, her hand coming up onto the back of my head. She likes it, so I do it again, just a little harder.

"Yes, Brady… yes."

My heart swells in my chest as she grinds out those three simple words. At least she knows it's me. She's not thinking about Mitch… and I can't describe how happy that makes me.

I lavish attention on her nipples, moving from one to the other, and every time I switch, she holds my head steady, like she doesn't want me to stop.

Eventually I have to. I need more, and I think she does, too.

I stand up straight, pushing down her thong, which she kicks off, before I remove my t-shirt. We're both naked, and while I'm aching to bury myself inside her, I also want to taste her. Properly. I've dreamed of it for so long, and I can't wait another second.

I turn around, backing her up to the couch, then lower her, pulling her forward so her ass is on the edge. She gazes up at me as I kneel, parting her legs, then raising them, letting my eyes drop to the triangle of blonde hair at the apex of her thighs.

"I always said you were the most beautiful woman in the world," I whisper, leaning closer, before I part her swollen lips with my fingers and lick her exposed clit. She tastes so sweet, I have to repeat that motion, and then I flick my tongue across that tight pearl.

"More," she groans. "Don't stop."

I'm not going to, and as she raises her legs a little higher, I insert a finger inside her, quickly adding a second. She bucks against me.

"G—Give me more," she stammers, so I add a third finger, stretching her, and her body shudders. I suck her clit into my mouth, working her pussy a little harder with my fingers, and the shudder becomes a tremor. A slight squeal leaves her lips and I tilt my head up, looking at her as she clamps her hand over her mouth, throws her head back, and comes... so damn hard.

She's keeping it quiet because of Addy, but I've never seen a woman come like this before. She's writhing, her body succumbing to pleasure on a whole new scale, and just as it subsides, I pull back, withdrawing my fingers, and kneel up, palming my cock. Her pussy is dripping, and I edge forward, rubbing the tip of my dick over her sensitized clit, which makes her quiver.

"Please," she whimpers, and I position my cock at her entrance. I dip the head inside, holding it there. She's tight, and I take a moment, watching the smile form on her lips, and then slowly thrust all the way home.

"Fuck... yes." I remember not to raise my voice, although it's a struggle, and I wrap my arms around her thighs, letting her legs hang over my elbows as pull her forward, her ass off the edge of the couch now. I pull back out, almost all the way, and wait.

She looks up at me. "Don't tease, Brady."

"You want me?"

"Yes."

I've died. I've died and gone to heaven. It's the only explanation.

I slam back into her, taking her hard, a film of sweat forming on my chest and back as I pound into her relentlessly.

She lets out a moan with every stroke, and then reaches down. I expect her to rub her clit, but she doesn't. She touches my dick, her fingers drifting along my length as I slide in and out of her. No-one's ever done that to me before, and there's something very intimate about it, like she's helping to join us together.

"You're really stretching me," she murmurs, her fingers alighting on her own flesh. She explores herself as I penetrate her, over and over.

"You wanna see what I can see?" I ask and she looks up at me like she doesn't understand.

"How?"

I glance around, but suddenly realize my mistake.

"Damn. I left my phone in the kitchen."

"Mine's behind you, on the table, but what do you need a phone for?"

I don't reply, but twist around, grabbing her phone, and then hold it out to her, so she can unlock it.

"What are you doing?" she says as I study the screen, finding the camera.

"Wait and see."

I raise her left leg again, then hold the phone in place, lining it up, and switch it to video as I start to move again. Laurel sighs.

"Are you taking pictures?"

"I'll show you in a second," I murmur, capturing a good couple of minutes of footage, my cock sinking deeper and deeper, glistening with her juices, stretching her wide.

Once I'm sure I've got enough, I switch the camera off and find the video, turning the phone around and showing it to Laurel.

"Press play," I whisper, and she taps the screen, her eyes fixed on it, as I keep moving, harder and harder, her breath shortening, her pussy tightening around my dick.

"That's so hot." Her voice is a murmur as she puts the phone down. "I can't believe how big you are."

"That's partly the perspective."

She shakes her head. "No, it's not."

I pull her even further forward so I can go deeper, and she lets out a low groan of satisfaction. "Rub your clit," I murmur. "I wanna watch you come."

"Again?"

"Of course."

She seems surprised, but moves her hand down, stopping at her clit this time, and circling it with her middle finger. She's done this before. That much is obvious. But I don't want to think about that. I don't want to think about anything that's gone before.

The circling becomes more of a rubbing.

"That's it, baby… make yourself come."

She stares at me, confusion warring with the hedonistic delight of her impending orgasm.

"It's too… It's gonna… Oh, Brady…"

She's incoherent, and I love it.

"Come for me. Let me watch you."

Her body tenses. She moves her free hand up, clamping it over her mouth, and I feel her tighten around me as she comes hard, her head thrashing from side to side, her body twisting and contracting. I keep moving, even though her squeal is in danger of becoming a scream. For a second, she removes her hand, draws breath, and then bites down on her knuckle, her eyes locking on mine, like she's asking for help, but begging for more.

Slowly, her orgasm subsides, her body convulsing as she calms, her hands dropping to her sides. She's spent, but I'm not done yet.

I lift her back up onto the couch, her legs still hooked over my arms, and I lean over her.

"Sit up," I whisper.

"Are you kidding?" She sounds a little drunk and I have to smile. She's so cute.

"No. Put your hands around my neck and sit up."

She takes a moment, but then raises her arms, doing exactly as I've said, and as she pulls herself up, I stand.

"What are you doing?"

There's just a hint of panic in her voice. I'm still inside her, and as I straighten, I impale her deeply.

"Getting comfortable."

She moans as I lift her up and bring her straight back down again, giving her my length.

"Oh… that's g—good."

"Yeah, it is."

"Are you sure this is comfortable?"

I turn, sitting down on the couch, with her on top of me, and smile. "Yes. Although it's nowhere near as comfortable as this."

She grins as I pull my arms out, releasing her legs and she lets them rest on either side of me, shifting her position. Her hands are still locked around the back of my neck, and she grinds her hips down onto me, her eyes fluttering closed.

"Oh, God… that's so deep."

"Take me, Laurel." Her eyes open wide, fixing on mine. "I'm yours."

I don't care if that's too much. It's the truth.

I don't know whether she understood my meaning, but she smiles, which is nice, and then raises herself up, moving her hands so they're on my shoulders, before she slams down again, letting out a guttural groan as she takes me deep inside her.

"Yes," she says, grinding out the word as she repeats her movements, over and over. I rest my hands on her hips, helping her. Up and down. Up and down.

She moves her right hand between us, and although I expect her to rub her clit again, she doesn't. She strokes my cock, just like she did before, as she slides back and forth.

"You like touching my dick?" I ask, and she nods her head.

"It's so big. I like how it feels."

Compliments like that, I can take any day, and I smile, lifting my hips off of the couch.

"I like how it feels too, baby."

We form a rhythm, hard and fast. She's slamming onto me, and after a while, she stops, moving her hand back to my shoulder, and leans forward. Her lips meet mine, our tongues clashing, and she rotates her hips in a slow clockwise dance, driving my cock crazy.

"You like being so deep inside me?" she whispers.

"I love being so deep inside you."

She smiles, grinding harder and harder, and then leans back, her hands behind her, resting on my thighs, as she rides me.

"Oh… oh, yes." She seems surprised by her own pleasure, and she nods her head, taking me faster.

"Please, Laurel… I'm gonna come."

"So… so…"

She throws her head back, and although she opens her mouth, nothing comes out. The sight of her glorious body, succumbing to pleasure yet again is too much for me, and even though I'm about as deep inside her as I can go, I raise my hips still further, struggling not to cry out… not to yell her name, and shout my love for her, as I fill her with everything I've got.

I've never felt anything like that in my life. It was like I gave her my entire body, my mind… my soul. My heart's been hers for years, and now I have nothing left to give. I'm hers. Entirely.

I lean back a little, letting out a sigh, still unable to believe this has really happened. We're here, at last. My dreams have all come true, and the wait was more than worth it.

Laurel's head is bent, and although she's leaning against me now, her arms have fallen to her sides, like she doesn't even have the energy to raise them. That thought makes me smile and I lean back further still, trying to put just a little space between us so I can see her face. She doesn't move, so I cup her cheek with my free hand, the touch sparking her to life.

She tries to sit up, to pull away from me.

"Whoa. Stop." She shakes her head, edging back. "Stop, Laurel. You need to take this gently, or it's gonna hurt."

I lift her off of me, taking my time over it, but the moment I have, she gets to her feet and stumbles backwards. I reach out, but she snatches her hand away. There's a bleak look in her eyes that tells me this isn't a dream come true at all. It's my worst nightmare, and I can't see any way in which it will end well.

"Laurel? What's wrong?"

She glances down at my cock, which is still surprisingly hard, considering what we've just done, and as I take that in, I suddenly realize what the problem is, and the magnitude of my felony... especially in her eyes.

I leap to my feet, but she steps back.

"I'm sorry. I'm so sorry. How could I have done that to you?"

"Done what?"

"Forgotten to use a condom." I feel like such a jerk. After the way things started out between her and Mitch, I couldn't have made a worse mistake if I'd tried.

"It's not that," she says, and I step closer.

"Are you on birth control?"

She shakes her head. "I've never been able to tolerate it, but after what happened... with Addy... Mitch always used condoms."

I guess that's something. He might have been cheating, he might have got Kaylee pregnant, but at least he was careful with Laurel. More careful than me, it seems.

"Okay, so..."

"I'm pretty sure the timing's out," she says, and although I want to ask for more details, like when she had her last period, or when the next one's due, I don't think I can. It might sound like I'm panicking, and I'm not.

"If you're wrong..."

"I can't do this," she says, raising her head at last and looking at me, the sadness in her eyes taking my breath away.

"Hey… you won't have to." I move closer. "Not alone."

She frowns. "What do you mean?"

"If you're pregnant, you won't be alone. I'll…"

"That's not what I'm talking about, Brady." Her voice is harsh, and it's my turn to take a step back.

"Would you like to explain?"

She takes a deep breath, and I brace myself. "No. I'd like you to leave."

"Excuse me?" I step closer again, my hand on her shoulder, although she shrugs it off.

"I said I'd like you to leave."

"After everything we've just done? You wanna throw me out?"

"I want you to l—leave," she says, her voice cracking.

"Why are you doing this? If it's because I forgot the condom, we can…"

"I told you, it's got nothing to do with that."

"Is it guilt, then? Is it something to do with Mitch?"

She steps closer, raising her eyes to mine. "I've asked you to leave, dammit. Will you just go?" Her voice is a low whisper, but I can tell she'd love to yell at me, and if Addy wasn't asleep upstairs, she would.

It feels like there's nothing left to be said, and I turn away, picking up my clothes from the floor and taking them with me to the lobby. I quickly put them on, out of her sight, and then I grab my phone from the kitchen, and leave, my heart in pieces.

Chapter Thirteen

Laurel

How can I still be so haunted by one night?

It doesn't make sense.

When I first slept with Mitch all those years ago, it didn't get to me like this, and that was my first time. Ever.

The truth is, what he and I did together was enjoyable, but it wasn't anything more than that.

I might have felt disappointed that he didn't want to make more of it, but that was the youthful romantic in me, and once I'd recovered from starry-eyed silliness, I wrote it off to experience in no time at all. Losing my virginity certainly hadn't been what I'd been led to believe, and if I hadn't found out I was pregnant, I'd probably never have given him another thought.

That's the God's honest truth.

No matter what became of us in the end, and no matter how our love grew from that strange starting point, there's no getting away from the fact that it was nothing more than an hour or so of rolling around in bed, and a mistake that changed both our lives.

Forever.

I'd enjoyed it. I've never denied that. But enjoyable is one thing…

What Brady did to me is something else entirely.

It's been exactly four weeks now, and instead of getting on with my life, trying to rebuild things after Mitch's death, all I can think about is how Brady touched me in a way I've never experienced before, how he made me come so hard I lost control… and the look in his eyes when I sent him away. It still haunts me, just like it did the moment he walked out the door that night, closing it so quietly behind him, *and* when I heard his car drive away, *and* as I tried to get to sleep, failing dismally, my body aching for him. I can't forget any of it, any more than I could the next morning, when I woke alone, wishing he could be there with me.

I can't think straight, even now.

I've done nothing about going through my law books, or talking to Ezra about a job. The money from the sale of the gym came through over a week ago, and at the very least I should look at my finances, but instead I'm sitting at the island unit, nursing a cup of cold coffee and thinking about Brady… no, Mitch… no, Brady.

"Oh, why does this have to be so complicated?"

Whatever 'this' is.

I can't think about that. Not while I'm still trying to work everything out. Not while I'm coming to terms with what I've done, and what I've lost.

Which would be Mitch… no, Brady.

"Oh, hell…"

I keep asking myself if it's guilt that's making me feel this way. It was at the time. Brady was right about that. The moment I came down from that last orgasmic high, for some reason, reality hit me. It hadn't after any of the others, but it did then.

I could feel his arousal still twitching inside me… see the look of contentment on his face, and I was wracked with guilt. That's why I threw him out. Because I couldn't face him.

It made sense then. But now?

Can this confusion and muddle… this indecision and longing all be about guilt?

I don't know.

After all, it was me who instigated what happened that night. I was the one who asked Brady to kiss me. I practically told him to kiss me. So why should I feel guilty? It was my idea.

I wanted him, and I won't deny it.

I can't.

I've got the video evidence of how much I wanted him. It might only be a couple of minutes long, but it's enough.

To be honest, I was so wrapped up in what had happened, and in beating myself up over it, I forgot about the video for a while, until I was taking some photographs of Addy. I happened to look back at them after she'd gone to bed, and that was when I noticed it. I played it. Not just once, but over and over, surprised still by how big Brady was, and how he stretched me, aroused by watching him slide in and out of me, my juices glistening on his shaft. I touched myself then, remembering how good it had felt to have him inside me, and although I hadn't done anything like that since before I met Mitch, I came in no time at all, my pussy dripping with need for him.

For him.

Not Mitch.

I shake my head.

What's wrong with me?

Quite a lot, it seems, because I've done that almost every evening since. It doesn't help, and it certainly doesn't make me feel better, but I can't seem to stop myself. When Addy's gone to bed, I sit and watch the video, and I make myself come. I tell myself I won't. All day, I remind myself I'm supposed to be in mourning, not lusting after another man, but when evening comes around, I'm like a moth being drawn to a flame, knowing it'll end badly, but unable to deny the overwhelming compulsion to do it, anyway.

It seems my need for Brady is greater than anything... even my guilt.

When I think about him, which I often do – not just when I'm touching myself – my body is filled with a longing for more. I yearn for his touch, for his tongue, his lips, his words... to feel him deep inside me. I used to want Mitch, but never like this... never like I couldn't breathe, couldn't think, couldn't function without him.

And that's got to be wrong, hasn't it?

Mitch was my husband. I'm still grieving for him. How can I possibly want Brady in the way I do?

I've told myself to regret it, but how can I regret something that felt so good?

How can I regret being with a man who looked into my eyes and said, 'I'm yours'?

I can't. And why should I?

It wasn't a mistake. I knew exactly what I was doing, and I wanted it, just like Brady did.

So, is it that I regret throwing him out? Is that what I feel guilty about?

I can't be sure. I didn't watch him leave. Instead, I stood with my back to him, waiting until I heard the front door close, and then I turned around, tears streaming down my cheeks, my body shaking, and pain coursing through me. I wanted to call him back. But how could I? I'd hurt him. Even I knew that.

And if I didn't, his silence has been a big enough clue for anyone to work it out.

Okay, so he hasn't been completely silent since that night.

He sent me a text message the following morning.

I'd only slept very fitfully, and had been awake for ages, regretting his absence, when when my phone beeped at six-thirty. I pulled it from the nightstand and squinted at the screen, seeing his name and trying not to hope as I tapped on the message, reading…

— *Are you okay?*

What had I expected? That he'd ask to come over? Say he wanted to talk? Beg me for a second chance?

Why would he?

After everything I'd said and done to him the previous night, he was being more than generous in asking if I was okay.

The problem was, I knew if I answered, he might take it as a sign that I wanted to start a conversation, and I wasn't sure I did, so I just put my phone back and left it.

I didn't expect to hear from him again… and I didn't.

Not for about ten days. I missed his lunchtime calls. I missed the sound of his voice, but I had no-one to blame, other than myself.

I was getting used to the silence when he contacted me again.

This time, I'd just stepped out of the shower. My phone was on the bed, and it beeped, although I never even thought about Brady. I guessed it would probably be Peony, or maybe even my mom or dad. I gasped when I saw his name, and sat on the edge of the mattress, a towel wrapped around me as I read…

— *Is everything okay? Or is it too soon to be asking?*

It seemed like an odd question, and I put my phone down, picking it up to read his message again before I remembered what we'd done, his words echoing around my head…

"If you're pregnant, you won't be alone."

Of course. He must have been tracking the dates, possibly worrying about the outcome, and because of that, I knew I had to reply.

— It's fine. I was right. The timing was out.

I wasn't about to tell him that my period had started five days after we'd made love, or that I'd felt weirdly disappointed when it had.

He didn't reply, and I haven't heard a thing from him since.

I can hardly blame him for that.

I treated him so badly, I don't deserve anything other than his silence. But what makes it worse is that I miss him so damn much.

I mean, how contrary is that? I threw him out, with no explanation... and I miss him.

It's not just his calls, or the sound of his voice, it's his friendship, his presence, the safety of knowing he's there, when I need him... and if I'm being honest, it's the romance of him. Because he was romantic, even before we kissed.

Although, speaking of kisses, I miss those too.

We might have only had one evening together, but I can't forget it.

I can't forget how he felt, or what he looked like, and from that perspective, having the video on my phone doesn't help.

I know I could delete it, but I can't.

I like the reminder that I could make a man feel like that. Because there's no denying, Brady was enormous, no matter what he said about perspectives. Mitch was never like that, and I guess that's another problem.

I hate myself for making comparisons.

It's not fair... but it's also not the only one.

Brady was bigger and better, but he was also kinder and more accepting.

I can still remember what Mitch said to me on the night I first moved in with him. I was lying naked on the bed, and he settled between my legs, shimmying downward, and letting out a sigh of what sounded like disappointment.

"Is something wrong?" I asked.

He looked up, a slight grimace on his face. "I don't do hairy pussies."

"I'm sorry?" I knew I was blushing and was grateful the light wasn't too bright.

"I like my women shaved."

I hadn't known women could be shaved there. He'd made love to me twice before and hadn't mentioned it. Although he hadn't gotten up close and personal on either occasion. Even so, he must have realized. And what did he expect me to do? I didn't know how to ask, but it transpired I didn't need to.

He changed position then, shifting from between my parted legs, to kneeling alongside me.

"You can still suck my dick," he said, like it was some kind of reward, and he tapped it against my lips until I opened my mouth, taking him inside. It occurred to me that he wasn't shaved, and that the hairs were tickling my nose, but I couldn't say very much at the time. I just got on with doing what he said, acting on his instructions. He used his fingers then, rubbing my clit until I came, and I forgot all about the inequity of his comments.

When he went to work the next morning, I showered and made sure to shave. It felt odd, and I wondered why he'd made such a thing about it, and whether my efforts would please him.

They did.

He came home from work that evening, and after we'd eaten, I told him what I'd done. He smiled and insisted I show him… there and then, in the kitchen. I felt self-conscious, but stripped off my clothes, and smiled when he let out a groan, and moved closer, dropping to his knees before me.

"That's perfect," he murmured, then he leaned in and kissed me, parting my lips with his fingers, and running his tongue over my clit. I came in no time at all, and from that day on, I made a point of keeping myself in trim… until his death.

I couldn't see the point after that.

But did Brady say anything?

No.

Did he mind?

It seemed not.

The way he made me come was incredible. I've never known anything like it… not just in the number of times, but the variety of ways in which he did it, and now, whenever I think about missing sex, missing having a man in my life and how it makes me feel, the man I'm thinking about isn't Mitch, it's Brady.

But that's wrong, isn't it?

How can I feel like that when Mitch has only been dead for five months?

"Mommy?"

I jump out of my skin and look down at Addy, who's standing beside me. Heaven knows how long she's been there, and I'm just relieved I've kept my thoughts to myself, rather than saying anything aloud.

"Yes, sweetheart."

She frowns. "Don't call me that."

"Why not?"

"Because Brady used to call me that, and he doesn't come here anymore."

She misses him so much, it makes me want to cry.

For the first week or so, she asked after him every day. She cried a lot too, and there were more tantrums than I want to think about. At times, I thought about calling him for her sake, if not for mine. I couldn't, though. It wouldn't have been fair… to any of us.

"I know, but that's only because he's busy."

"Too busy for us?"

She looks so sad, and I get down from my chair, crouching in front of her. "No. He's just busy."

I feel even worse now. Brady was good for Addy. He was like the father she had never had in Mitch, and I guess that's another thing for me to feel guilty about. No matter how much I loved Mitch, and how grateful I was to him for doing the right thing, he wasn't a very good father. I've tried to pretend he was, I've praised him to anyone who'll listen – including Brady – but there's no getting away from it, Mitch and fatherhood were not well matched. He was never here. He was a stranger to Addy and her response when he died made that obvious. She couldn't mourn someone she didn't know… but she's mourning now. For Brady.

He spent more time with Addy in the few weeks he was here than Mitch did in her entire life… and it shows.

Because Addy's so sad without him.

If only I hadn't asked him to kiss me, things could be as they were.

Does that mean I should regret what followed that kiss?

Or does it mean I should feel guilty about instigating it in the first place?

Or maybe both?

I pull Addy into a hug, wishing I could understand, or better still, turn back the clock and make it all right again… for both of us.

Or should I say for all of us?

Chapter Fourteen

Brady

Tomorrow, it'll be six weeks to the day since I made love with Laurel, and I miss her so much I can taste it. Sometimes I even think I can still taste her, but I know that's only my imagination playing tricks on me.

Sure, I could call her. I could even go over there and see her. But what would be the point?

She pushed me away and made it clear she wanted nothing to do with me… and I have to respect that. No matter how much I want to know what happened.

Because I'm damned if I can understand it.

I've contacted her twice, but I haven't asked her for an explanation. I haven't asked her anything, other than if she's okay. The first time I asked, she didn't reply, and in a way I wasn't surprised. She'd thrown me out less than twelve hours earlier. Why would she have wanted to talk to me? I might have hoped she'd say something, even if it was just 'yes', or 'no', so that we could have a conversation of sorts, but she'd made it clear she wasn't interested.

I thought about her every minute of every day, though, reliving our time together, torturing myself with the thought that, having made all my dreams come true, my life without her is now far worse than anything that came before.

I've touched her, felt her… been inside her, and knowing I'll never do any of that again doesn't bear thinking about.

The second time I sent her a message was nearly two weeks later. I'd been dumb enough not to use a condom and, even if she didn't want to talk to me, I had to know if there were any consequences to my actions.

I asked if *everything* was okay that time, and she replied, thank God. Her message might have been short and to the point, explaining that she'd been right, and that the timing was out, but at least I knew.

She wasn't pregnant.

I didn't know whether to feel relieved or disappointed.

The thought that I could have been as irresponsible as Mitch had been weighing on my mind. But if she'd been pregnant, at least I'd have had an excuse to be with her.

The thing was, I didn't want it to be like that. Sure, I loved the idea of us making a baby together… of becoming a family and living the life I'd always dreamed of. But I didn't want to be the man she had to settle for because it would make things look right. The thought of forcing her into a relationship with me, when she so clearly didn't want one, was abhorrent, so I swallowed my disappointment and left it at that.

I haven't stopped beating myself up, though.

Why would I?

If I'd waited, I could still call her every day, hear her voice, and go over there several times a week. What we had before might not have been perfect, but it was better than this.

Maybe I should have stayed… perhaps even told her she had nothing to feel guilty about. Because she was clearly overcome with guilt. Why else would she have behaved the way she did? I could have explained to her that Mitch was cheating… that he was leaving town with his pregnant girlfriend to start a new life somewhere else. She'd never have believed me, though. She'd have thought I was trying to score points, and in any case, I couldn't do that to her.

It would break her heart to know what Mitch was doing… that she and Addy meant so little to him.

No. I had to leave. I had to do as she asked. But sitting around at home every evening is killing me, even if I don't know what else I can do.

I grab my phone from the table in front of me, and look up Cooper's number. His Friday nights are usually spent with Meredith, as are his Saturdays and Sundays, but he won't mind me interrupting. And if he does, he won't answer.

"Hi," he says, and I struggle not to sigh out my relief.

"Hello."

"What's wrong?"

He can tell, just from my 'hello', and I almost smile. "Pretty much everything."

"Wow. It's that bad?"

"It's worse."

There's a slight pause. "I'd offer to come over, but…"

"But what?"

I hear a slight rustling, although I'm not sure what it is. "I've just had a massive fight with Meredith." He's lowered his voice, and I wonder if the noise I heard was him moving, so she wouldn't be able to hear what he's saying.

"What was it about this time?" Cooper is as laid-back as they come, so I imagine it was something to do with Meredith… or something Meredith's done. It usually is, and while I'm not saying he'll have been blameless, I doubt he'll have started it.

"A painting," he says, surprising me.

"A painting?"

"I know it sounds trivial, and it is… to me."

"But it's not to her?"

"Nothing about her art is ever trivial to Meredith."

"What happened?" I ask, keen to hear about someone else's problems for a change.

"She brought one of her paintings over last weekend. She'd been talking about it for ages, and although I'd never seen it, she'd made it sound like it would fit really well in the living room here."

"Can I guess it doesn't?"

"It might… if I had absolutely no taste whatsoever. It's totally fucking hideous."

I surprise myself by laughing. "You didn't say that to her face, did you?"

"Of course not. I'm not an idiot. I learned not to voice my opinions on her work when I first met her, but I thought she might have learned something too…"

"Namely, that your taste and hers don't align?" I say and he sighs loud enough for me to hear him.

"Something like that."

"But she brought the painting over, anyway?"

"Yeah. I took one look at it and knew it wouldn't work, but I made all the right noises and told her I'd hang it during the week."

"And you forgot?"

"No. I hung it. I knew she'd be mad if I didn't."

"Then what's the problem?"

"I hung it upside down." I laugh again, even louder this time. "It's not funny, Brady."

"Yeah, it is."

"No, it's not. She got here earlier this evening, and because I haven't seen her all week, we went straight to bed for a while. She got up to get a drink while I was still lying there recovering, and telling her about my receptionist, and the next thing I knew, Meredith was screaming at me, calling me a fucking philistine."

"That sounds a little extreme."

"You don't know Meredith."

It's true. I've only met her a few times, and we didn't warm to each other. I've always been amazed she and Coop have stayed together for as long as they have. They're like oil and water.

"Where is she now? Has she gone home?"

"No. I thought she was gonna storm off, like she usually does, but I think she's decided to make me suffer. She's in the bedroom, sulking. I'm sorry, man, but if I go out now, I think she'll probably freak out."

"It's okay," I say, even if it isn't.

"Do you wanna talk?"

Not over the phone. "No. It's fine. I—I think I'll go to Dawson's and drown my sorrows." It's got to be better than sitting here, dwelling on them.

"Okay. If I can iron things out with Meredith, I might join you there."

"Then you can tell me what's happened with your receptionist."

"Oh, that's nothing… except I think she's gonna hand in her resignation."

"Seriously? She hasn't been with you very long."

"I know, and to be honest, I could do without the hassle."

"I can understand that. You get enough from Meredith."

He chuckles and we end our call, and although I know there are no guarantees Coop will make it, I go out anyway, walking the short distance to the bar at the end of Maple Street, where I live.

Dawson's place might be close to my home, but I'm not exactly a regular here. Even so, Dawson knows me well enough, and greets me with his best effort at a smile. He's been miserable since his wife left him a while back, and I can sympathize… although I'm not about to say that.

I order a glass of red wine, and find a table, wondering as I sit whether this was such a good idea. I feel the need to get very, very drunk, but for a man in my position, that's something best done in the privacy of my own home, not in a bar, in public.

I drink my wine quickly, wishing I'd had something to eat before coming out, and although I know I ought to go straight home, I get up and wander to the bar, ordering a second.

Focusing on not making a fool of myself seems to help with not thinking about Laurel too much, and once I've finished the second glass, I order a third, telling myself with every sip that it'll be okay. I can handle it.

Of course I can.

"Hi."

I jump as a woman sits down in the chair opposite mine, and it takes a moment or two for my eyes to focus on her. She's not familiar, and I'm pretty sure I'd remember her if I'd seen her before. She's pretty enough… not beautiful, like Laurel, but pretty enough. Her long auburn hair falls in ringlets over her bare shoulders. She's wearing one of those tops with really thin straps, and it's clear she doesn't have a bra on underneath. The outline of her nipples is too prominent.

"I've been watching you," she says and I raise my eyes, noting how green hers are, and that she's smiling, her full mouth opening to reveal a line of brilliant white teeth.

"You have?"

"Yes. You look sad."

"I'm fine. Honestly. I was just going home."

I get up, because even though she's pretty, I'm not interested.

Outside, I'm surprised by how the wind's picked up. It's been hot for the last few days, but now it feels like it might rain, and

I'm pleased I brought a coat. I'm also pleased I didn't drive, because I've had too much to drink.

I'm about to set off for home when I feel a hand on my shoulder and I turn around. The woman is right behind me, the wind catching her hair. Now she's standing, I can see that not only is her top barely there, but she's also wearing a pair of denim shorts that don't really qualify for the name. They're practically non-existent.

"You're not fine," she says. "And I don't think it's very sensible for you to go home alone... not when we could go home together and have so much more fun."

I've never been propositioned before, and I'm not sure I like it. I open my mouth to say so when I remember Laurel asking me to kiss her. "Why don't you?" Those were her words, and she gazed into my eyes as she said them. Did she know where that kiss would lead? It felt like it at the time. It felt like she knew exactly where we were headed, and if that wasn't being propositioned, I don't know what it was. The thing was, I liked that. I liked every syllable of her come-on and every second of what happened afterwards. Her words made me feel wanted, but this... this is different.

"I'm sorry. Do I know you?" I say, and the woman shakes her head.

"I don't think so. I'm not from here."

"Where are you from?"

"Willmont Vale. I came here with my friend, but she's hooked up with some guy..." She waves her hand in the vague direction of the door, teetering on her four-inch heels, and I realize how drunk she is, and how young.

"I'd offer to take you back to Willmont Vale, but I walked here, and besides, I've had too much to drink. I can't drive."

Her eyes light up and she steps closer. "If you walked here, you can't live too far away, so why don't we just go back to your place?"

She's persistent. "No, thanks." I pull out my phone. "I can call you a cab to take you home, if you like?"

She turns and looks at the bar, as though she's considering her options, and I notice the back of her shorts. They're cut in such a way that most of her ass is revealed, making it clear she's either wearing a thong, or no underwear at all. That thought ought to elicit some kind of response, but all I can see is Laurel lying on the island unit in her kitchen, that thin scrap of lace doing nothing to hide her from me. I wanted her so much. I want her now, and I know I always will. There's no hunger in me for anyone else, and despite this young woman's obvious attractions, I can't feel anything... except old. She turns suddenly, shrugging her shoulders as she looks up at me. "Okay," she says and I take a moment to remember what we're talking about before I dial the number for the local cab company, the call being answered by Alison, who I've known all my life. She's about fifteen years older than me and owns the company with her husband, Derek.

"Ali? It's me, Brady."

"Oh, hi, honey. How are you?"

"I'm fine." I'm not, but she's the kind of woman who'd get my darkest secrets out of me in ten seconds flat, given the chance, so it's easier to pretend I don't have any.

"What can I do for you?"

"Have you got a cab available?"

"Sure."

"One with a female driver?"

"In about ten minutes," she says after a slight pause.

"Okay. Can you send it to Dawson's place? I've got a young lady here who needs to be taken to Willmont Vale. She'll give the driver the address."

"She's not gonna throw up in the back of the cab, is she?" Alison sounds wary.

"No. She'll be fine."

"Okay. I'll get Linda over there in ten minutes."

I thank her and we end the call before I replace my phone in my back pocket and look at the young woman again.

"A female driver?" she says, raising her eyebrows at me.

"Yes."

"Is that for my benefit?"

"Of course. I'm the sheriff here. It's my responsibility to…"

"Oh, shit. You mean I've just… I've just… with the local sheriff?"

I smile. "You didn't do anything… with anyone."

"Only because you said 'no'." She shakes her head. "I feel like such an idiot." Her eyes fix on mine and she moves a little closer. "You're not married as well, are you?"

"No."

She nods, relieved by my answer, I think. "Are you recently divorced then?"

"No."

She tilts her head. "There's someone, though, isn't there?"

Maybe she's not as drunk as I thought. "Yeah, there is."

She sighs, and shivers, and I remember how windy it is, removing my jacket and holding it out to her. I don't offer to help her put it on, and she hesitates for a second before she takes it, draping it around her shoulders. "Thanks," she murmurs, then looks up again. "I hope she knows how lucky she is."

On the contrary. She thinks she's better off without me.

"What's your name?" I ask, changing the subject.

"Why? Are you gonna arrest me?"

"No. You haven't committed a crime that I'm aware of. I'm just asking your name."

"It's Peyton. And you're Brady."

"How did you know that?"

"Because you told the lady at the cab company."

It's my turn to feel like an idiot now. "And how old are you?"

"Old enough." I raise my eyebrows and she lets out a sigh. "I'm twenty-two."

"Which makes me fifteen years older than you. Did you know that?"

She shrugs her shoulders, my jacket slipping slightly, although she pulls it back again. "I dig older men." I don't want to think about that, and I shake my head. "Who's the lucky lady?" she asks.

So much for changing the subject.

"She's a friend."

"With benefits?"

"Something like that."

She frowns, like she's thinking, and then her face clears. "Oh, I get it. You wanted more than benefits. You wanted forever."

She's stating a fact, not asking a question, but I nod my head, anyway.

"Yeah, I did. But she doesn't even want friendship anymore." No matter how many times I've thought that through in the last six weeks, it hurts to say it out loud.

Peyton moves closer, tilting her head back and looking up into my eyes. "I'm sorry."

"So am I, believe me."

She shakes her head. "I wasn't meaning about her. If she's too blind to see what she's throwing away, more fool her." She sucks in a breath, reaching out and placing a cool hand on my arm. "I meant I'm sorry about tonight. I genuinely thought you looked sad… as well as handsome, and sexy, and just my type."

"Even though I'm fifteen years older than you?"

"Like I say, I prefer older men. They know what they're doing."

"I'm not sure I do."

She smiles. "Yeah, you do. I've got a sixth sense about these things. You're hot, Brady, and you shouldn't waste your time on someone who doesn't appreciate you."

She moves her hand up to my chest. "It's not wasted," I murmur, stepping back so her hand falls to her side. "One day you'll fall in love, and then you'll understand that nothing is too much... not time, not pain, not anything."

She looks down. "It's just my luck. Not only are you the sheriff, but you're hopelessly in love."

Hopeless feels about right, because I can't see any future for Laurel and me.

In fact, I can't see any future at all.

Chapter Fifteen

Laurel

"You honestly can't see a thing from here, can't you?" Peony sits beside me on the shady terrace at the back of the house, craning her neck to get a view of Nate and Taylor's house. I know they've been coming up here more often, because Nate called when they got back from their honeymoon to say they were starting work on the interiors. It was kind of him to let me know, and he really didn't need to. I haven't seen them in person, although I guess that's not surprising. I haven't seen anyone, other than Peony, who invited herself over this afternoon.

"No. It's because of the dip."

"Is it finished yet?"

"Not quite, but I don't think it'll be long now."

She turns, her eyes alighting on Addy, who's playing on the grass a few feet away, before she focuses on me, raising her hand to shield her eyes from the sun.

"Are you okay?"

"I'm fine."

I'm very far from fine. I'm still haunted by what happened between me and Brady. The memories haven't faded. If anything, they've grown more intense over the last few days, but what can I say? If I told her, she'd think badly of me, and I couldn't handle that.

"How are the preparations going for Gabe and Remi's wedding?" I ask, and she narrows her eyes, knowing that's a deliberate change of subject.

"I think we're just about ready." She takes a sip of homemade lemonade, then rests her hand on her baby bump. It's much more substantial now, but she looks fantastic, especially given the heat. She's wearing a pale blue sundress, which is most unusual for Peony. She's normally a jeans and t-shirts kind of girl, but it's too hot for that. Her dress is almost identical to the one I put on today, and even if we didn't plan it that way, it made us laugh when she arrived. Addy said we looked like twins, and with the way my hair's grown out, it was hard to disagree.

"What are you going to do about work once the baby's born?"

"I'm hoping to be able to carry on with most of it. I've been resting quite a lot, and still been able to get everything done, and if I have to, I'll find someone to help part-time."

"Can you afford to?"

She smiles. "I can. I never thought I'd say this, but I'm actually doing quite well."

"Don't put yourself down."

She shakes her head. "It wasn't that long ago that I nearly lost everything. Sometimes I have to pinch myself just so I can remember this is really happening."

"Which part?"

"All of it. Ryan… getting married, having a baby, having Simeon to help around the farm…"

"How's that going?"

"Really well."

"What's he like?" Not having left the house for months, I haven't had the chance to meet him.

"He's quiet, but he gets the job done."

"And you don't mind taking a back seat?"

"Not at all. After all the problems we had last year, with the apple blight, it's good to have someone else who can take the strain."

"How's it looking this year?"

She crosses her fingers, holding them up. "A lot better, and this weather is definitely helping."

"It's good to see you so happy."

Her eyes sparkle, a smile tugging at her lips, although it quickly fades.

"You're not, though, are you? Happy, I mean. You say you're fine, but I know that's not true."

I sit forward, lowering my head. "My husband died, Peony."

"I know, and I'm not being insensitive, but to be honest, I thought you were getting better. A few weeks ago, you seemed to be almost back on track, and now…"

"Now what?"

She sighs. "It feels like you've gone backwards."

That's because I have. I miss Brady so damn much, but I can't tell you that.

"It's hard," I say instead, although that sounds so lame.

"I get that, but it's been nearly six months and you still haven't been outside the house."

"No."

She reaches over, putting her hand on my arm. "Even if you don't feel like sitting in a bar drinking soda water with me, why don't you treat yourself?"

"How?"

"Go to the beauty salon and get your hair cut."

"Is that your way of telling me I look a mess?" I don't need telling, to be honest. I know already, courtesy of the mirror in the bathroom.

"Of course not," she says, in the friendliest of lies. "But don't you think it's time you got back to being you?"

She's not wrong. I used to take so much pride in my appearance, and even though I've put on a summer dress, that's only because it's hot. I didn't give any thought to it, or to coordinating my underwear, or brushing my hair.

"I—I can't."

"Yes, you can. I'll stay with Addy, and…"

"You're suggesting I go now?"

"Why not?"

"It's Friday afternoon. They'll be busy."

"So? I'm sure they can squeeze you in."

"But…"

"Stop making excuses. And don't tell me you'll fix an appointment once I've gone, because we both know you won't." She lowers her voice, leaning a little closer. "It's a haircut, Laurel, and you'll feel a lot better once it's done."

"Are you sure about staying?"

"Of course. Addy and I will be fine." She shoos me away with her hand. "Go on."

I stand, my legs feeling a little unstable, but Peony isn't taking 'no' for an answer, and maybe she's right. Maybe I will feel better.

I don't think I could feel much worse…

I park directly outside the beauty salon, surprised that it's not busier in town. At this time on a Friday afternoon, I remember it being much more bustling than this. Still, I'm not complaining… not if it means I can sneak in and out of the salon unnoticed.

There's a bell above the door that announces my arrival, even though I wish it wouldn't, and the woman behind the reception desk looks up. I don't recognize her, but that's not a surprise. I haven't been here since before Christmas.

"Can I help?"

"Yes, I was just wondering…"

"Laurel? Is that you?"

I turn at the sound of my name to see Raelynn Tucker walking straight toward me. Her hair is a very unnatural shade of orange, but she wears it well, in a short pixie style. I've never known her age, but if I had to guess, I'd say she's around fifty, and unlike the people she employs here, she doesn't wear simple black clothes that don't get in the way while working. No, Raelynn is renowned for her flouncy sleeves and flowing skirts, neither of which are particularly practical.

I smile and nod my head as she comes over, giving me a hug.

"How are you?" she says and I open my mouth to answer, but before I can, she rolls her eyes. "That was a damn silly question." She takes my hand, leading me to the seats by the front window, where she sits me down, studying my hair with a pitying expression on her face. "We're slammed this afternoon, but don't you worry. I'll take care of you myself."

I know from experience how unusual it is for Raelynn to see a client personally these days, and I smile up at her.

"I can come back another time."

"I wouldn't hear of it. Just give me ten minutes."

She turns and dashes off toward the back of the salon. I feel honored in a way, but still a little nervous, and I grab a magazine from the table beside me, opening it in the middle, on an article about the menopause, which I pretend to read.

"It's such a shame, don't you think?"

I look up at the sound of the raised voice coming from the other side of the room, relieved to get some respite from a woman's account of weight gain, hot flushes, and mood swings.

Unfortunately, I can't see who's talking because there's a bank of mirrors running the length of the salon that are blocking my view.

"I know. Someone really ought to tell her."

Tell who? Tell them what?

I'd forgotten what a hotbed of gossip this place could be and I lower the magazine, unable to help myself.

"It's a bit late now."

"You think because he's dead it doesn't matter?"

"I don't think it'll do any good raking it up. That's all I'm saying."

Has someone else died? I wonder who… and why no-one told me.

"You're assuming she doesn't already know. Let's face it, everyone knew what Mitch was like."

Mitch? Did she just say Mitch?

"Yes, but not everyone knew he was sleeping with his receptionist." My blood turns to ice. I can't have heard that right. It's not possible. "I heard it had been going on for months," the woman continues.

"And they were leaving town together? Mitch and this young woman?"

"Evidently. They were gonna start again in Springfield."

What are they talking about? Springfield? Starting again? This can't be right.

Can it?

I stand, the magazine falling to the floor, and although the young woman behind the desk looks up, she doesn't understand.

Why would she?

She doesn't realize it's my husband they're talking about.

I can't stay here.

I can't…

I dart to the door, yanking it open, the words, "Excuse me?" ringing in my ears as I run out onto the street, and hurry straight to my car, wishing I'd come.

The drive home is a blur, and I park in front of the garage, practically falling through the front door.

"Laurel?" Peony comes out from the kitchen and I look up at her. "What's wrong? Why are you back already?"

"I—I…" My voice catches in my throat, and sensing something's wrong, she holds up a hand.

"I'll just check Addy's okay in the playroom. It got too hot outside."

She disappears, returning moments later, and leads me into my own kitchen, sitting me at the island unit. I'm in a daze, but I'm aware of her beside me.

"This can't be real," I whisper.

"What?" she asks, studying my hair for a second. "Was there a problem with the car? Did something happen?"

"Yes, but not with the car. It… it was something I heard."

"Where?"

"In the beauty salon. There were some women talking…"

"What did they say?"

I turn to look at her, trying to ground myself in the reality of our friendship.

"They said Mitch was sleeping with his receptionist." I hear her gasp, but I hold up my hand. I need to say this all at once, or I won't be able to say it at all. "They said it had been going on for months, and that they were moving away… to start again in Springfield."

"That can't be right." She shakes her head. "You know what people are like around here."

She has a point. People love to gossip. Hell… I even thought that myself, before I realized my husband was the subject of their tittle-tattle.

Except…

"Mitch was always working, wasn't he? At least, that's what he said he was doing. But if he'd wanted to, he could easily have afforded to employ someone else. And if he'd done that, he'd have been able to spend more time with us… not her."

"Hold on a second. You're letting your imagination run away with you. None of that proves he was having an affair," Peony says, trying to sound reasonable. "You didn't suspect him before you heard those women gossiping, did you?"

"No, but I wouldn't have known what to look for. Did you… Did you notice anything when Luca cheated on you?" I ask, still trying to make sense of it, although her eyes cloud over slightly and I feel guilty for bringing it up, especially in such a heartless way. "I'm sorry. That was insensitive of me."

She shakes her head. "It's okay. He's ancient history, and in answer to your question, no, I didn't notice a thing. He didn't change at all toward me, other than the fact that he stopped saying he loved me… although I didn't even realize that until after he'd left."

"You didn't?"

"No. I think it was something I took for granted. Our relationship hadn't altered. He still made love to me all the time, and made me feel loved, so I assumed he loved me… even though he didn't."

I try to think back to the last few months with Mitch and how often he said those words. Even on the day he died…

"Mitch never stopped," I say out loud. "He never stopped saying he loved me."

"In which case…"

"That doesn't mean it was true, though, does it?"

She sighs. "Are you sure you're not just looking for excuses… for reasons to believe the gossips?"

"Why would I? I don't want this to be true." I don't want my marriage to have been a lie, even though there have been a few surprises in it since Mitch died, and I shake my head, trying to think that through.

"What's wrong?" Peony asks.

"I'm just trying to work out if there might be a link."

"Between what?"

"Between this and his money… or rather, the lack of it."

She frowns, tilting her head. "You're not making sense, Laurel."

I sigh and lean forward, wondering if it might help to say it out loud. "When Mitch died, there was nothing left, other than the house and the gym. The money was all gone."

"All of it? I—I didn't realize."

"That's why I had to sell the gym," I explain.

"But surely there must have be—" Peony stops talking mid-word, raising her hand to her mouth.

"What is it? You've remembered something, haven't you? Is it to do with Mitch's business?"

She shakes her head. "No, and it's probably nothing."

"Tell me anyway."

She hesitates for a second or two and then leans a little closer. "Remi said she thought Mitch was flirting with her at our wedding."

"Your wedding?"

"Yeah. She dismissed it because Gabe told her he was happily married to you, but…"

"That was last December, Peony. Why didn't you tell me before now?"

"Because Remi and Gabe explained that she isn't very good at knowing when men are flirting. I think it caused a few issues between them when they first started dating." She puts her hand on my arm. "If I'd thought for one second, there might have been any truth…"

"It's okay. It's not your fault." I sit back and stare up at the ceiling. "How can this be happening? I thought I knew him better than anyone, but it feels like I didn't know him at all."

"You can't say that just because of a rumor and a misunderstanding."

"Except it's not just the rumor, or the misunderstanding, is it? There's the money, and…" I let my voice fade and Peony edges forward on her seat.

"And what?"

I look back at her. "I've always held Mitch up as the perfect man… the perfect husband."

"I know you have."

"Yes, but lately I've been wondering if I got that all wrong."

"Before today, you mean?"

I nod my head. "Even aside from all this, he spent so little time with Addy, and he could be really selfish sometimes, you know?"

"In what way?"

"You probably don't remember the two of us having a conversation not long after you came back from your honeymoon."

"A conversation about what?"

"About Mitch and his finances." She shakes her head, looking bewildered, and I can't blame her for that. It probably didn't register with her like it did with me. "We were discussing the fact that you'd put the farm in Ryan's name as well as yours, and that he'd added you to his bank accounts. I told you then that Mitch had never done anything like that for me."

"Oh, yes," she says, nodding her head. "I remember now."

"Do you remember me defending him?"

"Yes," she says, smiling. "But that wasn't unusual."

"Exactly. I defended him every time, no matter what."

"Of course you did. He was your husband."

"A husband who kept everything to himself... who shared nothing with me. Like you said, we should have been a team, but if I needed anything – even if it was for Addy – I had to ask him for it." She raises her eyebrows, but doesn't say anything. "It wasn't just that, though... it was other things, too."

"Like what?"

"Like in... in bed." I lower my voice to a whisper, but Peony stands now, moving closer to me.

"Did he hurt you?" she says, her concern obvious.

"No, but it was another example of how selfish he could be."

"I see... so what you're trying to say is that he wasn't very considerate."

"No. No, he wasn't."

She sucks in a breath. "Did you ever talk it through with him?"

"I thought what he was doing was perfectly normal. Now, with this affair, and..."

She holds up a hand. "You don't know there was an affair. You can't be sure about any of it. Not unless you get some answers."

"How am I supposed to do that?"

She frowns, like she's thinking. "There are several receptionists at the gym, aren't there?" she asks. "I know there used to be when Luca worked there."

"I don't know... not now the new owners are in charge. But I imagine there are. One person couldn't cover all the hours, and everyone who worked there was given the option to stay on when it was sold."

"Okay. So, why don't you go over there and ask?"

"Are you seriously suggesting I walk into the gym, go up to the reception desk, and ask which one of them was sleeping with my husband?"

"How else are you gonna find out the truth?"

"You think whoever it is will just confess?"

"Maybe not, but she might give herself away, or someone else might know the answer… one way or the other."

"How can I…?"

"How can you not? If you don't at least try to find out, you're just gonna sit here going crazy."

When she says it like that, it makes sense, and I get to my feet, grabbing my keys from the countertop.

"Can you stay?"

"Of course. I'll text Ryan to tell him I'll be late."

I nod my head, taking a deep breath. "If I don't go now, I'll lose my nerve."

"Then go now."

She smiles, and although I can't smile back, I appreciate the gesture, and run from the house.

The town seems even quieter now, and I park outside the gym, my hands damp with sweat, my stomach churning, as I go to the door and push it open.

It's cool inside, the air conditioning working to the max, and I clench my fists a couple of times before walking up to the reception desk. There's a brunette sitting there with her head bent, and she takes a moment to look up, although when she does, we both smile.

It's Freya, thank God. A friendly face. She worked for Mitch for as long as I knew him, and is in her mid-thirties, with a husband and two children. It can't be her… I'm sure of it.

"Hi," she says. "How are you?"

"I'm okay."

I'm not, and I think she knows it.

"How can I help?"

"I—I was just wondering, are there any other receptionists working here now, who were here when Mitch owned the place?"

She shakes her head. "No, I'm the only one left. They've taken on some new people, but they're not a patch on the team we had before."

Damn.

"Do you know what happened to all the others?"

"Ruth and Olivia left. They didn't like the hours the new bosses wanted us to work." She rolls her eyes. "As for Kaylee..." Her voice fades, and my skin prickles.

"Kaylee?" I try to picture her, but come up blank.

"Yes. You remember her, don't you? Kaylee Prentice. She started work here about... oh, about eight months before..."

"Before what?"

"Before she died."

"Sh—She died?"

"Yes."

"When was this?"

"It was..." She frowns. "It was the same day as Mitch, oddly enough. We weren't told very much about it, and to be honest, with Mitch dying too, it..."

My blood freezes for the second time today... and it has nothing to do with the air conditioning. "How did she die?"

"That was the really odd thing. She was killed in a road accident, too."

"On the same day as Mitch?"

"Yes. She wasn't from around here, so we weren't given any details. And she'd kept herself to herself all the while she'd worked here, so it wasn't like she was great friends with any of us. It was sad, though. She was..."

Alarm bells are ringing so loudly in my head I can't hear another word, and I back up toward the door.

"Th—Thanks," I murmur, bolting outside.

This can't be, can it?

Kaylee Prentice is a faceless woman to me, but she died on the same day, in a car accident, just like Mitch. And while that could be a coincidence, it could also mean they were leaving town together.

Couldn't it?

Or am I imagining things?

I can't be sure, and I need to be. I have to know the truth, and although I don't want to face him, I know there's only one person who can tell me…

I run across the street, straight to the sheriff's office, pulling open the door and stepping inside. This is a building with a lot of glass in its construction, which doesn't help when it's so warm. In fact, it's stifling, despite the fan rotating on the desk, and Deputy Jimmy Phillips looks up as I stride forward. He was in the year above me and Peony when we were at high school, but we didn't have very much to do with him. He always came across as patronizing, and charmless… and he still does.

"Mrs. Bradshaw." He says my name with something approaching disdain and looks down his nose at me. My mom and his mom were friends, and I've always had the impression she didn't approve of my marriage to Mitch. It's an attitude that seems to have rubbed off on her son.

"Hi, Jimmy." I could call him Deputy Phillips, but using his first name will annoy him. "Is the sheriff here?" I find it hard to say Brady's name without thinking about whispering it in the throes of a mind blowing orgasm, and that's too confusing right now.

"No. He's out, I'm afraid. Can I help?"

I doubt that very much. Brady seemed to handle everything to do with the accident, but I guess there's a chance Jimmy will know at least some of the details, or be able to look them up, perhaps. The problem is, how to ask. I can hardly come out with the question, but I guess I can call his bluff. If I'm wrong, I'll just end up looking silly, which won't be anything new in his eyes. If I'm right, he won't be able to deny it.

"I had a question about my husband's accident."

"Oh?"

"Yes. I understand Kaylee Prentice was involved."

He frowns. "I believe she was, but I'd have to check." He pauses. "Did you have a reason for wanting to know?"

"Only that she used to work at the gym, and I wanted to contact her family."

That sounds so lame, but he doesn't seem to notice. He nods his head, looking sympathetic. "I see. If you can give me a minute?"

"Sure."

He turns around, going through the door behind him and I glance to my left, noticing another closed door, which has Brady's name etched in black writing on the glass panel. It makes me think of him… but most things do, it seems.

"Here we are," Jimmy says, coming back through the door again, clutching a file in his hand, and opening it as he approaches the desk. "Hmm… they were in the same car, traveling on route 103, heading out of town." He glances up and I nod my head, even though my heart is struggling to beat. *They were together. The gossips were right. My husband was a cheat.* Jimmy flips over a page, his expression changing. "Oh, that's a shame. I didn't know that."

"Know what?"

He looks up. "Miss Prentice was pregnant."

My legs feel like they're going to give way and I lean over the counter slightly, just for support.

"P—Pregnant?"

"Yes."

He glances down at the file again. "There's not really much more I can tell you. I can't give you her parents' details… not without their permission. But I can…"

I hold up my hand, my stomach churning. "I—It's okay."

He looks confused, slamming the file closed. "Mrs. Bradshaw? Are you okay?"

I shake my head, bile rising in my throat. "I—I…"

I can't speak. My voice won't work.

I didn't want to be right, but I am.

My marriage hasn't just been a lie. It's been a joke.

In which case, why isn't this funny?

Chapter Sixteen

$\Rightarrow\!\!\Rightarrow\!\!\Rightarrow\!\!\Leftarrow\!\!\Leftarrow\!\!\Leftarrow$

Brady

I've spent the last two hours driving around the town. It's not that big a place, but I've filled the time, taking it slow.

I could easily walk, rather than driving, but then I might have to talk to people. I'd probably run into Cooper, too, and I've been avoiding him since our conversation last weekend.

He'd be bound to ask how I am, and I'm not in the mood for explaining. I'm especially not in the mood for telling him about what happened at Dawson's place.

I still feel embarrassed about that.

Peyton may have been pretty, and I can think of a lot of men who would have willingly taken her up on her invitation, but all she did was remind me how old I am… and how lonely my future looks without Laurel.

The cab came for her in the end, and although she renewed her invitation as she handed me back my coat, I declined, and watched as she drove away, before returning home.

My house seemed empty, but even as I leaned against the door, trying to picture what might have happened if I'd brought Peyton home with me, I couldn't imagine any such thing.

The idea of being with anyone but Laurel is fundamentally wrong.

I shake my head, indicating right and parking in my designated spot outside the sheriff's office. It's warm today and I take a moment to enjoy the air conditioning, knowing my office will be like a sauna, and then I get out, just as the main door opens, slamming back on itself. I'm about to call out that there's no need to take the thing off of its hinges, when I realize the person coming out is Laurel.

She's wearing a pale blue sundress that hugs her curves, making me ache for her, although I can't fail to notice she's in a daze, her face pale as she strides across the parking lot, making for the street.

Was she here to see me? Is that possible after all this time? I open my mouth to say her name when she turns for some reason, and spots me, my hopes dying when I see the fury in her eyes.

"Brady?" she yells, retracing her steps and coming to a stop right in front of me. My heart is beating so fast, I can hear it, and I long to take her in my arms. "How could you?"

"How could I what?" I try to keep calm, although I've got no idea what she's talking about.

She raises her clenched fist and slams it against my chest. "You know what."

"No, I don't. What have I done?"

She hits me again, and although I try to grab her arm, she takes a half step back, putting enough space between us to make it impossible.

"How can you pretend you don't know?"

"I'm not pretending."

"So you're saying you didn't know my husband was sleeping with Kaylee Prentice, that she was pregnant, and that she was in the car with Mitch when he died? You're saying you were ignorant of all that, even though your deputy just confirmed it?"

Shit…

Not this. Anything but this.

My world disintegrates before my eyes, a loud sob escaping Laurel's lips as she puts her hand to her mouth, her eyes boring into mine with nothing short of hatred.

"Laurel… please."

She shakes her head, then turns and runs, my heart stopping as she doesn't even pause, but sprints straight across Main Street without looking.

Dammit.

I step away from my car to go after her, just as she jumps into hers, which is parked outside the gym on the other side of the street. Within seconds, she reverses out of the space, and with a screech of tires, pulls away, barely in control of the vehicle.

On instinct, I leap back into my car. She's in the distance, driving like a wild woman, going way too fast, her steering all over the place, and I put my foot down, switching on the siren, and catching up to her in no time at all. She's barely half-way home when I pull her over to the side of the road.

My heart still hasn't slowed, and my legs don't feel like my own when I climb from the patrol car and walk up to her Lexus. The window is open, and she glares at me.

"What?"

"You can't drive like that."

"I'll do whatever I damn well please." She holds out her hand. "Give me a ticket, if you want, and let me go."

I rest my hands on the roof of the car, leaning over. "I'm not gonna give you a ticket, Laurel, but think about what you're doing here. Do you want Addy to be an orphan? Don't you care about yourself at all?"

She opens the door, forcing me to step back, then climbs out and slams it, leaning back against the side of the car, her arms folded across her chest. "Don't talk to me like that."

"Like what?"

"Don't make me sound irresponsible."

"I'm not. But I can't let you drive like that."

"Because it's illegal? I know that. I already said, give me a ticket, and leave me alone."

"I can't leave you alone. I care about you too much."

She narrows her eyes. "Really? Is that why you lied to me?"

"Of course it damn well is." I raise my voice and notice the way she jumps, inching backward, although she's got nowhere to go. I ought to stop, but I can't. Not now. "Why else do you think I kept it all from you?" I move closer, so I'm almost touching her, and she tips her head back, staring at me, her eyes filled with confusion and anger. "I've loved you all your adult life, Laurel. How the hell was I supposed to tell you your husband crashed his car because he was distracted by his pregnant girlfriend?"

She blinks, and although her eyes don't leave mine, I can't read them anymore. It's like she's lost all over again.

"Distracted?" she whispers.

"Yes."

"How?"

There's nothing to be gained by lying anymore. Not when she knows so much already. "When we found Kaylee, she had her skirt hitched up around her hips and she wasn't wearing any underwear. You can work out the rest for yourself." I move closer still, raising my hand to stroke her cheek, although she leans even further away, making it clear touching is out of the question. "I didn't want to tell you this, Laurel. None of it."

"I don't believe you," she says, narrowing her eyes at me.

"How can you say that? It's been eating away at me, having to keep it from you."

"That's not what I meant."

"What did you mean, then?"

"That I don't believe you found Mitch and Kaylee like that. I don't believe he was…"

"It's the truth." I raise my voice again, although she doesn't jump this time. "That's how Kaylee was found. I saw her myself."

"And you didn't tell me? Any of it?"

I step back, pushing my fingers through my hair. "You're the only woman I've ever loved. How was I supposed to tell you your husband was a lying, cheating asshole, when I knew you worshipped the ground he walked on?"

"I didn't worship him."

"Yes, you did. You did it all the fucking time. Every goddamn day. You kept telling me what a fabulous father he was, even though he was never there for you, or Addy, which he wasn't, because he was planning to leave you and take everything."

She pushes herself off of the car, stepping up to me. "Not everything. He left us the house and the gym."

"Jesus Christ. Even now, you're defending him. Even when you know what he was doing to you." I shake my head and step closer… so close I can see her pulse racing in her neck. "Think about it, Laurel. You told me yourself there was no cash left. That had to be because he was using it to to set up somewhere else with Kaylee."

She hesitates, biting on her lip. "Even so, he wouldn't have taken the house."

"Wouldn't he? You think the money he had would have been enough? It might have bought them a small property somewhere, or given him enough to start up in business again, but he'd have needed more… and fairly soon, I imagine. He didn't intend crashing his car, did he? He drove out of town with Kaylee that day, with something in mind that didn't involve dying."

She looks around, like she's desperate for a way out. "Maybe… Maybe he was just taking her somewhere?"

"Where?"

"I don't know." She glares at me. "Maybe he was taking her for a termination. The baby might not even have been his. He… He could have taken pity on her and offered to help. Perhaps that's where the money went." She sounds almost triumphant, but nothing she's said makes sense.

"You're clutching at straws, Laurel, and you know it. For one thing, terminations aren't that expensive. Besides, if he was just taking her for a termination as a friend, why didn't he tell you? Why didn't he explain? He'd have had no reason to keep it a secret from you, would he?"

"Well, no… but…"

"But nothing."

She stares at me, blinking hard, clearly trying not to cry, and I feel desperately sorry for her, wishing I'd found another way to say all of that. I reach out, but she steps back.

"Whatever else he was doing, he definitely wasn't gonna sell the gym," she says defiantly.

"How do you know that?" *And why are you still defending him?*

"He told me."

"When?" She blushes, and I move closer still. "When?" I repeat.

"The first time was years ago, when I asked him about us having another baby. He said he wanted to make changes at the gym, and we needed to wait until he'd done that."

"And the second time?" I ask.

"That was when we were fighting about him selling the land to Nate without telling me, and he said he needed the money from the sale to buy a new gym in Willmont Vale. I was mad because he'd kept his plans to himself and because I knew it meant we'd have to wait even longer, but he wasn't selling, Brady. He was expanding."

"And you believed him?"

"Of course I did."

"You didn't think it was odd that you wanted to have another baby with him, and he knew that, and yet he kept using the same excuses not to?"

"It… It wasn't like that."

"Wasn't it?"

She steps up, glaring into my eyes. "What else do you know, Brady?"

"Nothing."

"Then why shouldn't I have believed him?"

"You mean, aside from the fact that Mitch has been a consummate liar all his life?"

"That's not fair. He's not here to defend himself."

"Why the fuck does he need to be, when he's got you doing such a fantastic job for him?" *Shit*. I shouldn't have said that. "I'm sorry, Laurel. That was out of line. I—I just hate the way he treated you… the cheating, the deceit, the lies."

"He wouldn't," she says. "He wouldn't have lied to me about that. And he wouldn't have taken everything from us. I know…" Her voice fades and I wonder who she's trying to convince.

"It's the only thing that makes sense."

She looks up at me, tears welling in her eyes. "But that's… that's Addy's home. It's where we live."

Can it be? Is she finally accepting the truth? Is she finally acknowledging that Mitch wasn't who he said he was… who she thought he was.

"I know, but it was his, Laurel, not yours. You just said he kept his plans to himself, and you told me ages ago that he kept everything in his name. Think about what that means. He could have sold it anytime he wanted. He could have changed his will, too, if he'd had the chance, and there was nothing you could have done."

She shakes her head, her bottom lip trembling. "No!" Her voice comes out as a strangled scream. "No!" I reach out, but she slams her fist against my chest again. "No!" she bawls, hitting me with her other fist, both of them hammering down on me. I don't even attempt to stop her, or to step away, the blows raining hard and fast, her cries echoing in my ears.

Suddenly, she stops and stares at me, struggling to breathe, tears trickling down her cheeks. She opens her mouth, snaps it closed again, then turns and opens her car door, jumping inside. Before I can say a word, she's started it, and pulled out onto the highway.

I run to my car, wary of getting too close this time, just in case, and I follow her back to her house, making sure she's safe before I turn around and drive slowly back to town.

That's it now.

It's over.

I didn't have many hopes for the future, but even those I'd dared to harbor have been dashed.

I might have told her the truth, but I'm going to pay for it for the rest of my life… with my happiness.

Chapter Seventeen

Laurel

I clatter through the front door, barely able to breathe, and fall to my knees.

"Good God. What's happened?"

I feel Peony's arms around me, but I can't stand, and I look up at her, shaking my head before I curl in on myself again, my body trembling.

Even in my worst nightmares, it wasn't this bad.

"Laurel. Talk to me."

I can hear the fear in Peony's voice, and I slowly raise my head again. She's kneeling beside me now and she edges a little closer.

"H—He was…"

She looks into my eyes. "He was having an affair?" I nod my head, seeing the sadness on her face, the way her shoulders drop.

"Oh, Laurel."

"Th—That's not all."

She leans back. "Not all?"

I shake my head. "There's so much more to it than that."

"How much more? How do you know?"

"Brady told me."

I shudder, recalling his words, and the way he said them… the look in his eyes when he said I was defending Mitch, and when he said he loved me.

Oh, God…

Peony reaches out, but winces in pain. "I'm sorry. I can't kneel here like this. Can you stand?"

I nod my head, even though I'm not sure I can, and between us, we help each other to our feet.

"Where's Addy?" I ask, fear rising inside me.

"She's in the playroom."

I nod my head. "Okay. She can't hear any of this."

"I'll just go check on her, shall I?"

"Thanks."

Peony disappears toward the playroom, and I wander to the kitchen, my feet dragging along the floor, the sound of my scraping shoes bothering me enough that I kick them off halfway there.

Once I reach the island unit, I sit up on a chair, letting my head rest in my hands.

"She's fine," Peony says, and I look up at her as she sits beside me, pulling her seat a little closer. "Now, tell me what's happened."

My head is fully of Brady, but I guess I have to go back… to my conversation with Freya.

"I—I went to the gym, like you said."

"And?"

"And Freya told me there was a woman who used to work there called Kaylee Prentice."

"I don't remember her."

"No. Neither did I. She died on the same day as Mitch, but Freya didn't know anything about it, except that she'd also been in a car accident."

Peony frowns. "That's a bit of a coincidence."

"Not really. They were in the same car."

"How did Freya know that?"

"She didn't. I ran across the road to the sheriff's office and asked Jimmy Phillips."

"I thought you said you spoke to Brady."

"That happened later. I saw Jimmy to start with and he found the file, and told me Kaylee and Mitch had been in the same vehicle, leaving town on route 103."

"They were driving out of town?"

"Yeah."

"But that doesn't mean he was leaving you. It doesn't even mean they were having an affair. They could have been going somewhere to do with work."

I shake my head, even though it hurts. "She was pregnant, Peony."

Her face pales. "P—Pregnant?"

"Yes. Jimmy told me. It was in the file."

She sucks in a breath. "Okay, but that still doesn't mean anything. It could…"

"It means everything," I say through gritted teeth, struggling not to raise my voice, so Addy won't hear. "Brady told me."

She frowns. "When did you see Brady?"

"He arrived at the sheriff's office as I was leaving and I… I attacked him."

"You did what?"

"I was angry with him, Peony. He'd known about it, all of it, right from the start, and he'd kept it from me. I was so damn mad at him, I—I hit him."

"What did he do?"

"Nothing really. He didn't deny that he'd lied to me, and to be honest, I was too confused to hang around. I needed to get away… to get back here, so I ran."

"To your car?"

"Yes. Only he followed me and pulled me over."

"Because he wanted to explain?"

"Because I was driving like an idiot." I look up at her. "He said he loved me."

"Excuse me?"

"He said he'd loved me all my adult life, and that was why he hadn't told me about Mitch and Kaylee."

"Oh." She sits back a little, raising her eyebrows. "What did you say?"

"Nothing."

"Nothing?"

I shake my head. "I couldn't think straight. As well as telling me he loved me, he also said Mitch had crashed his car because he was distracted by his pregnant girlfriend."

"Distracted by his girlfriend doing what?" she asks.

"He didn't make that clear to start with, and even though I'd heard what he'd said about loving me, I needed to know what he meant about Mitch. So I asked."

"And?"

I turn, staring out the window. "H—He said they found Kaylee with her skirt hitched up and no underwear on."

"Oh, my God."

"I know. He didn't go into any further explanation, but he didn't need to, did he?"

"Not really." She puts her hand on my arm. "I'm so sorry, Laurel."

I look back at her. "I didn't want to believe him to start with. It was too much to take in. But he told me he'd seen it for himself. Then he said I was the only woman he'd ever loved."

His words echo around my head. How can he have loved me all this time, without me knowing?

Because he's good at keeping things to himself, I guess. Secrets, and lies… and love, it seems.

"He should've told me," I murmur.

"How?" Peony asks. "How was he supposed to tell you what Mitch had done when he loved you like that?"

That wasn't what I meant. I was talking about the love, not the secrets and lies. But I nod my head, even though I still can't help wishing he'd told me of his feelings before.

Would it have made a difference, knowing how he felt? I don't know. But I'd like to think so.

"What Brady said today, it confirmed everything I was thinking… everything we were saying earlier, about the money. He'd taken it all, hadn't he? Mitch, I mean. He'd taken it to start a new life with her."

"You can't know that was what he intended."

"Can't I? What else would he have been doing? And it's like Brady said just now, if Mitch had needed more money, he'd have… he'd have…"

"He'd have what?"

I shake my head, still struggling to come to terms with it. "He'd have sold the house and the gym."

"No. This is your home."

"I know. That's what I said to Brady."

"And you're right."

"Am I? Mitch didn't know he was going to die, did he?" I repeat Brady's words, finding they make so much more sense than anything I've been thinking until now. "He left here with almost all the cash. If I hadn't sold the gym, we'd have starved."

"No, you wouldn't. Ryan and I would have…"

"I get what you're saying, and to be honest, Brady was helping out anyway. But that's not the point. Can't you see? If Mitch had lived, do you honestly think he'd have let us carry on living here, in his house, while he set up his new family somewhere else?"

Peony bites on her bottom lip, and I know I'm right. If Mitch hadn't died, he'd have divorced me, changed his will, and forced us out… not necessarily in that order. Either way, though, Addy and I would be homeless by now. We'd have nothing.

"He couldn't have just thrown you out onto the streets," she says, like she's just read my mind. "He had responsibilities, for Addy, if nothing else."

"Maybe. But I'd have had to find him first." I let my head roll back, staring at the ceiling. "God… I feel like such a fool. To think, I've been mourning him all this time, painting him as the perfect husband and father… not to mention defending him to Brady. I mean… what does that say about me? I could hear every word he was saying just now, and I still tried to justify Mitch's behavior. All I could think was that I'd had a life I believed in." I let out a half-laugh, shaking my head. "Do you know, I wanted us to have another baby together? But it was never gonna happen, was it? Because he was too busy making babies with her." My voice cracks and I can't hold back the tears for a moment longer.

Peony's arms come around me. "Oh, Laurel. I—I didn't realize."

"Realize what?" I look up at her through my tears.

"That you wanted another baby." She puts her hand on her bump. "I'm sorry."

"It's not your fault."

She smiles, although it's a little half-hearted. "Did Mitch know how you felt?"

I nod my head. "Of course. We'd talked about it."

"And what did he say? A resounding 'no', I'm guessing…"

I shake my head, and she stops talking. "He was surprised to start with, but he agreed. He said he wanted another baby, too… only he thought we should plan it better this time. There were things he needed to do at the gym. That's what he said, and I believed him. Only I was a fool, wasn't I? Brady was right about that, too. It was just an excuse."

"You can't know that."

"Yes, I can. Mitch didn't do anything at the gym."

"You think he was seeing Kaylee, even then?"

"He can't have been. She only started working for him eight months before the accident." She frowns, like she doesn't understand. "It means there must have been others, Peony."

She shakes her head. "You can't go down that road."

"I think I can. You said yourself about him flirting with Remi. That would have been after he met Kaylee. Probably even after he got her pregnant. He obviously didn't understand the meaning of the word monogamy… and to think I've been beating myself up all this time."

There's a moment's silence as I realize what I've just said. It's too late to take it back, but I sit still and wait, hoping Peony didn't understand the significance of those few words.

"Beating yourself up over what?" she says. *So much for hopes.* I turn my head to face her. "What on earth have you got to beat yourself up over?"

I've gone this far. There's no point in trying to hide it any longer. "Promise you won't think badly of me?"

"What for?"

"For sleeping with Brady."

Her eyes widen. "When?"

"Seven weeks ago tomorrow."

Her lips tip up just a fraction. "That's very precise."

"I know. It's not something I'm gonna forget in a hurry."

"Why? Was it that bad?" I shake my head. "What happened?" Peony's voice has softened, and she tilts her head to one side. "Seven weeks ago? That was after he stopped staying here, wasn't it?"

"Yeah. Nothing happened all the while he was sleeping over. He behaved like a perfect gentleman then."

"But not when you slept with him?"

"Oh, no. He was pretty damn perfect then, too." She smiles fully. "Stop it."

"Stop what?"

"Smiling. It's not funny."

"I'm not saying it is, but you had nothing to beat yourself up over."

"I didn't know that at the time, did I? I've been feeling awful about it ever since, especially as…"

"Especially as what?"

I can't think how to phrase this. "Especially as that's how I know Mitch wasn't a very considerate lover."

"Because Brady was?"

I nod my head. "I only threw him out because…"

"Wait a second. You threw him out?"

"Yes. I felt so guilty for enjoying it, for betraying Mitch, for wanting Brady." I cover my face with my hands. "And now you're gonna hate me."

Peony grabs my wrists, pulling my hands away. "Of course I'm not. You were grieving. You wanted to feel loved."

"I did… although I didn't realize Brady loved me."

"He didn't say anything?"

"Not then. I suppose he might have done afterwards, if I'd given him the chance… if I hadn't been in such a hurry to get him out of here."

She shakes her head. "You were confused."

"Tell me about it."

"You probably felt like you'd cheated on Mitch… or at least on his memory."

"I did." Although that wasn't all of it.

"It's enough to confuse anyone."

"It is, but knowing what Mitch was doing, and how Brady really felt, it makes everything a hundred times worse."

"Maybe. But I hope you don't still blame Brady for any of it." She nudges in to me. "The guy's in love with you. According to what he said, he was in love with you before you even met Mitch, so you can't blame him for wanting to protect you from hearing about what Mitch had done."

"No, I know."

"And you can't blame him for wanting to be with you, either."

She raises her eyebrows, tipping her head, like she's waiting for something. Me, I think.

"Are you saying I owe him an apology?"

"A pretty big one, I'd have said. You hit him…"

"Several times. And I yelled at him. I can't even remember all the things I said, but none of it was pretty… or justified." I clamp my hand over my mouth.

"Do you wanna go speak with him?"

"Now? I can't. I mean… it's… it's late."

"Not that late. And besides, do you think it's fair to leave the poor guy hanging?"

"What about Addy?"

She pauses for a second or two. "Why don't I take her back to my place? She can run around the orchard for a while. Ryan can take her out on the tractor, and I'll make up a bed for her in the guest room."

"You mean you'll have her to stay?"

"Of course. If it helps." She raises her eyebrows again.

"I guess it might. If this goes wrong, I'll probably want to cry myself to sleep."

"And if it goes right?" she says with a smile.

"I don't wanna think about that."

"Why not? You said he was…"

"I know what I said, but what if he can't forgive me?"

She smiles. "He'll forgive you."

I wish I had her confidence, but even without it, I can't escape the inevitable. Like it or not, I have to face him. I have to apologize for everything I've said. I owe him that, and probably a lot more.

"I'll go tell Addy, shall I?" I say.

"Sure. I can put some things in a bag for her, so once you've told her what's going on, you can leave."

"Are you trying to get rid of me?"

"No. I'm trying to stop you from finding excuses to put off what needs to be done."

She's right, and I slide from the chair, smiling as she struggles down herself, and as she makes for the stairs, I head for the playroom.

Addy has tipped a couple of puzzles on to the floor, and is trying to piece them back together again. She has the patience of a saint with things like this and where other kids might throw a tantrum, she'll just keep trying.

"Hey," I say from the doorway, and she looks up with a smile on her face.

"Hi, Mommy." She frowns. "I thought you were getting a haircut."

"I was."

Her frown deepens. "It doesn't look any different."

"No. Something happened."

"Oh?"

"Yeah." I can't tell her what. I don't think I'll ever be able to do that. "How would you like to go stay with Aunty Peony and Uncle Ryan tonight?"

"At the apple orchard?"

"Yeah. Aunty Peony said Uncle Ryan might let you ride on the tractor, if you're good."

She leaps off of the floor and runs over, throwing her arms around my legs. "Thanks, Mommy." She leans back, looking up at me. "Will you be okay by yourself?"

"I'll be fine." *I hope.* She nods her head, happy with my answer. "Aunty Peony is upstairs, packing you some things."

"Shall I go help?"

"That's a good idea." She goes to run off, but I grab her, pulling her back. "Mommy's gotta go out again now, but I'll see you in the morning. Okay?"

"Okay, Mommy."

I hug her tight, giving her a kiss, and then she rushes off.

I hear her footsteps on the stairs and smile to myself as I make my way back to the kitchen, putting on my shoes as I pass them, and grab my keys, the sound of laughter and voices filtering down from upstairs as I close the front door behind me.

I take the drive back into town much more slowly, ashamed of the way I drove earlier. Brady was right. I was being irresponsible... and rude, and dismissive. I didn't even acknowledge what he said about loving me, although I know he said it twice.

Come to think of it, he said something before... on that evening seven weeks ago. He mentioned regrets. He said he regretted not taking his chances with me... not walking up to me and kissing me. It didn't register then because I was too busy thinking about where things were going between us. I was too preoccupied with getting him to kiss me in the here and now than with thinking about what he'd just said, and how he might be feeling.

How insensitive was that?

And how selfish?

He said he'd loved me all my adult life, which I'm guessing means since I was eighteen.

That's nine years.

He waited nine years?

What if it's too late now? What if he's done waiting?

I park outside the sheriff's office, noticing the patrol car he was driving earlier is still in the same spot it was when I yelled at him... before he came after me.

He must have driven back here.

But he would, wouldn't he? He's a man who does his duty... unlike Mitch.

I shake my head.

I refuse to think about Mitch. I can't. It makes me feel hurt, and angry, and so foolish for not seeing through him. There will be time enough for negative thoughts like that... but not right now.

I get out and stroll to the door, pulling it open, my heart flipping over in my chest when I see Brady standing behind the counter. There are two people talking to Chip McGuire, who's writing something down, and Brady is reading from a print-out, his head bent. He looks up as the door swishes closed behind me, and he frowns at me as I walk over.

That's not the most promising of starts, but as I get to him, I stand up on my tiptoes, putting my keys on the counter as I lean up over it. Then I reach for his face, holding it between my hands as I pull him closer and kiss him...

Chapter Eighteen

Brady

I'm stunned. But only for a second, no longer.

Then put my hand on the back of Laurel's neck, and I lean in, my tongue flicking against her lips. She opens and I delve inside, tasting her. I don't know which one of us is claiming the other, and I don't care. She's here. We're kissing, and that's the only thing that matters.

I change the angle of my head, and hear just the slightest of moans as I deepen the kiss, her fingers twisting into my hair.

She moans again, and then stops, pulling back.

A blush creeps up her cheeks and she glances to her right, where Chip is standing, along with the two tourists who came in a short while ago, looking for directions, which he had been writing down. He's grinning; they're standing, wide-eyed.

"Are you okay?" I ask, and Laurel turns back to me, nodding her head.

"I—I'm sorry."

"For the kiss?"

She smiles. "No. For everything else." I open my mouth to tell her she has nothing to be sorry for, but she holds up her hand.

"We can't talk here, but can you come to my place when you've finished work?"

"Of course. I'll be about an hour."

"Okay."

She smiles, her eyes dropping to my lips just for a second, like she's remembering that kiss. It's a kiss I'm never going to forget, but before I can say another word, she grabs her keys, turns around and leaves.

I feel like I'm in shock, although it's the best kind of shock I've ever known, and I stare at the door for a moment or two, until Chip clears his throat in a rather obvious way.

"Be quiet," I growl.

"I didn't say a word, boss."

"Keep it that way."

I don't look at him, or the tourists. Instead, I turn and go into my office, closing the door behind me. Unfortunately, there's too much glass in this building for me to jump for joy, but I sit at my desk, smiling, while I pretend to be busy on my computer.

In the end I give up pretending and sit back. Did that really just happen? I know it did. I can still feel Laurel's lips on mine, even though when I got back here earlier, I thought it was all over between us.

Jimmy was standing behind the desk, a file lying in front of him, and I knew straight away that he must have been the one to tell her.

"Is everything okay, boss?" he said.

"No." I glanced down at the file. "Did Mrs. Bradshaw want something in particular?"

"Yeah. She said she wanted to contact Kaylee Prentice's parents about the accident, but she left before I could explain…"

I held up my hand, and he stopped talking. "You told her Kaylee was involved in the accident?"

"She seemed to know already." That puzzled me, as did his frown. "I didn't realize she was pregnant, though."

"Kaylee?"

"Yeah."

"There was no reason for you to know," I snapped, and came into my office, slamming the door. Jimmy can be arrogant at times, but I couldn't blame him for what had happened. It was my fault, and no-one else's.

I was entirely to blame for my own misery.

Although I don't feel miserable anymore. I feel ecstatic... ecstatic and confused.

Laurel practically attacked me when I told her about Mitch and Kaylee, and his plans for the future... and now...

I get up, unable to wait a second longer to find out what's going on.

"I'm going home," I say as I exit my office.

Chip is still standing behind the counter, although there's no-one else here and he raises his eyebrows.

"Really?"

"I thought I told you to be quiet."

He smiles and I head for the door. "Have a good evening, boss."

I turn, smiling back. "I will."

At least, I hope I will.

I get to my car, hesitating for a second. Should I go home to change? Or should I just head straight for Laurel's place?

Changing out of my uniform will only take a few minutes, but I'm too impatient. I need to know what's happened, and if it means I have a future with Laurel, so I jump into my car, pulling out of the space and heading straight for her house.

Her Lexus is parked in front of the garage and I pull up behind it, getting out and turning to find she's waiting for me on the doorstep. She's still wearing that sexy blue sundress, her hair tied up in a ponytail behind her head, and I struggle for control as I walk over to her, my stomach churning. I'm a mixture of hope and fear, needing answers… and needing them now.

"Hi," I say, nerves almost capturing my voice.

"Hello."

We stare at each other and she tilts her head, biting on her bottom lip as she does. That's too much for me, and I grab her, pulling her close and crushing my lips to hers in a bruising kiss. She responds, her arms coming up around my neck, and I walk her backwards into the house, kicking the door closed before I push her back against the wall, holding her there with my body. I flex my hips, and she rolls hers at the same time, both of us moaning as I take her hands from behind my neck and hold them above her head, pinning them there with one of mine, while the other roams down her side, lingering over the swell of her breast. She arches her back and I move my hand further south, raising her skirt. I reach around behind her, groaning into her mouth when my fingers meet bare flesh, and I pull her onto me, grinding my hips into hers. She's not naked underneath her dress… she's wearing a thong, and I respond just how I should, my imagination going into overdrive. I need to be inside her, more than ever, to make up for all the lost time.

"I want…" I murmur, leaning back and looking into her eyes. "Oh, shit."

"What's wrong?" She frowns up at me as I take a half step back and her hands fall to her sides.

"Addy. I forgot about Addy," I say, bending to straighten her skirt. "I'm so sorry, Laurel." She giggles and I look up at her. "What's funny?"

"Nothing… except that Addy isn't here."

"She's not?"

"No. She's gone to stay with Peony and Ryan for the night."

"Really?"

"Yeah." She rests her hand on my chest and I hold it there with one of my own. "Tell me what you were gonna say. Tell me what you want."

"To be inside you." She takes a breath, nodding her head, and I have to smile. "You want that, too?"

"I do. But I think we should probably talk first, don't you?"

I'm torn. I need her more than anything, but I also need answers. "Promise you're not dismissing the idea?" I say, and she shakes her head.

"I promise."

"Okay."

She smiles and pushes herself off of the wall, heading for the kitchen, but I grab her hand, pulling her back.

"Kiss me."

She leans up, brushing her lips against mine. I keep it gentle, still holding her hand, and not doing anything else. If I do, I won't be able to stop... especially as I know we've got the place to ourselves.

She pulls back, looking up into my eyes, and I wonder if she feels the same. I'm not about to ask, though. She's right. We need to talk.

"Would you like something to eat?" she says and I smile.

"Okay."

We'll have to eat at some point this evening, and there's no reason we can't talk and eat at the same time, so keeping hold of my hand, she leads us into the kitchen, only releasing me when we get to the island unit.

"Take a seat," she says, wandering to the refrigerator.

I do as she says, watching as she pulls a few things out, putting them on the countertop.

"How did you find out?" I ask, cutting to the chase. There's no point sitting here in silence when we could be answering each other's questions. I'm sure she's got just as many as I have.

"Find out what?" She grabs the bell peppers, onion, and eggs from the countertop, bringing them over.

"About Mitch and Kaylee." She sucks in a breath, her shoulders rising and falling as she almost curls in on herself. "Don't you wanna talk about this, Laurel? I thought…"

"Yes," she says, interrupting me. "I think we have to. It's just… it's just hard hearing their names like that. Like they were a couple. But I guess they were, weren't they? They were gonna be a family."

"They were." I'm relieved she's not pretending anymore, and she nods her head and puts out a chopping board, reaching for the vegetables before she looks up at me.

"I heard about it at the beauty salon," she says, slicing into the onion.

"The beauty salon?"

"Yeah. Peony suggested I should get a haircut, and she was right." She smiles, shaking her head, her ponytail swishing back and forth. "I hadn't realized how much I'd let myself go… although obviously I didn't get around to doing anything about it, because I overheard the gossips."

I get up and wander around the island unit, standing behind her, my hands on her waist, my body pressed firmly against hers. I'm still hard and I let her know about it, grinding my hips into her ass. She moans, letting her head rock back onto my shoulder, and twisting slightly to look up at me.

"I thought we were gonna talk first."

"We are. I came around here to say you haven't let yourself go at all."

"You think?" She puts down the knife she's still holding and turns in my arms, so she's facing me. "I shower, Brady. That's about it. I've been wearing my hair in a ponytail because it so desperately needs cutting. I don't remember the last time I coordinated my clothes, and as for makeup…"

I clamp my finger over her lips to silence her, and she stares up at me.

"You're far too beautiful to spoil your face with makeup. As for your hair, I like ponytails." I lower my head, kissing her just briefly. "And what's the point in coordinating your clothes when I'm only gonna rip them off of you?" She giggles, and I have to smile, the sound making my skin tingle.

Our eyes lock for a moment, something binding us to each other, and then she blinks.

"Shall I get on with the dinner?"

I want to say 'no'. I want to take her in my arms and kiss her. Hard. I want to make love to her all night long. But there's so much still to be said.

"Okay." I step away and she turns around, getting back to slicing the onion. "What did the gossips say?" I ask, watching the way her shoulders sag.

"That Mitch was sleeping with someone from the gym… someone who worked there. He had been for ages, evidently. They said the two of them were leaving town together."

I can't say it doesn't hurt to hear that, and I lean back on the countertop behind me. "You mean, you'd heard that much already, but you still wouldn't believe me when I told you about it?"

She stops slicing, but doesn't turn around, the tension building in her shoulders.

"I guess I could pretend it was just gossip when they said it. But I knew you wouldn't lie. Not directly."

"Then why didn't you believe me?"

She drops the knife and spins around, tears welling in her eyes. "It wasn't that I didn't. It was that I couldn't. The truth made a mockery of my life, Brady. Everything I'd believed in became a joke. Mitch had tricked me and lied to me, and cheated on me in the worst way possible. It was bad enough losing my husband, but to discover he'd never been mine in the first place… that he wanted someone else more than me, and they were having a baby… I felt like such a… such a fool." Her voice cracks and a sob leaves her lips. I step forward, pulling her into my arms, and hold her close against me.

"Hey… I'm sorry. I should have thought." She pulls back a little, looking up at me. "It's just that once I realized you knew what he'd done, I wanted you to know all of it. I wanted you to see him for the asshole he was, to stop pining for him… stop defending him. He wasn't worth a second of your remorse, Laurel, but you gave him all of it. You gave him everything."

"I know. That's why I feel so stupid."

I pull her close again. "You're not stupid."

We stand for a while, and then she leans back, a little calmer. "I need to get dinner cooked, or we're never gonna eat."

I nod, smiling, and step away, walking back around to the other side of the island unit. Laurel goes back to slicing the onion, and then chopping the pepper. Once she's done, she puts the knife down again and stares across at me.

"I'm sorry," she says.

"What for?"

"For not believing you."

"It's okay. I understand."

She smiles, although it's a little half-hearted, and she carries the vegetables over to the stove, grabbing a pan and adding some oil.

"I want you to know something," she says, adding the onions and peppers and letting them sizzle.

"Oh?"

"Yeah. I—I don't regret what we did… here, that night."

We both know what she's talking about, and I have to shake my head, although she turns and sees me do it, frowning. "Are you serious?" I say, knowing I have to explain myself. "You practically threw me out of here. In fact, you did throw me out."

"I know, and I was wrong. I spent ages trying to work it out."

"Why? There was nothing to work out. You felt guilty."

"Except I didn't. Not in the way you mean."

"Really?"

I get up again, walking over to her and watching as she stirs the vegetables in the pan. "It wasn't about betraying Mitch," she murmurs, taking a deep breath.

"No?"

"No. At least it wasn't entirely about that. It was about what you did to me."

Jesus. What's she saying? I take her arm and she drops the wooden spoon she's holding as I spin her around so she's facing me. "About what I did? Christ, Laurel. Is this about me not using a condom? Or did I hurt you in some way? Was that it? Was I…?"

She raises her hand, placing her forefinger over my lips. "It was nothing to do with the condom. That was an accident with no consequences, and I know you'd have stood by me if anything had happened."

I reach up and pull her hand away. "Of course I would. But in that case, what…?"

"It was because everything you did to me was so… was so damn good."

"So I didn't hurt you? I wasn't too rough with you?"

She shakes her head. "It all felt incredible," she says. "All of it. That's what I felt so guilty about. I felt bad for enjoying it… for thinking it was better than it had ever been before. I know now that Mitch didn't deserve my loyalty, but at the time, it felt wrong to make comparisons. Especially ones where he came up wanting every time." I can't help smiling, and her lips twitch upward at the corners. "I beat myself up for thinking about you, when I should have been thinking about him."

I pull her close. "You had nothing to feel bad about."

"I know that now."

"I knew it then. I just wish I could have put you out of your misery."

She shakes her head, pulling away from me and going back to the vegetables, which are burning at the edges. "Damn. I need to concentrate on this."

I step back and she fetches the eggs, cracking them into a bowl, beating them and adding them to the pan. They bubble and she stirs them around a little before looking up at me.

"This is probably going to taste disgusting. I can't even think straight."

"Neither can I, so don't worry about it."

I open a bottle of wine and pour some out, then fetch some dishes, bringing them back, and she divides the mixture between the two plates before I carry them to the island unit.

"It was supposed to be a frittata," she says, sitting beside me and handing me a fork. "It looks more like scrambled eggs with burned vegetables."

"It doesn't matter what it was supposed to be, and the vegetables are charred, not burned. It's fine."

She takes a mouthful and tips her head. "Actually, it's not too bad."

"See? Stop worrying."

We both eat, then clink our glasses together, our eyes meeting as we take a sip of wine. There's still so much to be said, but I'm not sure where to start.

"Am I forgiven?" I ask, putting down my glass.

"What for?" She copies me, although she looks confused.

"For not telling you sooner. I didn't know how."

"I know. I understand." She doesn't mention my outburst this afternoon, or my revelations of having loved her all her adult life. I guess that's not a bad thing, though. This probably isn't the time or the place for that.

"So, am I forgiven?"

"Only if I am."

"There's nothing to forgive, Laurel."

She shakes her head. "Yes, there is. On so many levels."

I reach out, placing my hand over hers. "If you need me to forgive you, then you're forgiven, but you have nothing to feel bad about."

"Neither do you."

"I should have told you."

"How could you? And in any case, I'm not sure I'd have believed you if you'd said anything sooner."

"You wouldn't?"

She shakes her head. "You have to remember where I was... how I was feeling. At the beginning, I was too mired in grief to believe anything bad about Mitch, and on the night we... we..."

"Made love?" I say and she nods her head.

"On the night we made love, if you'd said anything then, I think I'd have wondered if you were trying to score points. Mitch couldn't defend himself, and I think I might have resented you for that."

"More than you resented me for making love to you?" I ask, and she frowns at me.

"I didn't resent you. I was confused by you."

"Are you confused by me now?"

She studies my face, gazing into my eyes, then focusing on my lips before letting her eyes drop to my chest and my arms. "No," she whispers, and I have to smile. "Although I still think it was better that I heard the truth about Mitch from someone else before I heard it from you."

"Even though you practically attacked me?"

She sighs, putting down her fork and twisting in her seat. I copy her, so we're facing each other, and she rests her hand on my chest.

"I'm sorry I did that. Are you okay?"

I place my hand over hers. "I've taken worse. And will you stop apologizing?"

She nods her head and I push our plates away, lifting her onto my lap, smiling when she puts her arms around my neck and clings to me.

"God, that feels good."

"Hmm… it does." She smiles up at me.

"I know we've kissed, and we've said we forgive each other, and I've told you what I want, but can you tell me what you want? I need to know, Laurel."

She rests her head on my shoulder, which feels promising. "I think the first thing I want is the truth."

"The truth?"

"Yes. I don't want any more surprises like the one I got at the beauty salon."

"About me, you mean?"

"No. About Mitch. I want you to tell me everything you know."

"I don't know very much, Laurel."

"Maybe not. But the only clue I've got – other than his affair with Kaylee – is that he flirted with Remi at Peony's wedding. What I need to know is, did he cheat on me all the time?"

"Excuse me… did you say he flirted with Remi?"

"Yes."

"And you knew about it?"

"No. Not until earlier today, when Peony told me. She'd written it off as a misunderstanding, because she assumed Mitch was happy with me, but…" She lets her voice fade, then coughs and takes a breath. "He clearly wasn't, was he?"

"That doesn't mean he had the right to flirt, or to cheat. If he was unhappy, he should have talked to you."

"I know. But that's the whole point. He didn't say a word. In fact, as far as I was concerned, everything was fine between us. I thought we had the perfect marriage, the perfect family, the perfect home…" She stops talking, then clamps her hand to her mouth, shaking her head.

"What's wrong?" I ask, and she stares at me for a second before she lowers her hand again.

"Do you think he ever brought her here?"

"Kaylee? I doubt it. When would he have had the chance? You and Addy were always here, weren't you? At least at night."

She shakes her head. "We stayed at Peony's place on the night before her wedding," she says. "He could have brought her here then."

"Maybe."

"She could have spent the night in our bed for all I know." She glances around the kitchen, like she's seeing it with fresh eyes.

"But he was all over you at the wedding, Laurel." She sucks in a breath, focusing on me again. "I remember it well. It hurt like hell to watch him paw you."

"He wasn't just pawing me. He was telling me all the things he wanted to do to me when we got home."

"I can't blame him for wanting you, Laurel, but the way he went about things was all wrong. It was like he thought he could pick you up and put you down whenever he pleased… like he thought he owned you. And no-one has the right to do that."

"Not even you?"

"No."

"Don't you want to own me?" she asks, sounding doubtful.

"No. I want to be yours."

She smiles. "That's good. Because I want to be yours, too."

I hold her close. "Which makes us equal. And that's how it should be. Always equal, Laurel. In everything."

She rests her head against my chest for a moment or two and then looks up into my eyes. "In that case, can you make us equal now? Can you share your knowledge with me and tell me what he did?"

"I don't know what he did with Kaylee. Until I found them together in his car, I didn't realize he was even seeing her."

"Okay… but before that? Did he cheat on me with anyone else?"

"I honestly can't say. If he did, he kept it quiet, because believe me, if I'd known about it, I'd have done something."

"You would?"

"Of course. Do you think I'd have stood by and let him do that to you?" She shakes her head, although she doesn't say a word. "I know he fooled around before you got married. A lot."

She leans back. "Really?"

"Yes. Didn't you know?"

"No. I asked him about his past once, and he said there wasn't much to tell. I believed him… like I always did."

"Well, that was another of his lies, I'm afraid."

"So he slept around?"

"Yes."

"With anyone I know?"

"There was a rumor he had an affair with Sabrina Pope while she was redecorating this place."

"Excuse me?" She sits up, staring at me. "Sabrina Pope?"

"Yes."

"But she was married to Tanner back then, wasn't she?"

"She was."

"Is that why they got divorced?"

"I don't think so, and I'm not about to ask him, either. Their divorce was messy enough, and like I say, it's only a rumor. If it wasn't true…" I let my voice fade and she nods her head.

"No. I see." She leans back against me again, and I put my arms around her. "I don't suppose it matters now, either way."

"No, it doesn't."

"Although it shows the kind of guy Mitch was. He didn't respect other people's marriages any more than his own." I can't argue with that, and we sit in silence for a moment before she looks up at me. "Do you know of anyone else?"

"Not specifically, and like I say, I don't know of anyone after your marriage, which is what really counts, isn't it?"

"I guess, although I suppose his behavior might make more sense of my parents' reaction to him. If they knew of the rumors, it would explain why they were so disappointed that he was Addy's father."

"Maybe."

She shakes her head. "How did I not know any of this?"

"Because you were too young to be interested before he left for college and the pro-football circuit. He probably didn't feature on your radar, and I can't imagine it would have been something your parents would have discussed with you at that age."

"No, they wouldn't. But what about when I came back, after he'd retired and I'd finished at college?"

I frown down at her. "There wasn't time for any fact-finding, was there? I mean, you slept with him almost immediately, didn't you?"

She blushes, then nods her head. "Yeah. I guess so." She sighs. "I was so stupid."

"No, you weren't. Mitch was good at that kind of thing."

"Clearly." She tilts her head. "Promise you'd tell me, if there was anything else? Anything after our marriage that you knew about?"

"I promise. I'll always regret not telling you about him and Kaylee, but I thought I was doing the right thing. It hurt so much, having to lie to you, and watch you grieve for him, but I didn't know what else to do. From here on in, I guarantee, I'll never keep anything from you, ever again."

She smiles. "Thank you."

"You don't have to thank me, but now we've gotten that out of the way, can you put me out of my misery and tell me what you want?"

"You," she says simply. "All of you."

"Sure?"

"Positive. I know people are gonna judge me and say it's too soon, but I don't care. I've been judged before."

"Who by?"

"Half the town."

"When?"

She shakes her head. "Are you being deliberately forgetful?"

"Not that I'm aware of."

"So you don't remember the way people talked when Mitch and I got married?"

"I do, but I wasn't in the mood for listening back then."

She sighs, resting her head against me. "No, I guess not."

"Did it bother you?" I ask, and she shrugs her shoulders.

"I expected it. I might have tried to dress up my relationship with Mitch, but it didn't take a genius to work out what had happened between us."

"Do you regret it? What happened between you, I mean?"

"I felt disappointed in myself, I guess. It was my first time, and…"

"It was your first time?" I can't hide my surprise.

"Yes."

I shake my head. "You got pregnant the first time you had sex?"

"Yes. But I got Addy out of it, and I can never regret that." She leans back, looking right at me. "I also got Mitch, and at the time I was grateful."

"Grateful?" I can't believe I just heard that. "Grateful? Jesus…"

"I know. But I thought we were happy, Brady. Try to remember that." I nod my head, although it's a struggle. "I—I didn't know how you felt about me back then," she murmurs.

"Would knowing have made a difference?"

"It's impossible to say." She lets out a long sigh, shaking her head. "What must you have thought when you found out I was expecting Mitch's baby?"

"I suppose my strongest emotion was probably disappointment."

"I thought you might say that," she says, the sadness in her eyes taking me by surprise. "I let you down."

"No, you didn't. It wasn't you I was disappointed in. It was the lost opportunities… the life I thought we'd never have. I didn't stop loving you, just because you'd slept with Mitch, or because you were pregnant with his child."

She frowns. "But surely…"

I hold her closer. "When you married Mitch and I found out you were pregnant, it broke my heart. I'm not gonna say it didn't. But I'd already loved you for four years by then. If Mitch hadn't stepped up, I'd have married you myself… in a heartbeat."

Her eyes widen, and she raises her hands, clasping my cheeks and gazing into my eyes. "Y—You'd have married me?"

"Yes."

"You'd have raised another man's daughter?"

"I would. I'd have given the town gossips something to really think about and said she was mine, if that was what you wanted."

Her eyes glisten with unshed tears. "You'd have done that? For me?"

"I'd do anything for you."

She closes the gap, her lips touching mine. "I'm sorry," she whispers.

"Don't, baby. Don't." Her shoulders shake and she starts to sob. "Don't cry, Laurel."

"But I got it so wrong."

"It doesn't matter. We can get it right now, can't we?"

She leans back slightly, tears hitting her cheeks. "You want to?"

"You know I do. More than anything."

Chapter Nineteen

Laurel

Brady leans forward, his lips hovering over mine, and I close my eyes, waiting for the moment of contact. It doesn't come, though, and I open my eyes again, looking up into his face.

"Is something wrong?"

He startles, like he was somewhere else for a moment, and then lets out a sigh. "Sorry. I just remembered something."

"Oh?"

He sits up slightly, pulling back. "Yeah. It's something I need to tell you."

This sounds worrying, and judging by his expression, it looks slightly scary, too. "What is it?" I ask.

"I was propositioned."

"You were what?"

"I was propositioned."

"When?"

He frowns. "Last Friday."

My heart quickens, my palms dampening as I prepare myself for the worst. "What happened?" I ask, although I know I have no right to question him. I rejected him. He was free to do whatever he wanted.

"Nothing," he says quickly, holding me close to him. "I promise. Absolutely nothing happened."

The relief is overwhelming, and holding it in is a challenge. I try my best, though. "Okay, then who propositioned you? Was it someone I know?" Is that why he's making such a big deal out of this? Because if nothing happened, I can't see why else he'd be telling me about it.

"No. Her name was Peyton." I definitely don't know anyone called Peyton, that's for sure, and I nod my head. "She came up to me at Dawson's bar."

"You were at Dawson's bar?"

"Yes. I was…" He stops talking for a second. "I was drowning my sorrows."

"About me?"

He nods. "Yeah."

"I'm sorry, Brady."

"Please stop saying that."

How can I, when I've made so many mistakes? I meant it when I said I don't regret having Addy, but I regret everything else… most especially hurting Brady. And I did hurt him, so many times.

Even so, apologizing won't get us anywhere. It won't get us to the end of his confession, that's for sure.

"How much had you had to drink?" I ask.

"I don't know. Three glasses of wine? It was enough that I couldn't drive, I know that much. But I hadn't taken my car, anyway, so it didn't matter."

"And Peyton? Did she have a car?"

"No. She suggested coming back to my place, though." I pull back, but he holds on to me. "I told you, nothing happened."

"You turned her down?"

"Yes. I told her about you. Not in any detail, but enough for her to guess I was taken… or hopelessly in love, as she put it."

I suck in a breath. He's said that so many times now, but I'm not sure I'll ever get used to hearing it.

"You weren't tempted?" I ask.

"No. I didn't want her. I wanted you. It might have been breaking my heart that you wouldn't even talk to me, but that didn't mean I was gonna jump into bed with anyone else."

I shift closer to him, feeling his arousal beneath me. "I didn't mean to break your heart."

"I know, but it's very fragile when it comes to you."

"Then I'll be sure to take good care of it."

He smiles and leans in, although it's my turn to pull back, and he frowns. "Is something the matter?"

"Only that I'm wondering why you told me about Peyton, if nothing happened between you."

"Because I promised never to keep anything from you again."

"In that case, thank you."

He leans in again, and this time, I close the gap myself, our lips clashing, our tongues colliding. We need this... both of us. There's been enough talk for now. We need to feel.

His arousal is pressing in to me and I grind my hips against him, which makes him groan into my mouth, his head tilting to one side as he deepens the kiss.

I want him so much. I need to feel him inside me, and I pull away, heaving in a breath, and looking up into his misted eyes.

"Do you want to move this to somewhere more comfortable?" I ask, surprised by how low and throaty my voice sounds.

"Sure." He stands with me in his arms, and lifts me onto the countertop, pushing the plates aside and sitting me back. "Is that comfortable?"

"I guess."

"Good."

He raises my skirt, exposing my thong, and sighs, pushing my thighs apart and rubbing his fingers over the thin lace material.

I moan softly and spread my legs further still, leaning back on my elbows.

"That feels good," I murmur, letting my head rock back.

"I can't see the point in this."

I raise my head again, staring at him. "In what?"

"In this." He puts his fingers in the top of my thong, tugging just gently. "It barely covers anything, and you're so wet the lace is soaked."

"I'm not sure the purpose of a thong is to cover. It's more to enhance, isn't it? And are you complaining about how wet I am?"

"Not at all…" He leans in, smiling. "But you don't need enhancing, baby." With that, he rips through my underwear, tearing the seam. "There. That's better."

He stares down at me, like a hungry man being offered a feast, and grabs my thighs, pulling me to the edge of the countertop before he bends his head and licks my clit. I shudder, lying back, and he raises my legs, pushing them up and holding them there as he flicks his tongue over and over me, driving me wild.

"More," I groan through gritted teeth, as I bring my hand down on the back of his head. "Give me more." He does as I ask, sucking and nibbling at me, alternating that with long slow licks and flicks until I'm so close, I know I can't hold back. "I'm gonna… I'm gonna…" I can't get the words out, and as he sucks me into his mouth once more, I tip over the edge, my body convulsing in a savage orgasm that rips through me. It's been so long since he did this to me, I scream his name, needing him to know that it's him… it's all him.

As I calm, he continues to caress me with his tongue, only stopping as the last quiver of my climax leaves my body. He stands then, looking down at me, licking his lips.

"Man, you taste good."

I smile. "That felt amazing."

"It sounded like it."

"Hmm… it was nice to be able to make some noise."

He holds out his hand and I take it, letting him sit me up. "I don't mind if we have to be quiet, just so long as we can keep doing this."

"We can," I whisper, and he smiles, then lifts me off of the countertop, into his arms. I wrap my legs around him, clutching his shoulders, and he walks through to the living room. The evening sun is blazing in through the back window, straight across the couch, and he sits down in the center of it, with me on his lap.

His arousal is bone hard against my core, and while I could just sit here and rock against it for a while, I want more than that.

As he leans in to kiss me, I pull back, shimmying away from him and then sliding downward to the floor.

"Where are you going?" he asks.

"Nowhere." I kneel at his feet, reaching up for his belt buckle. "You might look as sexy as sin in your uniform, but I'd rather see you naked."

He smiles. "Here… let me." He removes his holster first, putting it aside, and then undoes his pants before tilting his head at me. I take over, lowering his zipper and then tugging on his pants. He raises his butt and I lower them, along with his trunks, moving back while I pull them off completely and throw them to one side. He kicks off his shoes and I remove his socks, raising my head, my eyes fixing on his erection. It's even bigger than I remember it, and I lick my lips, which makes him smile.

"Is it still mine?" I ask as I move closer again, reaching out to clasp it around the base.

He sucks in a breath. "Both it and me. We're all yours."

I smile, and keeping my eyes fixed on his, I settle between his legs and take him in my mouth. He closes his eyes, his head rocking back as he lets out a sigh, my tongue swirling around the head of his arousal, before I swallow down the first two or three inches of him. The problem is, he's so big, he fills my mouth, and that's about as much as I can take. He seems to like it though, flexing his hips a little, and as I bob up and down, I use my hand to stroke him at the same time.

"Fuck…" He opens his eyes again, gazing at me. "Oh, God… the sight of you with my cock in your mouth, it's…" He stops talking, his breathing ragged all of a sudden. "Stop, Laurel… stop. Or I'm gonna come."

I release him from my mouth, although I keep my hand around him. He twitches against me, and I see the concentration on his face, wondering if I left it too late. He seems to swell slightly, and he moans, but nothing happens, and after a second or two, he nods his head, like the moment has passed, and I pull my hand away.

"That was close," he whispers.

"Would it have been the end of the world?"

"If I'd come in your mouth?" He sits forward, smiling, and I nod my head. "No, but I'd rather not. Not tonight."

"Tomorrow then?"

He grins. "Maybe. Or the next day."

He bends and kisses me, his tongue searching for mine. There's a slightly sweet taste to him now, and I suddenly remember what that is, and pull back from him.

"You taste of me," I whisper.

"Is that a problem?"

"No."

"Good… because I've gotta say, you taste incredible." He leans in again, but then stops. "Can I ask you something?"

"Of course."

"Was that something you did with him?"

"Oral sex, you mean?" He nods his head. "Yes, it was. Although I think he preferred getting to giving."

"Why doesn't that surprise me?" he mutters, shaking his head, which makes me smile.

"Why do you ask?"

"Because you were surprised when I tasted of you. I wondered if that was something new to you."

"It was."

He frowns. "But you just said…"

"I know, but Mitch had… how can I put this? Mitch had routines."

"Routines? With sex?"

"Yes. One of those routines meant he never used to kiss me after he'd… you know…"

Brady frowns. "Really?"

"Yeah. It's like he'd never kiss me, or lick me… down there, if I wasn't shaved. And I mean shaved. If he found so much as a hair out of place, he'd stop."

He pulls back. "Are you serious?"

"Absolutely."

"The guy was an idiot." I can't help smiling and I rest my hands on his bare thighs. "Does that mean you used to be shaved?" he asks.

"It does. Why? Would you prefer me to be that way now?"

"Not unless it's what you want."

He puts his hands over mine, and I notice a faraway look in his eyes. It's gone almost as soon as it got there, but I can't help wondering about it.

"What are you thinking?"

"Nothing."

I kneel up, getting closer to him. "You said you wouldn't keep things from me."

"I'm not."

"Then tell me what you were thinking just then."

"How do you know I was thinking anything?"

"I saw it in your eyes."

He sighs. "It was just something to do with the accident, that's all."

"Mitch's accident?"

"Yeah." He pulls me up, lifting me onto his lap so I'm straddling him and holds me there, his hands on my ass. The look in his eyes tells me he doesn't want to say anything more, but I need to know.

"Was it something to do with her? With Kaylee?"

"It was."

I think for a second, but that's all it takes for me to remember what Brady said about the way she was dressed, and I lean back slightly. "Was she shaved?"

He sighs. "Yeah, she was."

I shake my head. "Knowing Mitch, he probably made her. He probably…"

He pulls his hand around, placing his finger over my lips. "Don't," he says. "Don't start down the road of wondering what he said to her, or what she did for him. It won't help."

He's right. And no matter how much I hate the thought of Mitch's deception, I need to forget about it. He's not worth it.

I reach out and unfasten the bottom button of his shirt, working my way up. Brady watches me as I push it apart and then from his shoulders, sitting forward so I can lower it down his arms. Unlike when he was here in the winter, he's not wearing a t-shirt. He's naked, and utterly glorious, and I study his tattoo again, paying it a little more attention than I did before.

"What made you choose this design?" I ask, tracing my fingers over the leaves and across the rose petals. There's no color to the tattoo. It's all in black, but it's beautiful, nonetheless.

"What do you think?"

I lean back a little and frown at him. "How should I know?"

"Look at the flowers." I do as he says.

"They're roses."

"Exactly. And the leaves?"

I shake my head. "They're leaves."

He smiles. "They're laurel leaves."

"Laurel leaves and roses?"

"Yeah." He stares at me, and I let those words swirl around my head for a second, before I realize the meaning behind them.

"My name?"

He nods his head. "What else?"

"But you said you had this done nine years ago."

"Yes. When I realized there was no-one else for me but you. I could hardly have your name tattooed on my chest. Not when you were so much younger than me, and seemingly so out of reach. But I could do the next best thing. Obviously, when you married Mitch, I was even more relieved I hadn't done anything too blatant."

"And no-one's ever realized the connection?"

"To be honest, it's not something I show off to the world at large, but if anyone has worked out what it's about, they've never mentioned it." He studies my face. "Do you like it?"

"I do. I think it makes you look…"

"What?" He's smiling.

"Masculine."

"You think I need the help of a tattoo?"

"No." I run my fingers over his chest, tracing the lines of the leaves up onto his shoulder. "I just think it enhances what's already there."

I let my hands wander a little further, down his arms and then across his abdomen.

"I think you're a little overdressed," he whispers, his eyes twinkling.

"Maybe you need to do something about that."

He feels for the zipper at the back of my dress, pulling it down to reveal my naked breasts.

"I could get used to this no underwear thing," he says, leaning in and licking my nipples… the left one first and then the right, which he bites on just gently.

"I had trouble coordinating my panties and bra this morning, so I gave up," I say, trying to concentrate.

"Glad to hear it. Who needs coordinated underwear, anyway? In fact, who needs underwear?" He raises my skirt, his hands making contact with my bare ass. "I much prefer you naked."

"But I'm not naked."

"You will be."

He twists in his seat, then flips me onto my back, pulling my dress down over my hips. I raise my ass, and he completes his mission, dropping it to the floor.

"Is that better?" I say, gazing up at him, and he changes position, settling between my legs.

"Much."

He takes my right leg, raising it onto the back of the couch, then stops.

"What's wrong?"

He smiles. "I forgot something."

He leans over, searching the floor, then stands, bending to pick up his pants and delve into the pocket, pulling out his wallet, which he opens, retrieving a condom.

"You're being cautious this time, are you?" I raise myself up on my elbows, watching as he tears into the pack and rolls the condom over his length, our eyes meeting as he looks down at me before he resumes his position between my legs.

"Yeah, I am." He leans in, taking his weight on his elbows. "I'm sorry about what happened last time… about forgetting."

"It was okay."

"I know it was, but I should have been more careful, and I'm going to be from now on."

I rest my hands on his biceps, and then move them to his chest. "Until we're ready not to be?" I say in a whisper, holding my breath.

He smiles. "Yeah. Until we're ready not to be."

I let out that breath, moving my hands up, around the back of his neck and into his hair, my fingers knotting there. "That will happen, will it?"

"Hell... yeah."

Can it be? Can I really be this lucky?

I grin at him, and he nods his head, sucking in a breath as he reaches between us, holding his erection in his hand and rubbing it against me. It feels sublime, and every time it hits my clit, I shudder, parting my legs a little further.

"Please, Brady... stop teasing me."

He smiles, finding my entrance on his next stroke, and entering me.

"Fuck..." he whispers, groaning loudly. "Fuck, yes..."

He pulls out, then pushes back inside. "Do that again," I mutter. "Again."

He does as I say, penetrating me afresh with every single stroke. The feeling is like nothing else, and I love every second of it, taking his length deep inside me.

I reach down, parting my lips with my fingers, and circling them over my clit.

"That's so hot," he says, taking me just a little harder. "Is that something you did before?"

"Before? With Mitch, you mean?"

He shakes his head, his eyes darkening. "No. Before him." He stills, most of the way inside me, waiting for my answer and I feel myself blush, keeping my hand where it is although my fingers aren't moving anymore. "What's this?" he says with a smile on his lips. "Is there something you wanna tell me?"

"Maybe."

He pushes all the way inside, but holds still, waiting again. "Go on then."

"I—I used to do this before I met him." I've realized that saying Mitch's name isn't a good idea… not when we're making love, anyway. The look on Brady's face was enough to tell me that.

"Oh, yes?"

"Yes."

"But you didn't do it after you met him?" I'm surprised he's asked, but I can't fail to notice he didn't say Mitch's name either.

"No, I didn't."

"Was there a reason for that?"

"It wasn't that he was spectacularly good at making me come, if that's what you're wondering." He smiles and pulls almost all the way out of me before he plunges back in again, making me moan.

"I'm glad to hear it," he says. "But if it wasn't his prowess, what was the reason?"

"If you must know, he didn't like it."

"He didn't like you touching yourself?" I nod my head. "Why not?"

I shrug my shoulders. "Don't ask me. I tried it once, and he told me not to."

"That's just plain dumb. I could sit here and watch you all night long." I smile, feeling that blush return. "Why is that embarrassing?" he asks. "I enjoy watching you."

"I know. And that's not what's embarrassing."

"Okay. What is?"

"The fact that I've been doing it by myself."

"You have?"

"Yes."

"Since he died, you mean?"

"No. Well, yes. But it wasn't about him. It was about you. I only started after we made love." He smiles. "Being with you was so good, and I missed it. I missed you. I wanted you."

His smile widens. "I wanted you, too."

"I—I remembered the video you recorded on my phone, and I played it, and…"

"It turned you on?" he says, positively grinning now.

"Yeah."

"I'm not surprised. You looked amazing."

"So did you."

He starts to move again, groaning loudly with every thrust. There's something about that… about his obvious need, and I let my fingers play over my hardened clit again, my body responding.

"Make yourself come," he whispers. "Show me what you can do."

I rub a little harder, arching my back as I feel that familiar tightening inside and he leans up, changing the angle slightly. That's all it takes to push me over the edge, my body spiraling down through wave upon wave of ecstasy. I'm screaming with pleasure, crying out his name and he keeps hammering into me, harder and harder, until I can't take any more.

"Stop," I mutter. "I can't…"

"Yes, you can. We're not done yet."

He pulls out of me, flipping me over onto my front. I feel spent, like a rag doll, but I want him still, and as he settles behind me, I raise my ass off of the couch, whimpering with pleasure as he slams into me.

"Yes… please, yes."

"I thought you wanted to stop."

"Don't listen to me. I don't know what I'm saying."

He chuckles, taking me harder still, putting his foot up on the couch so he can raise himself slightly, changing the angle. I buck against him, and he slows.

"Take it easy, baby. This is gonna be deep and I don't wanna hurt you."

He wants me to take it easy? Now?

I push backwards again, and he leans over me, his lips beside my ear.

"I thought you were gonna take it easy."

"I—I can't. I need you."

"You've got me, baby. I'm yours."

"What you're doing, Brady... it's... it's..."

"It's what?"

"It's driving me wild."

"Good."

He straightens up again, and grabs my ponytail. It feels like he's wrapping it around his hand and although it's not tight enough to hurt, he's letting me know he's in control... and I love it.

I love him.

I really do.

He tugs, just slightly, pulling my head back. "You want my dick?"

"Yes!"

He rams it home, and without warning, I come around him, so damn hard.

"Fuck!" he yells and I feel him swell inside me, his body stiffening as he tugs my hair just a little harder, and then he howls my name, the sound filling the room as he fills me...

*

All I can hear is our breathing. I've collapsed onto the couch, unable to move, although that's possibly because there's something heavy on me, holding me down.

"Relax, baby," Brady whispers in my ear. He must be lying on top of me, and although I don't think I could be any more relaxed, I make a conscious effort to breathe out, to let my body luxuriate in the moment. Speech is too complicated, but the weight lifts as he pulls out of me, taking it very slow. "Give me five minutes. And don't move a muscle."

"I can't," I whisper, and he chuckles.

I hear his footsteps leaving the room, but try as I might, I still can't even turn over, let alone sit up. So I lie, face down, drained…

"Do you want a hug?" I raise my head at the sound of his voice right beside me.

"Did I fall asleep?"

"I don't know. Did you?"

"I think I must have done."

He sits by my head, and although I try to shimmy closer, I can't. "Here… let me." Brady lifts me onto his lap, turning me over, and I snuggle against him, his erection prodding into me as I shift, trying to get comfortable.

"Is that normal?" I say, looking down at it.

"It is with you."

He kisses me, his tongue caressing mine, his hands soothing my skin as they roam over my body, nowhere left untouched.

"I love you," I whisper, right at the moment his fingers brush against my inner thigh.

He stops, pulling back, and stares into my eyes. "Excuse me? Did you just say…?"

"I love you," I repeat and for a second or two, he studies my face, like he's never seen me before, like every feature is new to him.

"You mean that?"

"Yes. You've said it so many times, and I realized just now that I feel the same. I love you, Brady."

He smiles. "When exactly did you realize this?"

"If I'm being honest, it was when you grabbed my ponytail."

He laughs, throwing his head back. "I told you I liked ponytails."

"I can see why now."

"I love you so much," he growls, devouring my lips in a heated kiss. My body's on fire and as his tongue flicks against mine, I grind my hips into him, which makes him chuckle. "You want more?" he says, breaking the kiss.

"If you're offering."

He nods his head, then tips it to one side. "I know I said I wouldn't come in your mouth tonight, but…"

"You've changed your mind?"

"Only if it's what you want." I nod, and he grins, watching as I slide from his lap. "Not like that," he says, and I stand, frowning down at him.

"How then?"

He lifts his legs, twisting around and lying out on the couch. "You go on top."

"But I thought we were…"

"We are."

"I don't under—"

He grabs my hand, pulling me closer. "Straddle me, baby."

"Straddle you? Where? How? If I'm gonna…"

He chuckles and I stop talking. "I love this."

"Love what?"

"That you don't know what to do."

I pull my hand from his. "Don't make fun of me."

He sits up again, retrieving my hand, and pulls me down beside him. "I'm not. Honestly. I just love the fact that you've obviously never done this before. It means we get at least one first."

"One? You think we only get one?"

He frowns. "Why? What else is new to you?"

I'm starting to wish I hadn't said anything now… except it's nice to share things like this with Brady and for him to know what it all means to me.

"There's the list of ways in which you make me come."

"A list?"

"There are so many, I think it's list-worthy."

He chuckles. "We'll have to write them down, so I don't forget them."

"I don't think that's likely, do you?"

He shakes his head, then kisses me, holding my neck, his lips brushing mine in the gentlest caress. "Feeling you come on my cock is incredible, Laurel. Actually, watching you come is one of the greatest gifts in life… which is why I love doing it as often as possible."

"Hmm… that's another thing I didn't realize."

"What is?"

"How many times I can come. It's exhausting."

"But worth it?"

"Definitely."

He nods his head. "Speaking of coming…"

I tilt my head, smiling, and he lies back again, waiting for me to stand before he puts his feet up on the couch.

"What am I supposed to do?"

"Straddle me."

He said that before, but considering what we're supposed to be doing, I can't see how it's going to help. Even so, I put one knee on either side of his legs, looking up at him, and noting the grin on his face.

"What's the matter?"

"You're the wrong way round."

I contemplate what he's saying for a moment or two. "You want me with my back to you?"

"For this, yeah."

"You mean you want to… you know… while I…?"

He chuckles. "Why are you so shy all of a sudden? This is me you're talking to. Why can't you just say you want me to eat your beautiful pussy while you suck on my cock?"

"Okay. I want you to eat my pussy while I suck your beautiful cock."

He reaches up, puts his hand behind my neck and pulls me down. "That's not exactly what I said, is it?"

"No. But it's close enough. And it's accurate."

"I'll be the judge of that." He kisses me, then lets me go. "Switch around, baby, then move back up here. I need to taste you."

My body shudders and I take no time at all to flip around, so I'm facing his feet, and then shimmy back until I'm above his face, feeling the heat of his breath on my core.

"Lower yourself down a little," he says, so I do, sucking in a breath when I feel his tongue flick across my clit. I drop my hips just a little further and he nips at me with his teeth, sucking me into his mouth. It feels so good, and I rock against him, my hands resting on his rippling abs, my eyes settling on his straining erection.

I lean over, clasping it around the base, and take it in my mouth. He groans, bucking his hips off of the couch, and although my first instinct is to move my head back and forth, I don't. I hold still, letting him take me.

He's careful not to go too deep, although he hits the back of my throat every so often, and I remove my hand, giving him full control… because I like it that way. He seems to appreciate it, taking my mouth a little faster, as he inserts a finger into me, moving it in and out. My body's quivering, his tongue flickering over me, his finger working its magic, which feels incredible, until he adds a second…

It's too much. Something flips and I become a mass of nerves, all popping and detonating at the same time. I'm trembling and shuddering, out of control, and just as I hit the peak, he swells in my mouth, letting out a loud groan as a spurt of hot liquid hits the back of my throat. It's followed by another, and another. I swallow them down, barely able to focus, as my body writhes through pleasure that's so intense it almost hurts.

I can't take anymore. I can't.

I ease forward slightly, breaking the contact between his tongue and my clit, to get some relief. His orgasm is over, but I'm still twitching through the end of mine, and I feel him gently remove his fingers from me, and then slide from underneath my burned-out body.

He must realize I'm incapable of movement, and he tips me onto my side, against the back of the couch, then lies beside me, pulling me in to him, so we're facing each other.

"That was amazing," I whisper, surprised by how drunk I sound.

"It was."

He kisses the tip of my nose, then my forehead, then my cheeks, and finally my lips, taking his time over them.

Everything he does is so intense… from this most gentle of kisses, to each and every mind-blowing orgasm, and I realize as he puts his hand on my ass, pulling me close to him, that I never want this to end. I break the kiss and lean back, looking up at him, wondering how to say that without sounding clingy, when he frowns and lets out a sigh. What's this?

"I guess I should go home," he says.

"No. Please don't. Please stay." I've never sounded more clingy in my life, but I don't care anymore. He smiles, brushing his fingertips down my cheeks.

"What about Addy?"

"She's not here. Remember?"

"I know, baby. But what will happen if Peony brings her back early tomorrow and she finds me here?"

"Nothing will happen. You've slept here before."

"In very different circumstances."

"Maybe, but I don't want you to go."

He smiles. "I don't wanna go either."

"Then stay."

He sits up, bringing me with him, so we're both on the edge of the couch, and then he stands, holding out his hand. I take it and he helps me to my feet. My legs are a little wobbly and he puts his arms around me, holding me up, and looking down into my face.

"I'll get up early and leave before Addy comes home."

I shake my head. "No. No, Brady. When I said I don't want you to go, I meant it."

He frowns, leaning back just slightly, although he keeps a hold of me. "What are you saying, Laurel?"

"I'm asking you to stay."

"For the night?"

I shake my head. "No."

"How long for?" It feels like he already knows the answer to that question, but he needs me to say it, and I will. Because I need it too.

"Forever," I whisper. "I know it's early days, and we've got a lot to consider – especially with Addy – but I can't bear the thought of you walking away from me."

He smiles. "You're serious?"

"Yes. I love you, and I need you, and I feel like we've spent too much time apart."

"So do I, but… but are you sure this is what you want? You're sure you're ready?"

"Yes. I think Addy is too. She missed you so much when you weren't here."

"I missed her too," he says, pulling me closer again. "Not as much as I missed her mom, but I definitely missed her."

He dips his head, kissing me, his arousal pressing against me, and I smile. "Shall we go upstairs?"

"Sure."

He releases me and bends, gathering up our clothes and putting them over his arm, his holster on top, before he takes my hand and leads me from the room.

I climb the stairs ahead of him, by-passing the room I used to share with Mitch and continuing on to the one I've made my own, although Brady pulls me back before we reach the door.

"Where are you going?" he asks, looking puzzled.

"In here." I tip my head backwards toward the guest bedroom.

He moves closer, looking down into my eyes. "If you want us to sleep together, we can sleep in your bedroom. It's okay. I'm not gonna…"

"This is my bedroom now."

"You mean you switched rooms?"

"Yes. I couldn't sleep in there anymore." I glance at the door to the room I used to share with Mitch, and Brady steps back slightly.

"Because it reminded you of him?"

"No." I move closer, resting my hand on his bare chest. "It had nothing to do with that."

"Then why did you make the change?"

"Because I've always hated that room. The way it's decorated is so drab. The colors are so depressing and morbid."

"I know. You said. I remember you telling me about it, and how Mitch liked it that way."

"He did, and I know I could have changed it since he died, but I haven't had the energy. Once you stopped sleeping here, it just seemed easier to switch rooms."

"Can I assume you didn't move your clothes in here?" he says, nodding to the guest room.

That seems like an odd question, and I shake my head. "No. I moved them in. Why do you ask?"

He blushes, which is kinda cute, and then looks down for a moment before he raises his eyes to mine. "Didn't you notice Mitch's things were missing?"

"Excuse me?"

"Mitch's clothes... he'd taken some of them with him. A few pairs of jeans, tops, sweaters, shirts. Didn't you notice they were gone?"

"No. We have... We had separate closet space. I haven't even looked at his since he died. I wish I had, though. Maybe I could have worked things out sooner."

He cups my face with his hand and gazes into my eyes. "Hey... it doesn't matter now. You're happy, aren't you?"

"I am." I smile up at him and step closer, inhaling deeply, a memory stirring. "It's odd, but when I first switched bedrooms, the guest room smelled of you."

"I guess that's not surprising. I'd been sleeping in it for quite a while."

"I know. I liked it."

"You did?"

"Of course I did."

He frowns, looking confused. "Why? I mean, why would it have even registered with you all those months ago? I thought we were just friends back then… at least as far as you were concerned."

"We were. But I missed having you here. I'd gotten used to you."

"Then why did you ask me to stop coming? I would have carried on, you know? I'd have done whatever you needed… whatever you asked of me."

"I know, and I'll always be grateful for what you did, but… but I had to ask you to stay away."

"Why?" He frowns.

"It wasn't personal, Brady. It wasn't anything you'd done wrong."

"Then what was it?"

"Peony."

His brow furrows. "Peony?"

"Yes. At the time, I was so jealous of her being pregnant. I couldn't handle seeing her all the time, knowing Mitch and I had been talking about…" I let my voice fade, realizing *we* hadn't been talking about it at all. *I* had. He'd been putting my words into action with someone else… and I'll never forgive him for that. Never.

"Are you okay?" Brady asks.

"No. I was just thinking about Mitch, and Kaylee, and her being pregnant."

He pulls me close. "I know."

"I can't forgive him, Brady."

"You don't have to. What he did was…" He shakes his head. "I can't think of the words to describe what he did to you, but you don't have to forgive him, or feel bad about that."

I rest my head against his chest, relieved at being given permission to feel the way I do. It makes it easier..

"I'm sorry," I say, looking up at him again. "We were talking about Peony, weren't we?"

"Yes. But you can talk to me about anything, you know that."

I smile up at him. "I do. But I need to explain this to you."

"About why you asked me to stop coming over?"

"Yes. It was nothing to do with you. It was just that I couldn't ask Peony not to come anymore without offending her, so I asked both of you. I made it sound like I was coping, even though I wasn't."

"Why didn't you just talk to me separately?"

"Because I didn't want you to think I was using you."

"Using me? Sending me away felt like you were punishing me."

I put my arms around his waist and lean against him, my head on his chest again. "I'm sorry."

"Don't be." He reaches down, raising my face to his. "Will you do two things for me?"

"Of course."

He smiles. "Will you remember that, whatever you say, and whatever you do, I will never judge you. I'll always listen, and I'll do my best to help, if I can. Okay?"

I nod my head. "What's the second thing?"

"Try to bear in mind that you have nothing to feel jealous of. Peony and Ryan are happy and we all know you don't begrudge them that. I know it was your plans with Mitch that made you feel that way, but they were your plans, not his."

"I know. I was just thinking that."

He smiles. "Good. I'm glad you worked it out. I meant what I said, baby. You're entitled to feel angry and used by him, but he's history now, and he's not worthy of a moment of your time."

"No, he's not. I think I'd rather forget the past." He smiles and I take his hand, pulling him toward the bedroom door. "Will you be okay in here?" I ask.

"Of course. I slept in here before."

"I know, but you were on your own then, and the bed is quite small."

He grins as I open the door. "I'm sure we'll cope."

I'm too warm, and I push back the covers, aware of something tickling against the back of my neck. I brush it away and settle into the pillow, only for it to start up again.

I pull away. "Stop it."

"If you insist."

My eyes shoot open and I flip over to be faced with Brady. He's lying on his side, propped up on one elbow, smiling down at me, and looking absolutely gorgeous. "I'm sorry. Was that you?"

"Of course. I was kissing your neck… only you didn't seem to like it."

"I did. Honestly. It's just I'm not used to waking up with anyone."

He frowns. "You're not?"

"No. Mitch was never here in the mornings, and…"

He places a finger over my lips. "I am," he says firmly. "I'm here."

"I know. Sorry I mentioned him. It's just…"

"It's okay. He might be in the past, but you were married to him for five years. Even if he didn't deserve five minutes of your time, he's still Addy's father. He's gonna come up in conversation from time to time. I get that. Doesn't mean I have to like it… but I'll live with it." He takes my hand, holding it against his chest. "I don't want you to feel you have to apologize every time his name is mentioned, though. It's gonna happen."

"But you'd rather it didn't happen when we're making love?" I say and he lets out a sigh.

"You noticed, did you?"

"Yeah." I smile up at him and he smiles back.

"I'm not jealous, Laurel. I just hate what he did to you, and I hate him for doing it. But I get that it might happen, and if it does, I don't want you to feel bad. Okay?" I nod my head. "We'll work around it, and in the meantime I'll do my best to remember you're not great with being kissed in the mornings."

His smile widens as he finishes speaking and I shuffle over, so I'm closer to him.

"I am. Really, I am."

"Wanna prove it?"

I move closer still and lean up, kissing his lips. He rolls me onto my back, growling into my mouth, and parts my legs with his, his erection pressing against my core.

"You said kissing." I smile up at him, caressing his chest.

"I lied."

He dips his head, licking my nipples, sucking them into his mouth, and biting on them, until I'm writhing beneath him.

"More… please, Brady. I…"

A phone beeps in the distance, and we both startle.

"Is that yours?" he says. "Because mine's up here."

"It must be."

"Where is it?" He kneels up, and I let my eyes drop to his erection, licking my lips.

"Where's what?"

"Your phone."

I raise my eyes to his. He's grinning, and I have to smile. "Sorry. I was distracted."

"Good. I like you being distracted, and I'll do it some more in a minute… once you've told me where your phone is."

"In the kitchen."

"Okay."

He climbs off of the bed and I watch him stride to the door, admiring his perfectly formed ass.

My body feels worn out, but somehow I still want more of him. No… I crave more of him. I wouldn't have thought that possible after everything we did last night, but I do.

It didn't stop with what we did downstairs, either.

Once we got up here, we climbed into bed, laughing at how small it was. We decided it would be easiest to lie with my back to his front, and once we'd gotten comfortable, he held me for a while before he nudged the tip of his erection into me.

"More?" I said.

"I just need to be inside you. We don't have to do anything."

Of course we did, though. Just the feeling of being stretched by him was enough to make me want more myself, and I wriggled back in to him, making him laugh. He pushed me over onto my front, my legs closed, as he straddled me and took me hard. I'd never felt anything like it, but the way he pounded into me was something else.

I came really hard, and could feel him getting close, too… but he remembered he hadn't used a condom and pulled out just in time.

"That was close," he whispered as he fell to the mattress beside me and I turned my head, smiling at him.

"It was. But it felt so good. I prefer it that way."

"So do I."

He leaned in and kissed me, and then jumped out of bed, dashing to the bathroom, and returning with a towel, which he used to clean my ass and back, before turning me over and pulling me into his arms again.

Neither of us said another word.

I don't think we were capable.

"You've got a message," he says, coming back into the room. He's still hard, and it's difficult not to be distracted by how magnificent he looks.

"Who from?"

"Peony."

I sit up. "Has something happened?"

He smiles. "I don't know. Your phone's locked so I can't see the message. But I doubt it. She'd have called."

That's true. He hands me my phone and I unlock it, going straight to my messages and clicking on the one at the top.

Brady walks around the bed, getting back in, and sits beside me.

"Well?" he says.

"She's asking when they should bring Addy back."

"Have they had enough already?" he asks, and although I don't look up, I can hear him smiling.

"No. She says Addy can stay for as long as we need. They're re-arranging the baby's clothes, evidently."

"Poor Peony. I wonder if that was something she wanted to do this morning."

"Probably not." I look up at him. "What shall I tell her?"

"An hour?" he says.

I nod my head. "Okay."

I tap out a message to Peony, putting my phone on the bed as he pulls me into his arms.

"I know we started something earlier, but now we're on the clock, shall we move it to the shower?"

"That sounds perfect."

"It will be."

I lean back, then kneel and straddle him, capturing his face between my hands. "Thank you."

"What for?"

"I couldn't possibly say. The list is way too long."

Chapter Twenty

Brady

Laurel has absolutely nothing to thank me for. Especially not after that shower.

I hand her a towel from the shelf, wrapping it around her, and take one for myself, trying not to smile so much. Although I don't see why I shouldn't.

I'm the happiest man alive, after all.

Yesterday afternoon, I'd lost all hope of there ever being anything between Laurel and me, and now it seems she wants forever. And so do I. She loves me, and I love her, and nothing could be more perfect.

Absolutely nothing.

"Are you ever not hard?" she says, snatching me from my thoughts, and I look down at her to see she's gazing at my hard-on, her eyes wide.

"Sometimes. But never when you're in the room."

She giggles, and I wrap the towel around my hips and pull her in for a hug, kissing her forehead.

"Has it always been like that?" she asks, leaning back and looking up at me. "When you've been with other women, I mean?"

"You wouldn't be fishing, by any chance?"

"I might."

"I thought you said you wanted to forget the past."

"That was my past, not yours."

"I see. So, what is it you want to know?" I said she could talk to me about anything, and I meant it.

"Has it always been like this?" she says, repeating her original question.

"No."

"And did you really wait nine years?"

I tip my head to the right, and then the left. "That depends on your definition of waiting."

"Did you see other women?"

"From time to time. But only after you'd married Mitch." I hate saying his name, but like I explained to her earlier, there will be times when we'll have to, and it seems easier just to accept it. It's not like I can change what's gone before.

"Does that mean you didn't see anyone for the first four years?"

"It does." Her mouth drops open and I push it closed again, my finger beneath her chin. "You were away at college, and I lived for the times you came home… for the moments we got to spend together. Once you were married, I didn't feel I had anything worth waiting for." She shakes her head, letting out a sigh, and opens her mouth. "Don't even think about saying sorry again."

She looks up. "Okay. I won't. I'll just think it."

"Why? There's nothing to be sorry for."

"I—I wish I'd known."

"So do I, but we can't change the things that happened back then."

"No, we can't."

Her eyes mist with tears, and I know she's not thinking about us anymore. "Don't, Laurel. Don't let what he did cast shadows over our future. We have so much to look forward to, baby."

As I'm speaking, I step back slightly and move my hand down, resting it on her flat stomach, which makes her smile, and I hold her close because I know we're both thinking about what just happened...

The choice not to bring a condom into the shower was unspoken, but mutual. After what we did last night, I don't think either of us wanted any barriers between us.

Everything that happened next was entirely Laurel's decision.

I'd pushed her up against the tiled wall almost as soon as she turned on the water, and she gazed up at me, biting on her lip.

"I know we don't have much time, but..."

"But what?"

"Can you make me come?"

I smiled. "Of course. I've got every intention of doing so." I raised her leg, but she shook her head and I lowered it again. "What's wrong?"

"I—I want it to be like it was in the kitchen."

"In the kitchen?" I thought back to last night, to lying her on the countertop and tasting her. "You want me to lick your pussy?"

She shook her head again. "No. I mean, the time before."

It would have been so much easier if she'd just said what she wanted, but I thought back to the only other time we'd done anything in her kitchen, and I smiled down at her. "You want me to make you squirt?"

"If that's what it's called, then yes."

"That's mostly down to you, babe, but I'll see what I can do."

I kicked her feet apart a little and took her hands, holding them above her head in one of mine, while the other roamed south, my fingers sliding through her slick folds. She flexed her hips, and I leaned closer.

"Keep still."

She looked up, nodding her head, gasping as I inserted two fingers inside her.

"Yes, yes," she breathed, and I gently brushed my thumb against her clit. It wasn't a necessary part of what I was about to do, but it made her breasts heave and her back arch, and I did it again, and again, and then I started to move my fingers, back and forth, rather than in and out, building to an almost brutal speed. She kept her eyes fixed on mine, and although neither of us said a word, I loved the fact that she trusted me enough not to hurt her, and to ask for what she wanted. Before long, she was straining, her body fighting the tension inside her as her nipples tightened to hard pebbles and she closed her eyes, shuddering, struggling to breathe.

"Come for me, baby. Show me what you've got." She opened her eyes again, tipping her head forward. "Don't fight it, Laurel."

It was like she had to make a conscious decision to go with it, but when she did, I saw the moment she gave in, the pressure mounting, and then subsiding, and then mounting again until she finally came... spectacularly. An arc of clear fluid shot across the shower as she screamed my name, her body shaking, and I released her hands, putting my arm around her waist to hold her up. I didn't relent, though. I kept moving my fingers, squeezing every last drop out of her, until she collapsed against me.

"Oh, God... oh, God..." she whispered.

"Was that what you wanted?"

She looked up at me, her eyes a little glazed. "Yes. I don't know how you do that, but..."

"Like I say, it's mostly you."

"Then why has it never happened before?"

I lowered my lips to hers, to distract her. "I don't know. And we're not gonna talk about that. We're just gonna enjoy it. Okay?"

"Okay." She breathed in and out a couple of times, resting her head on my shoulder, and then leaned back and looked up at me. "Can we agree on one thing?"

"Sure."

"Can we agree to limit that to the shower… and maybe the kitchen?"

"If you insist."

She smiled. "It's just easier to clean up, that's all."

I laughed, unable to help myself, and then I kissed her, my tongue seeking entrance, which she granted, her moans almost drowning out my sighs as the water cascaded between us and I pushed her back against the wall once more, as I raised her leg, bending it over my arm, and entered her.

"That feels so good," she whispered, breaking the kiss and clutching my shoulders.

It did. It felt like the first time… only better.

I took her hard and fast, hammering into her, and she came within minutes, clinging on to me as her orgasm wracked through her body. I hung on, wanting a little longer, but as her third climax built, I knew I wouldn't be able to last much longer.

"I'm gonna come."

"I know."

There was a look in her eyes… a kind of pleading, and as I went to pull out, she shook her head, and lowered her hands to my butt, grabbing me and pulling me back in.

"Laurel? Let me go. I'm gonna come. I can't…"

"Yes, you can."

I stilled, my cock throbbing. "You want me inside you? Is that what you're saying?"

"Yes."

"You mean that?" I had to know, and fast.

"Yes!" She screamed the word, and I slammed into her, once… twice. On the third time, I plunged in as deep as I could, filling her with everything I had as she came around me, her body trembling.

It took a while before we could speak, but when we could, I lowered her leg to the floor, pulling out of her, although I held her tight in my arms, pushing her wet hair away from her face.

"You realize what we've just done?"

She nodded, smiling. "Of course. And before you ask, I have no idea about the timing."

I thought back. "Well, it's seven weeks today since we last did this. Do you remember when your period started?"

"Not without checking, and I've had another one since, not that I know when that one started, either. And to be honest, I don't care."

Had I heard that right? "Are you saying what I think you're saying?"

"I'm saying I want us to have a baby together. Maybe more than one, if we're lucky." She frowned suddenly, pulling back as far as the wall would allow. "Is that a problem? You said last night we could—"

"It's not a problem. I want us to have a baby, too. I just wasn't sure you were ready yet. Let's face it, we haven't even told Addy about us, have we?"

"No, but she'll love having a brother or sister to play with, just as much as she'll love having you here."

I couldn't help smiling then, and I kissed her. Hard.

I've been smiling ever since. And who can blame me? I've got everything I've ever wanted.

And more…

"You don't regret it?" Laurel says, bringing me back to the present as she places her hand over mine on her stomach. "What we just did, I mean."

"Not in the slightest." She smiles and I bend my head and kiss her, although she breaks the kiss and frowns up at me.

"You were telling me about the women you used to see…"

We're back here again? I pull her close, wondering if she's feeling a little insecure… if maybe she wants some kind of reassurance that I'm not like Mitch.

"No, I wasn't. But if you want to know, then I'll tell you." She nods and I dip my head, brushing my fingers down her cheek. "After you got married, I started dating again. Not straight away, but eventually. I slept with a few of the women I saw. Not all of them, but some."

She nods her head. "And? Was there anyone special?"

I stifle a half laugh. "Special? No, babe. Spending time with other women only confirmed that I loved you more than I could ever hope to like anyone else."

She tips her head back, looking into my eyes, and then leans up and kisses me. I deepen the kiss, pushing her back against the wall, and I pull my towel away, doing the same with hers, our slightly damp naked bodies pressed hard against each other.

She moans into my mouth and I take her hands, holding them above her head as I break the kiss and bend, biting gently on her nipples.

She arches her back and I stand up and switch both of her hands into one of mine, letting the other roam down between her legs, which she parts, giving me access to her soaking clit.

"You're so wet," I murmur.

"You just came inside me."

"Yeah… inside you. It's your clit that's dripping."

"Because I want you."

"I want you, too, babe."

I circle my finger around that most sensitive spot and her breath catches, her body convulsing. She's close already, and I press a little harder, kissing her neck, feeling her pulse quicken against my lips as she strains and tenses, then lets out a squeal of pleasure, crying my name as she comes hard, for the fourth time this morning.

Before she's even calmed, I take my hand away, leaving her panting, and palm my cock, rubbing it against her drenched clit, making her shudder.

"You want more?"

"Yes."

I smile and flip her around, pulling her away from the wall.

"Grab the basin and don't let go."

She does as I say, bending over and offering me her delectable ass, as I step between her legs, kicking her feet a little further apart. I line up my cock at her entrance just as she stands again, twisting around to face me.

"We can't."

"We can't?"

"No. Addy will be home any minute."

"Oh, shit."

She smiles. "I'm sorry."

"Hey… it's okay." I lean in and kiss her. "I'll wait."

"You will? That doesn't seem fair."

"You're forgetting… I'm good at waiting for you."

It doesn't take us long to dress, and we've just cleared up the kitchen, which we failed to do last night, when we hear a car approach the house. By the time we get to the door, Addy's already climbing from Ryan's black Mercedes. She reaches back into the car to grab something, and then turns around, frowning when she sees me standing beside her mom.

"Brady?" Addy stares at me, and I nod my head, wondering if we got this wrong, but then she drops the doll she was holding, and rushes straight at me and I bend, catching her as she throws herself into my arms. "You're back," she says as I stand up again, with her clinging to my neck.

"I sure am, sweetheart. I'm sorry I went away."

She leans back. "That's okay. Mommy said you were busy."

"Well... I'm not gonna be busy anymore."

She grins and turns to Laurel. "That's good... because Mommy and I really missed you, didn't we, Mommy?"

Laurel's eyes are glistening, but she moves closer, leaning against me and I shift Addy, resting her on my hip, so I can put my arm around Laurel.

"We did, baby girl," Laurel says, and I smile at her, giving her a wink.

Ryan and Peony walk over. He's holding a small pink rucksack, and the doll Addy just dropped, and Laurel takes them both from him.

"Thank you so much for having her last night."

"That's no problem," Peony says. "We had fun."

"Uncle Ryan took me out on the tractor," Addy says, talking to me.

"It's okay," Ryan adds. "I was really careful with her." I notice he's talking to me, and for a second, I wonder if that's because I'm wearing my uniform... until I notice the smile on his face, and realize being the sheriff has nothing to do with it.

"I'm sure you were."

He puts his arm around Peony. "Are we going to Concord or not?"

"We are." She turns and looks at Laurel. "We're gonna buy more baby clothes."

Laurel smiles, and my heart flips over, wondering how soon we might be doing that for ourselves.

"Re-arranging them this morning has made Peony realize there's no such thing as too many rompers," Ryan says.

"I'm nesting." Peony nudges into him. "So sue me."

He hugs her a little tighter. "What worries me is that the nest won't be big enough for all the things you keep trying to put into it."

"Is it my fault you didn't want to know the sex of the baby?"

"No. But that doesn't mean we have to buy enough for twins."

She turns, slapping him gently on the chest, and then looks at Laurel. "We'll catch up next week, shall we?"

I know exactly what they're going to catch up about, and I don't mind in the slightest. Peony isn't a gossip, but even if she were, I still wouldn't care.

"Sure," Laurel replies. "Although I have another favor to ask." Everyone turns to face her, including me.

"Oh, yes?" It's Peony who speaks first, because she's the one being asked to do something, although none of us know what.

"Would you be able to come over on Monday and sit with Addy so I can go get a haircut? It didn't work out yesterday, and…"

"What are you saying?" I interrupt her. "It worked out perfectly… in the end."

"Not for my hair."

"Who cares about your hair?"

Laurel chuckles and leans a little closer. I kiss the top of her head and turn to Ryan and Peony, who are both smiling at us.

"I'll call you on Monday, and you can let me know when you need me," she says.

"Thanks," Laurel replies, and Peony and Ryan head back to his car. "And thanks for everything you did yesterday," Laurel calls after them.

"You don't have to thank me," Peony says as Ryan holds the door open for her. "Just be happy together."

"We will," I reply and she smiles, getting into the car, with a little difficulty.

Ryan closes the door and walks around to the driver's side, giving us a wave as he climbs in himself, and then he turns the car and drives off.

"What are we gonna do today?" Addy says as we all walk back into the house and I close the door behind us. "Have you got to work?"

I shake my head, loving how happy she is to see me.

"No. I'm not working today. In fact, Mommy and I haven't even had breakfast yet."

I set her down on the floor as I'm speaking and she folds her arms across her chest, shaking her head at me. "What have you been doing?"

I stifle a laugh, although Laurel chuckles, and I crouch down in front of Addy. "Would you like some pancakes?"

"Ryan made us scrambled eggs and bacon, but if you're making pancakes, I'm sure I could eat some."

"Okay." I stand and take her hand. "You sit with your mom and I'll make breakfast."

Addy grabs her doll, bringing it into the kitchen with her, and while she and Laurel get comfortable at the island unit, I set about fixing the breakfast, giving priority to making coffee. I pass Laurel a cup, and she looks up from her phone to thank me, while I pour some milk for Addy, who thanks me politely and then turns to her mom.

"This is better, isn't it?" she says and I have to smile.

"It's much better." There's a moment's pause and then Laurel puts down her phone and says, "Would you like it to be like this every day?"

I stop mixing the pancakes and hold my breath, wondering what Addy will say.

"You mean Brady being here for breakfast?"

"I mean Brady being here all the time."

There's another pause, and I turn, needing to see Addy's reactions. She's thinking. That much is obvious, and she raises her head, looking at me.

"Are you coming to live with us?"

"Only if that's what you want."

"If you do, will you promise not to leave us again?"

Oh, God… my heart.

Putting down the bowl and whisk, I walk around the island unit, sitting beside her and taking her hand in mine. "I promise, sweetheart. I'm never gonna leave again."

She pulls her hand from mine and throws her arms around my neck. I lift her onto my lap and hold her close, looking at Laurel, who's struggling to hold it together.

"I'd like that," Addy says against my chest. "I'd really like that."

Laurel lets out a slight sob, and I take her hand and pull her to her feet. She steps closer, and I put my arm around her, holding them both close to me… right where they belong.

"Brady has to go home," Laurel says as Addy helps herself to a third pancake.

She drops her fork, looking up at her mother. "Oh, but…"

"Let me finish," Laurel says, smiling at me over the top of Addy's head. "Brady has to go home to change out of his uniform, and then he's gonna come back again."

Addy nods her head and then turns to me, with the cutest of frowns on her face. "Are you gonna do that every day?"

"No," Laurel says before I can answer. "No, he's not. He's gonna bring some clothes back with him, so he doesn't need to keep going home every morning." She raises her eyebrows at me, and I nod my head. As ever, I'll go along with whatever she wants… whatever she needs.

"Okay," Addy says and picks up her fork again.

"After that," Laurel says, "I thought we could all go for a picnic."

Addy drops her fork yet again, and bounces so hard in her seat, I have to hang on to her to stop her from falling.

"I think she likes that idea," I whisper, as Laurel puts her hand on Addy's shoulder to calm her.

"Do you?" she asks me. "Do you like that idea, too?"

"Of course."

Addy pushes her plate aside. "Can I get down now, Mommy?"

"Don't you want to finish that last pancake?"

"No. I wanna go play with my dolls."

"Okay."

I help Addy down and she grins up at me, then runs from the room. Once she's gone, I shift into her seat, bringing my coffee with me.

"Are you sure about the picnic?"

Laurel tilts her head. "Why wouldn't I be?"

"Because you haven't been out since… since the accident."

"I'll be fine. You'll be there."

I lift her onto my lap, and she giggles, leaning against me, although a thought occurs and I pull back slightly. "Is this okay?"

"It's perfect."

"No. I mean, is it okay for me to sit you on my lap? For us to be intimate when Addy's around? Or should I keep my distance?"

"No. We're together now. I know we haven't explained that to her properly yet, but I'm not gonna pretend. I thought maybe we could tell her about us while we having our picnic."

"What will we say?"

She shrugs her shoulders, resting her head on mine. "I don't know. I was thinking something like Mommy loves Brady and Brady loves Mommy. It's simple, but honest."

"That's true. Although I think we should add in something else."

"Oh? What's that?"

"I think we should tell her we both love her, too." She gasps, her eyes brimming with tears, even though she's grinning.

"Y—You mean that?"

"Of course. Every word. I couldn't lie to her, anymore than I could lie to you. But we're making some big changes in her life, and I think she needs to know she's safe and loved. Because she is, Laurel. You both are. I won't let anything happen to either of you ever again."

"Do you have any idea how much I love you?" she breathes, and I smile.

"However much it is, I love you more." I lean in and kiss her, sighing as her tongue flicks against mine, and I grab her ponytail, tipping her head back, to deepen the kiss. She puts her arms around my neck and moans into me as another thought occurs, and I pull back. "There's just one thing…"

"Oh?"

"Yeah. You know you said about getting a haircut on Monday?"

"Um… yeah. What about it?"

"You weren't thinking about having it cut too short, were you?"

She smiles. "Are you asking if I'll still be able to put it up in a ponytail?"

"Yes."

"I imagine so."

"Good. I like your ponytail."

"Hmm… so do I."

I wrap it around my hand and tug just slightly, so she's looking up at me. "You'd let me know if there was anything I did that you didn't like, wouldn't you?"

"Yes," she says and I lean in, but just before our lips meet, she smiles. "You're full of surprises, you know?"

"I am?"

"Yeah. I've known you all my life, but I never would have thought you'd be the way you are."

"The way I am? What does that mean?"

"It's just that you're… you're quite controlling."

I'm not sure I like the sound of that, and I lean back, gazing down at her. "Controlling?"

"In a good way," she says, setting my mind at rest. "I'm only talking about the way you are when we're… intimate."

"And is that a problem?"

"God, no. I love it. I love everything you do to me, Brady."

"I don't do anything to you. I do all kinds of things with you, baby. If I ever overstep the mark, though, tell me."

"You don't think you'd know that yourself?"

I shrug my shoulders. "It's hard to say. You might think I'm controlling, but the reality is, when I'm around you, I have no control whatsoever."

She smiles. "I like that. I like the fact that I can do that to you… and I trust you not to go too far."

"Good."

She nestles against me. "I love you so much, Brady Hanson. I love who you are and what you do with me, and how you make me feel. I love that you give me the kind of life I never had before. You give Addy the kind of life she never had before, either… just by being here."

I never expected her to say that, and I whisper, "Thank you," pulling her closer. "Thank you for making me a part of this… a part of your life."

She leans back, staring up at me. "Don't thank me. I've been such a fool. I trusted…"

"Don't. We're done looking back."

She sighs and sits up, looking around the room. "Do you know… I don't think I want to live here anymore."

I didn't expect that either, and I sit up myself, studying the modern lines of her expensive and enormous kitchen. "Is that because of Mitch?"

"Of course it is. I'll never know whether he brought Kaylee here, but even if he didn't, I can't bear the thought that he might have been screwing the woman who decorated the place." I smile at her turn of phrase. It's most unlike her, but I like it. I like her speaking her mind, but before I can tell her that, she adds, "Even if I've changed the decor, being here is a reminder of the kind of man he was, and of how little Addy and I meant to him." She shakes her head. "It all feels tainted now."

"Then sell it."

"And live where?" She looks back at me, shaking her head.

"With me. My house might not be on this scale, but I've got three bedrooms, even if one of them is little more than a closet. I'm sure with some careful re-arranging of…" She frowns, and I stop talking. That wasn't the reaction I was hoping for. "Did I say the wrong thing?" I ask.

"No." She rests her hands on my chest. "Sorry. I was just thinking."

"What about?"

"About the fact that I don't want to keep moving Addy around."

I'm beyond confused now. "Why would you have to? We could just move out of here and into my place. It wouldn't be…"

"Please don't take this the wrong way…"

"Take what the wrong way?"

"What I'm about to say."

"Are you gonna tell me you don't want us to live together anymore?"

"No. I'm gonna tell you I'd like us to stay here."

I'm so confused…

"But I thought you just said…"

"I'd like us to stay here until we can sell this place… and yours."

"You want me to sell my house?"

"Yes. So we can buy somewhere new… together."

I was right about one thing. When I'm around her, I lose control… and right now, I've lost control of my lips. They're smiling… and there's not a damn thing I can do about it. "I think I'd like that."

"You won't mind staying here, just for a while?"

"Of course not. As long as you're okay with it?"

"I'm sure I'll cope. It's Addy's home, and I think we need to give her a chance to get used to us being together before we make any more changes."

I nod my head. "Speaking of changes…"

"Yeah?"

"Do you think you might consider making just one more?"

"Of course." My smile becomes a grin. "What is it?" she asks.

"Do you think you might consider changing your last name again?"

She gasps. "A—Are you…?"

"I'm asking you to marry me." I lift her off of my lap and get to my feet, holding her hands between us and gazing into her eyes. "It may not be the most romantic proposal ever, but I love you, Laurel, and I want to marry you so damn much. We can wait, if it's easier. I just…"

"Yes," she says, interrupting me. "Yes… yes, please."

"You want to marry me?"

"Yes. And I don't want to wait."

"Good. I don't either. I just said that because it sounded better."

She giggles and I release her hands, putting mine on her waist and pulling her in for a hug. She wraps her arms around me and I do the same, both of us just melting into the moment.

"I guess I should go home and get changed," I say when she finally pulls away, only she keeps a hold of me, like she doesn't want me to leave.

"You can't. Not yet. I've got a couple more things I need to say. Only I'm not sure which order to say them in."

"Does it matter?"

"I don't know." She frowns, then takes a deep breath. "Okay," she says like she's made a decision, and she steps back slightly, although I grab her hands, so she can't go too far.

"What is it, Laurel?"

"I—I was looking at the dates on my phone while you were fixing the breakfast."

"Right."

"And I've worked out I'm in the middle of my cycle."

The penny drops and I realize what 'dates' she's talking about, pulling her back to me again, so her body's hard against mine.

"The middle?"

"Yes."

"So you could be…?"

"It's possible."

I kiss her so hard it almost hurts, my heart swelling in my chest. "If it were true…" I say, breaking the kiss. "If you were pregnant, how would you feel? It wouldn't be like… it wouldn't feel like…?"

She shakes her head. "It would be nothing like that, Brady. I was so scared when I found out I was pregnant with Addy. This time around, if it happened, I'd be happier than I ever thought possible." She smiles up at me. "What about you? How would you feel?"

"The same. Maybe more so." She grins and sighs, like she's relieved, and I capture her face between my hands, locking my eyes with hers. "The thing is, I don't wanna go back now. If you're not pregnant this time, I wanna keep trying until you are."

"You mean that? You're not just saying it because you know it's what I want?"

"I mean it, babe. It's what I want, too."

She smiles, lighting up my world. "Does this make us crazy?"

"Probably. But at least we'll go crazy together." I chuckle at that wondrous thought. "What was the other thing you wanted to say?"

It can't get any better than that, so I brace myself for something worse, and the look on her face gives me cause for concern. It's a mixture of worry and doubt, and I hold her close, for both our sakes.

"It's about Addy," she says.

"What about her? If you're worried I won't treat her the same as a child of our own, then you don't need to. I..."

"That's just it. I know you'll be the perfect father to her. You already are, and that's why I want to ask if you'll let me change her last name, too."

"Change her name? What to?"

She shakes her head. "Hanson. What else?"

It's like everything in my universe has suddenly gone slightly off kilter. "A—Are you asking me to adopt her... to be her father?"

"I am."

I lift Laurel into my arms and swing her around, unable to speak, although she giggles, throwing her head back.

"Do you agree?" she says as I lower her to the floor.

"It would be my privilege. My honor. As long as it's what Addy wants."

She nods. "We'll ask her. Maybe not today, though. We're gonna be bombarding her with enough information for one day. But maybe tomorrow…"

"Or the next day," I murmur, resting my forehead against hers. "There's no rush."

"There might be… if I'm pregnant."

I frown down at her, the meaning of her words lost on me.

"Why does that make a difference?"

"Because I don't want Addy to be a Bradshaw if everyone else in the house is gonna be called Hanson."

"Oh. I see what you mean." I kiss her forehead. "Don't worry. We'll talk it through with her, and I'll look into how long it takes."

"Thank you." She rests her hands on my chest.

"You don't have to thank me. You've made me so damn happy, Laurel."

"Any happiness we have is entirely because of you," she says, looking up at me.

"Is there anything else you wanna tell me, or can I go home and change now?"

"You can go, just so long as you hurry back."

"Why? Are you gonna miss me?"

"Madly. I hate waiting for you."

"I hate waiting for you, too. And I've had more practice."

She looks up at me, then captures my face between her hands, looking into my eyes. "We're done with that now, though, aren't we?"

"We sure are, baby. We sure are."

The End

Thank you for reading *Being with Brady*. I hope you enjoyed it, and if you did, I hope you'll take the time to leave a short review.

We'll be back in Hart's Creek soon, in the next story –
Teaching Tanner – a love at first sight, age-gap romance.
Tanner Pope owns the local bookstore, and since his divorce, he juggles working there with caring for his son, Nash. He's lonely, and doesn't mind admitting it, but what's a guy to do when the trust has been sapped out of him?
Concentrate on where he's walking be a good idea...
But if he'd done that, he'd never have bumped right into the woman of his dreams. Now he has, though, he just needs to figure out how to make something of it.

Printed in Great Britain
by Amazon